SAFE HARBOUR

A Beaver Island Mystery

Book Five

MAIA ROSS

D1736970

Lazy Beaver
PRESS

FOR JOHN

CONTENTS

ONE — IRMA

There had been no way to know in advance that the Beaver Island gardening competition banquet would end in bloodshed. On the other hand, it would have been churlish to complain about my front row seat.

It was that seat I was currently defending. My little clan and I had only just arrived at the banquet, but my island nemesis, Snookie Smith, had already sent no fewer than three minions to try to oust me from my perch.

As we were seated at my family table, located near the front of the salon where the banquet was taking place—but still tucked into a corner where I could see each point of ingress and egress—I had every intention of staying put.

Beside me, my current houseguest and resident brainiac, Violet Blackheart, scratched nervously at her arm. She was forty-three but looked years younger—and semi-vampiric—most likely because she'd spent most of her life indoors, as nerds tended to do. Tonight she was wearing a lovely pale pink tea-length summer dress that fluttered when she

1

walked. Violet had never been a girly girl, and it had taken some time to wrestle
her into the ensemble.

Metaphorically speaking, of course.

Dr. Julian Harper, island doctor and formerly eligible bachelor, was on her left. To my right, Boris Andropov, a gentleman friend of mine, was trying to make me laugh, probably to take my mind off Snookie Smith's shenanigans.

"Stop that," I murmured to him. Violet raised her head to see if I was speaking to her. After I shook my head, she let out a sigh of relief, and Boris signalled the waiter for a beverage. I could not deny that at certain times in Boris's past as a Bulgarian intelligence agent, his drink might have come laced with an unpleasant additive, but luckily no such thing would happen tonight at the Beaver Island Country Club—*the club* to most islanders.

Hopefully.

Boris must have sensed my trepidation because he hoisted his glass, raised an eyebrow at me, and took a generous sip. "It will be a wonderful evening, Irma."

"Yes, it will," Violet whispered. "As long as you don't kill anyone."

"Don't be so pushy, dear," I said to her with a wink. Violet and her new beau, Dr. Julian Harper, were holding hands under the table in an attempt to hide their budding relationship from me, so perhaps she could be forgiven for her bossiness.

Julian's blue-green eyes met mine, and I sent him an encouraging smile. I'd known him ever since he was a pipsqueak in short pants. Such a good boy.

"You still haven't agreed not to kill Snookie." Violet sounded like she was trying to be accusatory, but the wine was helping to blunt her tone. Well, that was a good Chablis for you.

"I will not be killing Snookie tonight," I said mildly. "Right, Boris?" I nudged him under the table, and he covered his snicker with a cough. I briefly contemplated drowning him in our table's centrepiece—decapitated lipstick roses bobbing in a bowl so big it could double as a cistern—but decided to hold off. Too many witnesses.

"Okay, good, because your arch enemy, Snookie Smith, has sent her garden gnomes to our table like ten times to get us to move to a table at the back," Violet said before adding, "And I know how much that kind of thing irks you."

She was quite correct that Snookie wanted to banish us to the social Siberia at the back of the salon. I had a bit of experience with the real Siberia, on behalf of Queen and country, which was why I still had an English accent that most people couldn't quite place.

"Never fear, Violet," I said. "We're not going anywhere. And I definitely don't want to get blood on this outfit."

"Excuse me, Mrs. Abercrombie."

I looked up. Another one of Snookie Smith's emissaries was hovering behind Violet.

"Yes, dear?"

The newcomer was a twenty-something Asian woman with enormous eyes and a Cupid's bow mouth, and pleasant chestnut hair pulled back in an updo that was perhaps too complex for an evening that wasn't the Oscars. Her ensemble was a lovely lilac maxi dress that covered her shoes. I could only hope they weren't weaponized in some way, since tackling her to verify that detail was a no-go, considering all the eyeballs in the room at the moment.

"Uh…" A bout of handwringing from the young lady ensued, and I passed the time by partaking of some more Chablis. Eventually, she said, "I was, uh, wondering if you, uh, could maybe…think about moving to the back—"

"No, thank you, dear." To Boris, I said, "We have to get some of this wine for home."

"Excellent idea," he replied with a winning smile. He was in his late sixties or early seventies— with so many identities, who could know for sure?— with a steel-grey goatee and an aftershave I was becoming ever more fond of.

Thankfully, this evening he had eschewed his normal eye-blanching Hawaiian shirts for a bespoke suit that matched the lovely blue of his eyes. I wasn't certain what parts of his ensemble contained weapons—perhaps his shiny cufflinks, or maybe one

4

of his shoes—but I knew they were there somewhere. If the young woman in front of me *was* trying to kill us, they'd come in quite handy, although I was spring-loaded with a few surprises of my own.

"Uh…"

"What's your name, dear?" I asked.

"Ryeleigh. R-y-e-l-e-i-g-h," the girl said quietly.

"I'm Irma Abercrombie."

"N-nice to meet you."

"And you as well," I said. "I'm not sure how familiar you are with the club's inner workings, but this is my family table. Has been for many years. So we're all set."

"Oh."

Julian excused himself to go chat with some friends after giving Violet's hand a charming little squeeze.

I turned my focus back to Ryeleigh. "Perhaps you could tell me what the issue is, exactly? Then we can work together to find a solution." I said all this even though I knew full well that the problem with my location was that Snookie Smith didn't want to have to look at me while she was winning all those awards.

I supposed it made sense: Snookie had filed grievance after grievance to get the island's normally July-held gardening contest moved all the way into August. And then she'd cleaned up, winning the grand prize, since so many on the island—including myself—already had plans of our own that late in the summer.

Before making Beaver Island my permanent retirement home, I'd always spent my summer vacations here, taking up residence at my family estate on this tiny slice of land nestled in Lake Ontario, reachable only by air or boat.

Following in Mother's footsteps, I'd always spent a considerable amount of time working on my gardens during those summers, and I'd always won something or other in the island's annual competition.

But not this year. This year, Violet and I had been embroiled in a plot to wipe out an entire island family, and an old friend had been gravely injured during that particular operation. Happily, she was now on the mend.

"I'm, uh, not exactly sure," Ryeleigh said.

"Would you like me to speak to Snookie? I'm sure we can come to an agreement about what to do." And I *was* sure, in that I was certain that a quick blow to the back of Snookie's neck would bring all this nonsense to a very pleasing conclusion. Because then I'd be able to watch the tribute the club had organized on behalf of my mother's contributions to the island's gardening culture in peace, the real reason everyone at my table was here tonight.

"Uh. No." The poor thing looked like she'd sweated off ten pounds just talking to us.

"Would you like to sit down and join us for a drink, dear?"

In the background, I could hear Snookie hissing, *Ryeleeeeeeighhhhh.*

Theresa Ferrari, the club's head bartender, must have sensed something was amiss and sidled up to our table. "Hi there," she said to Ryeleigh. "What can I get you?"

The little thing twitched, then straightened her shoulders. "A double Glenfiddich, neat, with a water back, please," she said.

Boris threw me an amused look.

"Sit here," Violet said, patting Julian's empty seat.

Ryeleigh plunked herself down and let out a sigh. Her back was to Snookie, who was wearing a truly hideous muddy green and black polka dot dress.

"Ms. Smith has a restraining order out against you. That's why she wants you to move," she said quietly. Politely.

"Pish posh," I said with a laugh. "She's suing me, and she certainly *wants* a restraining order, but she does not actually have one." Snookie had conjured up a tractor-related injury back in June and blamed it on me, but she was faking the whole thing. And I knew that given enough time, that truth would come to light.

"Irma," Violet said, a warning in her voice.

Theresa deposited Ryeleigh's drink on the table with a little flourish.

"Thanks, Theresa," I said. "How are the kids?"

She rolled her eyes. "With any luck, they'll have cannibalised each other while I'm here and I can finally get some peace and quiet."

We all laughed. Ryeleigh looked like she was relaxing a bit, and good for her. Under the table, Boris's hand suddenly tensed in mine.

"Ouch," I said in Bulgarian.

"Sorry," Boris answered in the same tongue, a gentle tone in his voice that hadn't been there in our younger days. Of course, we'd been on opposite sides of the Cold War back then, and he'd once been tasked with killing me. Well, no one was perfect, as Violet would say.

"What's wrong?" I asked in the same language.

Violet leaned closer to Ryeleigh, trying to engage her in conversation. Violet claimed not to be an overly social creature, but she'd really bloomed on the island. She even had freckles now, due in no small amount to my efforts to drag her into the great outdoors. If there was anything Beaver Island was good at, it was water sports and spraying sunshine on nerds.

"Who is that man?" Boris asked, then took a small sip of his drink.

I followed his eye line, spotting the stranger almost immediately.

He was late-fifties, maybe older. A certain amount of hard living had etched itself into his features, and he was wearing a borrowed suit that didn't quite fit, a summer blue that pinched in his shoulders but bagged in his nether regions. Someone had obviously tarted him up so he would fit into the club's aesthetic. His hair had been slicked back, someone had taken a razor to his sideburns, and had missed a few spots. But it wasn't all that that bothered me.

He was trying not to be noticed.

As if sensing our gaze, he started to swivel his head toward us. Boris leaned forward and whispered a few sweet nothings into my ear, and I smiled like he'd just told me he loved me. Perhaps one day soon, he might even do so. I still wasn't quite certain how to feel about that, but after our summer romance had bloomed so sweetly, I was perhaps warming to the idea.

The strange man's gaze rested on Boris and myself before moving on.

"Private security?" Boris murmured into my ear.

"I don't think so," I said, meeting his eyes. Boris flashed me an impish smile that I'd always adored. "Doesn't feel quite right."

"Perhaps," Boris said. "But he's no civilian."

"Agreed. What if you got your hands on his wallet and—"

"Irma," Boris said, hoisting my right hand and planting a smooch on it before curling it into his own. "We should only observe this man. We are here to have a nice dinner, just as you said."

"Of course." Plus, the Abercrombies had participated in the island's garden competition from the very beginning, which was why Mother was being celebrated tonight as part of the banquet festivities.

The man from across the room had finished his drink while Boris and I were making kissy faces at each other, and was now heading in the direction of the loo. I could feel Boris focus on him.

"Excuse me, ladies," he said gallantly. To me, he raised an eyebrow. "*Obratno skoro.*" *Back soon.*

"Wonderful," I said, sighing happily as I watched him go. If the interloper was a threat, Boris would neutralise him in no time and then we could have a nice pre-dinner cocktail.

Suddenly, a hand was laid on my shoulder. I slapped one of my own over it, ready to catapult my attacker onto our table. What a shame. So many lovely glasses of spirits that hadn't yet been drunk, the linen starched to within an inch of its life, the about-to-be-served dinner scenting the air. But then a different perfume hit my nose and I relaxed a little as I turned my head.

"Irma," Imogene Flores, the club's general manager, squeaked. "May I please speak to you?"

"Of course, dear. Sorry about all the grabbing."

"I'm used to it," she said, letting out a breath.

"Take a seat."

Imogene looked around nervously, although to be fair, that was how she did everything.

"What's wrong?" I asked. "Snookie told you to make me move?"

"No." She picked up my water glass and helped herself to the entirety of its contents, which was most unlike her. "We, uh… We have a problem."

TWO — VIOLET

Irma was up to something, I could feel it. Of course, she was never *not* up to something, but tonight before we'd left the house, her head had been tilted the way it did when she had a plan up her sleeve. As a result, I'd decided that my current life goals were: survive the evening, keep Irma from killing Snookie, eat some delicious food.

The girl sitting beside me shuddered again. *Ryeleigh*, she'd said her name was. "So, how do you know Snookie?" I asked politely. I normally kept to myself in front of strangers, but the poor kid was wigging out with nervousness. I could relate. The club could be an intimidating place if you hadn't been born with a silver spoon clutched in each hand.

On the good side, the food and drink here were always over-the-top excellent, and I was a woman who liked to eat. And observe people. I'd always enjoyed learning new things, especially if they came with a side of wagyu beef and a few fancy cocktails.

Imogene Flores, the club's general manager, was holding a huddle with Irma at our table that had been going on for a while. After giving me a look that could have meant about a million different things, Irma let herself be whisked away. Elegantly, of course. Irma had old world charm and sophistication by the yard. Her silver bob was perfectly in place tonight, her barely five-foot figure was draped in what looked like vintage Dior, and all her jewels were real. So were her guns, although she hopefully hadn't brought any tonight.

"Ms. Smith hired me to help out with tonight's presentation."

"Help out how?"

"I edited some video footage for her. She had a film crew follow her around while she prepared for the gardening competition. They tagged me to put it all together, and I had to get her to sign off on the final reel."

"So, that's how you got suckered into it." I grinned. "Do you live here?"

"Just visiting. My sister and her fiancé have rented this huge place on the west side of the island. We're here until Labour Day."

"Is this your normal job, video editing?"

"I'm an accountant, actually. I just do this as a side gig."

"Ah, numbers. That's fascinating."

Ryeleigh threw me a half-glance, like she wasn't sure if I was serious or not. But I was. As an engineer, I always enjoyed numbers, measurements, numerical results. Unlike people, numbers could be relied on. They also made a lot more sense.

"I'm Violet Blackheart, by the way." I held out my hand to shake hers.

Ryeleigh's eyebrows shot to her hairline.

"What?" I asked.

"That's a pretty unique name," she said slowly. "You don't happen to be from Toronto?"

"Yeah."

"Do you know Maura Wong-Kent?"

I smiled. "Sure do. She used to work for me." I owned a Toronto tech business with my partner, Max, and Maura Wong-Kent had been our director of HR for a couple of years. Basically, she was sunshine in people form. Always upbeat, always throwing quirky celebrations, always happy, and always hugging the staff. That last one we'd had to talk her out of, lest someone sue us for an HR violation.

"She's my sister. Half-sister, actually."

"Oh, it's great to meet you," I said. "I was so sorry Maura had to move on. She was headed to Montreal, right?"

Ryeleigh raised her shoulders in the beginning of a shrug. "She was there for a bit, but she came back to Toronto. Well, actually, she's here on the island now."

"That's awesome! Did she come tonight? I'd love to see her."

Ryeleigh shook her head. "She doesn't get out much these days." I couldn't quite decipher the look on her face, and for a minute I wasn't thrilled that Boris and Irma weren't here to interpret it for me.

"What's wrong with Maura?" I blurted, then winced. Irma had been trying to groom me to improve my interrogation skills, to focus on finesse and subtlety. Let's just say we hadn't had a huge amount of success.

"Um…nothing?"

It was hard to believe her. Normally, I'd have just left her alone, but I was bothered by the thought of Maura not smiling like she'd just taken twenty edibles. It wasn't like her. "Are you guys here all together? Where are you staying?"

"Her fiancé rented some fancy estate. Can't remember the name."

"Oh, she's engaged!" I exclaimed. At the Solar Shoppe, we regularly hosted after-work drinks on Fridays, with friends and spouses welcome. I'd spent a fair number of Fridays with her boyfriend, Brandon Ott, and I liked him. But he was a registered nurse, so how he'd be able to come up with the kind of money needed to rent one of Beaver Island's fancy-shmancy estates was a bit of a mystery.

"Yeah, she is, and he's uh-ma*zing*. The engagement party is going to really slap. But she mentioned the other day that you haven't RSVP'd yet."

Slap? "Weird. I never got an invitation." I hit my forehead. "But I've been here all summer. If the invite went to my Toronto apartment, it hasn't been forwarded yet. Can you tell Maura to call or text me, please? She's got all my numbers. I'd love to see her while she's here."

"Yeah, sure." Shyly, Ryeleigh added, "She always speaks so highly of you."

"Well, she's pretty awesome, herself."

"I was wondering…" Big sigh. "I've been thinking of going back to school to get a degree in computer science, and now I'm wondering if I could…I dunno…take you out for dinner or something while I'm here. Maybe I could pick your brain a bit?"

"Sure, I'd love to. There's a great little pub on Main Street—Mandy McGuire's. Have you heard of it?"

"I almost lost my eyebrows eating her wings last week, they were so hot."

"That's the one." I took a business card out of my purse, and Ryeleigh snapped a picture of it with her phone. After that we returned to our drinks. I didn't mind silence, and Ryeleigh looked like she hadn't had any rest ever since she was dragged into editing Snookie's Big Special Moments Movie.

I took a moment to survey the room while we sipped. It was full of folks in high-end summer duds, some so hideous that they had to be monthly-mortgage-payment expensive. Ryeleigh was wearing a nice long dress that covered her shoes even though she was only about five-seven. Of course, that meant she would tower over Irma's not quite five feet.

Irma…who was still off somewhere with Imogene after giving me that look. What had it meant? Run? We were all going to die? She was changing her shoes? Irma was an enigma even when we were in normal places doing normal things.

On the bright side, I seemed to be developing some sort of emotional callus that helped shield me from her Irma-ness. We'd had a lot of adventures together this summer and I'd always come back alive—mostly—so maybe I was trying to pretend that things would always work out in the end. I couldn't wait to hear what my Toronto therapist thought about all that. Maybe we should start doing video sessions.

A voice behind us shrieked, "There you are!"

I snorted white wine up one nostril and into my frontal lobe. Ryeleigh seemed to have done something similar and was coughing into a starched napkin that had probably cost more than my shoes.

After we recovered, we turned to see Snookie Smith standing over us, glowering. Although, to be fair, I'd never seen her *not* glowering. Snookie's hair looked more like steel wool than usual tonight, and her dress was some sort of poufy neck-tie thing dappled with unbelievably ugly polka dots. The colour was probably something fancy, but I was just going to call it puke green. In her late sixties, she was tall and stick-thin, and looked like she really needed a massage.

"Hello, Ms. Smith," Ryeleigh managed to get out.

"I'd like to understand why you're not helping us set up the projector, Ms. Kent."

Ryeleigh looked down at the table in front of us: the crisp white tablecloth, the polished silverware, the fancy glasses, the baby pink roses bobbing in a bowl bigger than my childhood bathtub. "Actually, Ms. Smith," she said slowly, "we agreed I'd put the video together for you to review earlier this week, which we did. We never made any plans for me to do any work this evening."

Snookie made a low, guttural noise that I'd only ever heard from really spoiled people. A not-getting-my-way noise. I hid my smile in another sip of Chablis—Irma really did have excellent taste. I tried not to think of where she was or what she was up to right now. At least nobody was screaming.

Yet.

"I'm so sorry to interrupt your fun," Snookie said, making the word *fun* sound like Ryeleigh and I had been up to our elbows in satanic rituals when she found us. "But we have a problem that needs to be fixed."

Ryeleigh opened her mouth to reply, but I put my hand on hers, trying not to think about how Irma always used this exact trick on me. "What's the problem?" I asked, meeting Snookie's eyes.

Her mouth curled downwards. "It's a technical issue."

"That's awesome, because I'm an engineer with a master's degree from one of the best universities in the country. How can I help?" I didn't love getting all braggy-pants on Snookie, but my education was my most prized possession. And I'd had it with her. She was a bully and a sneak, and I didn't like either. For a moment, I thought about telling Irma that it was okay to kill her after all. It was something to think about.

Snookie looked momentarily flustered. "Well...I don't know for sure. It's with the projector."

"No worries," I said, my professional tone and smile perfectly aligned, for once. The wine helped. "The club's staff are the only ones who should be dealing with that. It's an insurance thing. Hey, Viggo!" I said, waving to the club's IT tech lead, whom I'd met a while back when I was helping the club sort out their automated—and very hackable—irrigation system.

Viggo's glasses were so thick they kept sliding down his nose, but he seemed to have decided to just live with it. He was wearing neat dress pants and a pale green collared shirt that looked like it might be choking him, poor kid. He was twenty-six but still looked like a teenager. We'd even played online video games together a few times; he was quick and merciless. Irma loved him, obviously.

He sent me an awkward wave from across the room. "See, there he is. Viggo can help you." When Snookie didn't leave, I added, "Ryeleigh and I were just discussing a project we're working on together. A confidential one, actually. I'm sorry, I can't let her go right now."

"Sorry," Ryeleigh echoed softly.

Snookie rested a gnarled hand on her chest. "I...well..."

I motioned for Viggo to come get Snookie, pantomiming getting a drink afterwards. A big one. He made a face, but eventually steered Irma's nemesis away from us.

"Wow," Ryeleigh said when she was gone. "I've been trying to get away from her for days. She keeps calling me."

"Just block her number. Seriously."

She laughed, then drained her glass.

"You're welcome to eat with us."

"It's okay. You only have four chairs. And your boyfriend is sitting in this one."

I tried not to barf on the table when she said *boyfriend.* Julian and I had just started seeing each other. I glanced at him. He was on the other side of the room, huddled with some friends, standing about a half a head taller than them. He was slender but still substantial, with sandy hair that often stuck out at the crown, still boyishly handsome at thirty-six.

But we were not boyfriending and girlfriending yet.

Julian noticed me looking and raised his glass, a smile in his eyes.

...or were we?

I swallowed hard, then cleared my throat. "We can get another chair. You should stay. The food here really helps make up for all the crazy. I promise."

Viggo, fresh from being yelled at by Snookie, sauntered over.

"Sorry about siccing her on you," I said.

Viggo grabbed a drink from a passing tray and plunked himself down beside Ryeleigh. "I'm used to it," he said.

"Yeah, sorry," Ryeleigh echoed.

"I'm Viggo," he said, smiling goofily at her. "I'm the head of IT here." But he wasn't bragging. Viggo was a good kid, a hard worker who'd realized he enjoyed sticking forks into electrical outlets at a young age. I could relate.

"Ryeleigh," she said softly.

I was glad Irma wasn't here. After retiring from intelligence work, she seemed to have developed a late-in-life urge toward matchmaking. I shuddered, thinking of her nudging a couple to the altar with one of the handguns she pulled out of her purse every so often.

"Did you get everything worked out?" I asked him.

But Viggo, who was staring dreamily at Ryeleigh, said nothing.

I cleared my throat.

"Um...what?" he asked.

"With Snookie?" I said. "Everything okay? She was trying to rope Ryeleigh into helping out."

Viggo picked up one of Ryeleigh's hands and stroked it. "Don't worry," he assured her, "that lady won't bother you again." Then he kissed her hand. Seriously, *kissed* it!

She flushed all the way to her ears.

What was I watching? Some sort of GenZ mating ritual? A secret Beaver Island greeting? Basic insanity?

"Your drink is empty," he said, signalling Theresa. "Let's get you another."

"Okay," Ryeleigh said breathily. The two of them got up as if they were one and shuffled off, their phones both out and ready to exchange deets.

A moment later, Julian rested his hand on my shoulder, and I interlaced my fingers with his briefly before letting go. He sat down and grinned at me. "What'd I miss?"

I leaned forward and said, "Boris followed some strange dude to the bathroom, probably to kill him. Irma's up to something, and I think those two literally just fell in love right in front of me."

Julian smiled again.

Just as one of the club's alarms started to *ping*.

THREE — IRMA

After getting mobbed by club members who just wanted to chat, Imogene eventually got us into her office and closed the door. As she turned, she blew some wayward hair out of her face.

Ping!

"Is that the fire alarm?" I asked, my nose wrinkling. The *ping!* was a soothing noise I'd never heard before, but the back of my neck was cold, never a good sign.

Imogene, who was somewhat ageless, between fifty and sixty, looked like she was about to have a breakdown. More so than usual. She opened a drawer, pulled out a walkie-talkie, and barked into it, asking what was going on. Immediately, some chatter came back.

"It's our new announcement chime, Irma," she said.

"What is the club announcing?"

She sighed heavily. "Nothing. The chime has been going off all week, but we still haven't figured out why. It's broken."

I wondered briefly if the pinging was actually penetration testing, or an enemy incursion, although I couldn't smell anything aflame yet, which was nice.

"I'm still not quite clear what problem you wanted to talk to me about, dear." Imogene and I had been stopped by so many people on the way to her office that we hadn't even started our conversation yet.

Her lips thinned until they disappeared and then kept going. In a minute or two, her whole face was going to vanish. "I've had to pull your mother's tribute out of the presentations tonight."

Ping!

"Oh?"

"Snookie has lodged a formal grievance against it."

"I do wonder if her pantyhose is too tight these days," I said, trying to keep my voice light. "Why would remembering Mother's contributions to the island's gardening culture cause a grievance?" A smile. "I mean, this is the gardening competition banquet. Mother was very active with the competition. Ergo, it would make sense to celebrate her at this very banquet."

Ping!

Imogene's fingers origami'd themselves together into what might have been a duck, and her pulse was thumping at the base of her neck. After picking up the walkie and barking some more orders into it, she set it down carefully.

Ping!

"Is everything all right, Imogene?" I said. She was a twitchy woman normally, but now that I looked a bit closer, I could see the dark circles under her eyes, artfully covered in makeup but still very much there. Of course, Snookie did have that effect on people.

Ping!

The walkie squawked and Imogene's frown deepened. She cleared her throat. "Everything is quite well, Irma. Thank you so very much for your concern."

She'd done a good job with her denial. She'd used all the right words in all the right order. But they were a pack of lies.

I gave her a look that had been honed over years of experience. Imogene didn't know all of the ups and downs of my career, but she was well aware of my family's military experience. Mother and Dad had always sat on the club's board of directors, with a focus on security. Naturally, I'd taken up that mantle after their untimely deaths. Imogene knew that I made her nervous, but since everything made her nervous, she was paradoxically less suspicious of me, which was always nice.

Ping!

"Snookie is driving me mad," Imogene blurted out, then slumped over her desk, squishing her hairdo, and most likely smudging some lipstick onto her old-fashioned blotter. I really did want Mother's

25

tribute to be included in tonight's program, but with Imogene this distressed, I simply couldn't bring myself to push her too much.

When the walkie squawked again, she reached out, pulled it toward her mouth, then told whoever was on the other end—Viggo Rossi, it sounded like—to fix the issue immediately or she'd just burn the club down. Then she reiterated the same threat in a morose Basque-accented Spanish for good measure. She always had been a talented polyglot.

"The evening will be over in a few hours, and then hopefully you can calm down somewhat," I said with sympathy.

"I'm going on vacation tomorrow," she moaned.

"Won't that be nice?"

"Irma," she said, still face-down on her desk, "please just let us honour your mother at another time. We'll have some audio-visual presentations on Labour Day weekend. We could include it then."

Ping!

Ping!

Ping!

Labour Day was the anniversary of Mother's and Dad's deaths, always a time of year that squeezed my heart closed for a few days. I normally spent it at home, in quiet contemplation.

Imogene let out a strangled noise.

I had no desire for Snookie to feel like she'd scored a victory if I agreed to the change. But it was always important to support those who had supported me, especially if they were on the verge of a nervous breakdown. And even more so if they were in the habit of not bothering me with a lot of questions, as was the happy state of affairs between myself and Imogene.

"Of course," I said eventually, patting her hand. She grabbed on to my arm and squeezed. "Ouch," I said quietly. Nervous people really did have some sort of demonic reserve strength.

"Thank you, Irma."

"Those pinging noises appear to have stopped."

"Thank heavens," Imogene murmured.

"See?" I said. "Everything's going to turn out just fine." I wanted to snatch the words back as soon as they were floating in the air, but I couldn't. Well, hopefully everything *would* turn out fine and Boris hadn't accidentally kneecapped that stranger we'd spied, like he had back in Riga in '82. If he had, we'd definitely require some cleanup, a resource I no longer had access to. I wondered, briefly, if he did.

Outside the window, a motorcycle revved up. *A sport bike?* I thought as it peeled out of the club's parking lot.

Imogene finally sat back in her chair. Her blotter now held a misshapen lip print and perhaps some eye makeup, but she still looked quite good. "Thank you, Irma. I'm sorry about all this. I owe you one."

I got to my feet, slipping my pocketbook under one arm. "Wonderful." Accumulating favours was my very favourite currency.

Leaving Imogene to collect herself, I made my way back to our table. Violet and Julian were sitting beside each other, heads together. Ryeleigh appeared to have taken her leave, and Boris was on the other side of the table, pretending to be texting someone so the young couple in front of him could have some privacy.

"What did I miss?" I asked.

"Some sort of alarm," Boris said, still looking down at his cellular telephone, finally hitting *send*. "Not quite sure why."

"It's the new announcement chime," I said. "Apparently, they've been having problems with it all week." Boris's mien indicated that the noise hadn't been caused by him, so I decided to accept Imogene's explanation about the system being buggy.

"Snookie was mean to Ryeleigh. And I think Ryeleigh and Viggo Rossi are in love now," Violet said, pointing at two young people across the room.

"What a nice couple they'll make!" I said, taking a seat beside Boris.

"Even accountants need romance," Violet said drily.

"They certainly do. Why was Snookie mean to Ryeleigh?" I asked. "She seems like a lovely young lady."

"Because Snookie is the worst?" Violet said.

"Well, there's that." I made sure not to flinch when one of the club's servers jumped out of nowhere and re-set my napkin on my lap, although it wasn't easy. To Boris, I whispered, "What happened? Did you—"

"Good evening, everyone." Imogene, now looking somewhat refreshed, stood at the front of the room and gestured for quiet. After thanking us all for coming, she repeated the same remarks about the island's gardening competition that she made every year, then mentioned how Snookie was the island's current grand prize winner.

An irritated noise fluttered through the crowd. *Interesting.* Obviously, I was not the only one who'd been annoyed at Snookie's machinations to transplant the competition from early July into August, thereby impacting the state of all our gardens, seeing as how different plants bloomed at different times of the year.

And I was not the only one who'd had to drop out due to a scheduling conflict, either. In my case, I'd been hunting for a miscreant who'd been wreaking havoc on the island. But other people had children, grandchildren, and other obligations to wrestle with.

Slowly, so very slowly, Snookie hobbled toward the podium at the front of the room, leaning heavily on a cane and flinching at each step like she was in extreme pain. Extreme pain caused by me running her over with a tractor back in June, of course.

She still refused to admit that the tractor I'd been driving at the time had been hacked by a murderer, and I was trying to *stop* it, not run her over, and that she could have easily moved two feet to the left and avoided the whole thing.

The audience coughed, rustling their Dolce duds. Still, Snookie hobbled. Viggo stepped up to try to help her and she batted him off like he was a bill collector.

At the next table over, Agnes O'Muffin, the town's head librarian and chief bosser-arounder, threw me a look I wasn't quite sure how to interpret. The two of us had recently chatted about Snookie's shenanigans, so I knew Agnes was less than impressed with her. Although, to be fair, Agnes had always been pretty hard to impress.

Snookie finally arrived at the lectern, those bloody reading glasses already perched on the edge of her nose. Then she took out a sheaf of papers and clacked them on the lectern long enough for dinner to have been served and eaten.

I could smell the delicious scents of the meal that was waiting in the wings: pistachio-crusted rack of lamb, whipped parsnips with a hint of nutmeg, baby carrots in a citrus glaze, and pencil-thin *haricots vert* that would be served with Farmer Ezekiel's artisanal butter. Violet was practically drooling on the table, and who could blame her?

"Good evening, everyone," Snookie said, leaning down to the microphone like a vulture, grimacing when it squawked. The look she threw poor Viggo could have stopped ten clocks. After taking a sip of water, she continued, "I am so happy that today is one of my good days, and my health is well enough for me to be able to attend this wonderful event."

"And we're all so very happy for her," Violet said, her mouth barely moving. I was quietly thrilled that our ventriloquist lessons were going so well.

"As many of you know, this has been a very difficult summer for me." Snookie was looking in my direction. But she wasn't looking at me. In fact, it looked like she was doing everything she could to not look at me. Which was how she planned on letting anyone in town who weren't already aware of Tractor-gate—which was nobody—know that it had been all my fault. "Earlier this summer, I was grievously injured—"

There was a noise in the crowd that I could swear in court did not come from me. Of course, truth-telling hadn't exactly been the focus of my life's work, but still. The noise was one of disbelief. Irritation.

Snookie had stepped on pretty much everyone in the room at one point or another. She'd made the Patels relinquish their boat slip at the club because their new sailboat put *her* boat in too much shade, even though they'd had that spot for years. She'd tried to taint Mandy McGuire's catering business by spreading rumours about mad cow burgers. She'd let the air out of Kendelle Chang's tires, making her miss a chess competition that she'd been the favourite to win at—turned out that Snookie had a niece in the same tournament. And so on. Snookie was a mini menace. And both Violet and my best friend Stuart Barker had told me I wasn't allowed to kill her, which was such a bother.

"—grievously…" Snookie fixed us all in her gaze, those reading glasses so very precarious on the end of her nose. "…harmed during an altercation earlier this summer which has left me disabled and unable to function in my daily life…"

Snookie worked at the local credit union. She sat all day long, every day.

"…which has been very emotionally difficult for me."

Violet tipped her head back and drank.

"Luckily, I've had the gardening competition to look forward to. Which has been such a comfort." She glanced up briefly. "Many of you have expressed support for my concerns with the event judging and able-ism—"

On the other side of the room, a clutch of club members started muttering to each other.

Snookie straightened the papers again, then glared at the noisemakers. An icy silence ensued. "…with the event judging, which led the gardening committee to accommodate my disabilities and move the competition into August. Happily, so did the *Toronto Star*, and *Home & Garden Canada*, who both wrote extensive articles about my gardens, which I invite all of you to peruse."

My current houseguest twitched in her chair. "I'd like to invite her to—"

I put a hand on Violet's arm and she silenced herself. It wasn't that I wasn't enjoying her anti-Snookie rhetoric; I just wanted to hear what Snookie herself had to say.

"Some of you have asked to come and view my prize-winning gardens while they are still in bloom. I would normally love to accommodate all of you, as keeping the island beautiful is one of my great passions in life…"

A lone cougher broke the silence.

"…but I have spent most of the summer lying in bed and gathering my strength so I could garden for just a few hours every day, and—"

The tractor had very slightly tapped her derriere. I'd bet good money that she hadn't even gotten a bruise.

"Thankfully, the gardening competition committee was gracious enough to move the competition forward a few days…"

Three weeks and four days—twenty-five days in total. An entirely different growing season.

"…to accommodate my…" After coughing like a tubercular orphan, Snookie continued speaking. "…wounded condition. Unfortunately, the severe injuries resulting from me being run down by a tractor commandeered by Irma Abercrombie—"

"Thank you so much, Snookie!" Imogene said, smoothly stepping beside her. And had she nudged Snookie with her hip a little? Well done, Imogene.

33

"Now, we all have a treat. Snookie had a camera crew embedded with her..."

"Embedded?" Violet mouthed.

I leaned forward. "Yes, dear. Like in Desert Storm."

"...to capture the thrilling lead-up to the competition. We are so lucky to be the first to see this mini-documentary."

A sparse sort of clapping emanated from the crowd.

Boris leaned forward. "In Bulgaria, when I was young, people sometimes clapped like this for party leaders who sent their mistresses to the gulag after they were bored with them."

When Snookie finally met my eyes, I nodded at her, making sure to transmit the ire I was feeling about Mother's celebration being bumped off the night's schedule.

She blanched.

"Without further ado, I give you *Snookie Smith: A Summer of Fun*," Imogene said.

Julian made an odd throat-clearing noise.

The room darkened, making me happy that our table was located so perfectly that nobody could sneak up behind us, and that I had a good eye-line to all the exits.

"What happened in the loo?" I whispered to Boris.

He finished his sip and set his heavy glass down carefully. "I do not know where that gentleman went—I lost him. And he has not returned to the ballroom. Perhaps he decided his luck was up."

"Perhaps," I said slowly, glancing around the room to make sure he was really gone.

A large screen was now in place at the front of the room, and the opening of Snookie's mini-movie started to roll. Snookie's house was a semi-Gothic mansion downtown, with a generous yard and good soil. I had never personally enjoyed her gardens—too stiff and formal for my taste—but I had to admit she had some lovely features, like the koi pond that was now showing on-screen.

In a voiceover, Snookie droned on about keeping raccoons away from the koi, as they would eat them. Sometimes I wished that dinosaurs were still roaming the planet and that one of them would eat Snookie.

The production looked professional, with good lighting and steady camerawork. A glance at the rest of the crowd seemed to indicate that they weren't exactly on the edge of their seats, but that Snookie's cinematic debut was a semi-pleasant diversion before dinner.

The scene shifted to the rest of the back yard, a slow pan of overstuffed hanging baskets with dahlias and periwinkle, flowering climbing vines, and some Baltic Ivy that I hoped would someday come to life and strangle Snookie in her sleep.

Snookie moved slowly into frame, limping, a set of crutches under her arms. She started to wax poetic about the ballerina pink miniflora roses that sat at the foot of the garden. I had always liked those roses.

Then, in the video, Snookie toppled over.

"I'm so sorry," movie-Snookie gasped. "I simply haven't been able to get around. You know, ever since being hit by that tractor earlier this summer."

Violet lifted her glass again and drained its contents. Another was set in its place. Luckily, Boris was my designated driver this evening, although an enterprising young club member had started a business shuttling people home from the club, as long as he could stow his bicycle in their trunk. It was an excellent way for him to work on his cardiovascular fitness, and I used his services as often as reasonably possible.

Big Screen Snookie sighed heavily. "If you observe the Baltic ivy—"

The movie jolted to a halt. And then something else appeared.

Four — Violet

It was incredible how a country club's staff could replace a glass of wine you didn't even know you'd finished. I wasn't much of a drinker before coming to Beaver Island, but I was definitely picking up the habit. My business partner, Max McCorkle, had even told me I should be drinking *more*. Our company was on summer hours, we were doing well, and I actually had enough time these days to sit down with an adult beverage. It was nice.

And so was the image in front of me.

"What on earth?" Irma said.

On screen, Snookie's telenovela had ground to a halt. Instead, she was boogieing around her living room, accompanied by incredibly loud big band music—with a little quickstep every now and then—her crutches hoisted in the air as she pranced around. The quality of the video looked different, and seemed to have been shot from outside the house. It was just too bad for Snookie that she had those big patio doors.

"Is she doing a rumba?" Julian asked.

"Jitterbug," Irma and I said at the same time, and I put a hand over my mouth. A fascinated sort of horror had lodged in my chest.

In her seat at the front of the club's banquet room, Snookie looked like she was about to crawl under the table. On screen, Snookie chucked one of her crutches into the air, twirled around, and caught it.

"She's got some moves," Julian observed. Boris snorted.

I looked around the room. Most people's mouths were hanging open. Some were laughing. A few little old ladies looked like they were about to barf all over their Chanel. Irma obviously wasn't the only one who'd been annoyed at Snookie for forcing the competition into August.

Movie Snookie was now partnering with an enormous birdcage on wheels, zinging it around her living room, which looked like it was from the late 1800s. Stuffy, uncomfortable-looking furniture, fussy wallpaper, frills as far as the eye could see.

"But here's my question," Julian said. "Is Snookie leading or following?"

I tilted my head to the side, still taking it all in. "When you're dancing with a bird…I just don't know if it matters."

Video Snookie was doing a bit of a free-form shimmy thing now, punctuated by a series of kicks that would have done the Rockettes proud. She was about five seconds away from breakdancing.

"I just ask because you're the dance expert," Julian said.

He wasn't exactly wrong, but then again, I wasn't sure how to tell him that after the one summer I'd spent here at the island ballet academy, I'd had to leave all that behind and focus on my university career. Julian came from money. Old island money. I hadn't even seen his house yet, but I was very sure my tiny Toronto condo would fit inside his vestibule. Before I came here, I hadn't even known what a vestibule was.

"This is totally unacceptable!" Snookie shrieked from the dais.

The video changed to a new image: Snookie, night-time, and a shovel. After checking to see if the coast was clear, Movie Snookie thrust the shovel into the dirt in front of a fancy-looking flowering bush, then lifted it out of the ground. The camera work was shaky, like someone was following her.

"So *that's* where my *Crocus sativus* went!"

I turned my head, expecting to see a little old lady hollering about her petunias. Instead, a twenty-something woman with enormous biceps and an even bigger scowl stood at the back of the room, hands on hips. Her hair was buzzcut-short and she was wearing a tailored black suit.

"Oh dear," Irma said.

Snookie rose to her feet, using Imogene's shoulder to help her up like she was a piece of furniture.

"You made everybody move into August and you were fine the whole time?" a little old lady hollered at Snookie.

Onscreen, Snookie was dragging the bush behind her. I spotted Ryeleigh across the room. Her mouth was hanging open, and her eyes were the size of dinner plates.

"I had a hip replacement last spring, and I was able to get my garden ready in time, you bloody thief!" another retiree hollered. Beside her sat Gertrude Romano, a delightful older lady who was a friend of Irma's, and Simone Summers, a wedding planner I'd met earlier in the summer. Beside them sat Mandy McGuire, purveyor of those famous hot wings. All three gave me adorable little waves, which I returned. After smiling sweetly at me, they resumed glaring at Snookie.

"I never...I just..." Snookie muttered. Then, one hand on her forehead, the other gripping a cane—not that she was using it—she started walking toward our table. Toward Irma. "What have you done?" Snookie hissed at her.

Irma's face had been pretty neutral up until now. Almost pleasant. And if you didn't know her, you wouldn't realise anything had changed. But her head was on the slightest of tilts, her shoulders were flexed, and she was doing that thing with her ankles that meant she was about to leap on top of you.

Against all my instincts, I felt sorry for Snookie.

"Why are you always ruining everything for me?" she shrieked at Irma.

...although it was a fleeting moment.

Then Snookie threw her cane at us. Which made a certain kind of sense, seeing as how she didn't really need it. Irma, as was her way, caught that cane, then hooked it over the back of her chair. She mouthed something that looked an awful lot like *Come and get it*, but it was hard to tell for sure.

Snookie let out a whimper before crashing to the floor.

"Is Angelique here?" Irma asked, referring to one of the island's other doctors.

"She's at her mom's for dinner," Julian said. Then sighed.

"I see," Irma said, setting her napkin on the table.

"No," Julian said, holding up a hand. "Don't go. She'll probably *extra* sue you if you touch her."

"I do see your point, dear," Irma said quietly. But there was a little twinkle in her eyes. I spent a long moment wondering if Irma had somehow organized all that extra footage. I'd known she was up to something when we left the house earlier, but I'd hoped her plans were more along the line of getting me two desserts.

Irma's amused expression was matched by an inhabitant of the next table over. Agnes O'Muffin, librarian extraordinaire, had the slightest of smiles on her face. She wasn't someone who ran around town smiling a lot, so it was unusual.

Julian was at Snookie's side now, murmuring something generically comforting while he ran through his usual are-you-still-alive drills with her.

Imogene knelt beside them, wringing her hands. Sometimes I wanted to suggest yoga to her, but I didn't know enough social niceties to be sure how she'd react.

"I'm gonna visit the ladies'," I said. I wasn't sad to have seen Snookie's dirty secrets revealed, but it was a lot of commotion and people and people commotioning, and I needed a quiet moment.

"And miss all this?" Irma said. She had a fresh drink in one hand and was holding Boris's hand in the other. I tried to think of the last time I'd seen her look so happy, and couldn't. Well, it was nice that she had a boyfriend. Helped keep her attention off me.

After a shrug, I set my napkin on my chair and headed to the bathroom. The hallways were empty, everyone probably having gathered in the ballroom to watch Snookie get taken out in an ambulance. Twenty bucks said she was going to suddenly acquire a new injury as a result of her faux-fainting spell. I wouldn't be surprised if she tried to blame that on Irma too.

There were a few bathrooms on the club's main floor. The biggest was a huge, fancy place where someone gave you hand towels and asked if you were having a nice day. I screamed every single time they came up behind me. Plus, I'd gotten hit with a selfie stick in there last Thursday.

So I headed to the small employee bathroom near the staff offices. I'd used it when I was working on the club's automated sprinkler system, and it suited me just fine.

Happily, it was empty. I set my purse on the counter, splashed some water on my face, and used the facilities. After wrestling with my Spanx for what felt like way too much time, I finally exited the stall.

There were no fluffy towels for me to dry my hands on, just a worn-out hand drier and some paper towels. I slapped on a bit more lipstick, straightened a few stray hairs, and sighed.

The shoes I was wearing tonight were high-heeled sandals I'd bought a while back for attending one of Irma's endless social events. I'd told her they would hurt my feet, but she'd assured me they wouldn't, and like so many other times, she'd been right. I decided to keep the thought to myself, and headed back to the ballroom. Hopefully, Julian wouldn't have to go to the clinic with Snookie and take care of her pretend injuries. We were supposed to hang out at Irma's after dinner—which smelled amazing—was over.

Viggo was leaning against the doorway to the banquet room, watching the scene inside. Julian was still attending to Snookie, who was lying on the floor with the back of one hand on her forehead.

"Hey," Viggo said, smiling broadly. "Was it you?"

"Was it me what?"

"Are you the one who spliced that film?"

"I'm a hundred percent sure that video was digital. So, you know, no splicing necessary."

His smile grew. "You know what I mean."

"Wasn't me." I decided not to mention my suspicions that while it hadn't been me, it might have been someone who lived in the same house as me.

"Seriously?"

"Yup."

An ambulance had shown up in my absence, the lights flashing on the wall in front of us. The EMTs blew past us and started settling Snookie onto a stretcher, and Julian stood, pulling nitrile gloves off his hands with a snap. He spoke to one of the EMTs, then slapped him on the back the way that men do. I tried not to stare at him, but it was hard. He was nerdy-cute when he did doctor stuff.

"Excuse me." A young dude passing by bumped into me, knocking my clutch out of my hand and onto the floor. I took my eyes off Julian and leaned down to pick it up—at the same time as the bumper did. Our heads clanged together and I closed my eyes in pain. I'd acquired a mild concussion recently as payment for helping Irma foil yet another island madman, and I didn't want any more brain damage than was absolutely necessary.

I was still seeing stars when the man pressed the clutch back into my hands. "Sorry about that," he said ruefully, and that's when I started paying attention.

"Brandon? Brandon Ott?"

Maura's boyfriend-fiancé blinked. "Whoa—Violet! What are you doing here?"

Viggo shoved his hand out for Brandon to shake. After a quick pump, the two disengaged.

"It's a long story," I said, grinning. "But congrats! I bumped into Ryeleigh earlier and found out you and Maura got engaged. I've been here all summer visiting a friend, and my invitation to the engagement party hasn't shown up yet. But, yay!"

Brandon licked his lips and glanced from left to right. He was in his late twenties and conventionally handsome, with a smile that was almost as nice as Maura's. "Maura is marrying someone else," he finally said.

"What?"

He motioned for us to move away from the brouhaha of the banquet room. When we were alone, he said, "And you can't tell her I'm here tonight."

"Why?"

"It'll take too long to explain right now," he said. "I'll give you a call. But please don't say anything until you've heard from me." And then he was off, striding toward the club's main exit.

I collected myself and rejoined Viggo at his post outside the banquet room. Snookie, arms still flailing, was being rolled out, right past the table I'd been sitting at with Irma and the gang. One of her arms snaked out and she grabbed at the tablecloth. From this angle, I could see her perfectly, right up to the three tiny dots of blood on her collar.

"Oh man," Viggo muttered.

Then, Snookie, still holding on to that tablecloth, rolled toward me and Viggo. Everything on the table came off in a crash of china and finely edged crystal. Irma and Boris had seen her coming, obviously, and already had that huge vase safely secured.

"You're wheeling me too quickly!" Snookie snapped at Jake, one of the EMTs, who I knew for a fact was a nice guy. After he adjusted his speed, she wailed, "Now it's too slow!"

Thankfully, she had a handkerchief draped across her eyes when she passed me, so I didn't get a surprise gut punch from her on the way out.

"Who was that guy?" Viggo said.

"What guy?" I asked, watching Snookie as Jake accidentally tapped one corner of the stretcher on the club's front doors.

"Oh, my leg!" Snookie wailed.

"That guy who just bumped into you."

"He used to date one of my employees." I slid my clutch under one arm. "And I'm pretty sure you're the one who messed up Snookie's presentation, not me."

Viggo burst into laughter. And given how great the acoustics were in the club, that laughter echoed out over the ballroom. People seemed to cheer up then and started mingling between tables.

"Nope, not me," he said.

"Of course," I said slowly, "it could have been Ryeleigh. She edited that file for Snookie."

Viggo's eyebrows lifted. "I've always liked bad girls."

I snorted.

Irma stretched, then looped an arm around Boris's. He leaned forward and said something that made her laugh.

Julian caught my eye and came over.

"Snookie gonna live?" Viggo drawled, shaking his hand.

Julian nodded.

"Glad to hear it," Viggo said. After giving me a jaunty salute, he ambled off.

"What's wrong with Snookie?" I asked.

"All her vitals are good," Julian said drily.

"So, nothing's wrong with her?"

"I mean, mentally, there's a lot wrong with her," he said.

"How are you two doing?" Irma asked, suddenly—noiselessly—appearing at Julian's elbow. I felt proud of myself for not shrieking in surprise.

"Fine," I said, then added, "And stop doing that."

"Of course, dear. Shall we eat?"

They had started serving dinner in a haze of delicious smells. Imogene organized another table for us, the room settled down, and we all devoured our meals—rack of lamb, fluffy mashed parsnips, green beans with a sweet crunch—along with a few more drinks. There was a nice feeling in the air now, festive and lighthearted. It was amazing how much things perked up when Snookie Smith was elsewhere.

After a chocolate chunk bread pudding that was served with a warm Irish whiskey sauce, Irma folded her napkin neatly, then announced, "Boris has to go see his nephew now."

"Is that some kind of code?" I asked quietly.

She grinned, then pointed at a young guy across the room whose features echoed Boris's. "Do you mind driving me home, dear?" she asked Julian.

"I was planning on coming over anyway," he said.

Irma smiled. "Well, isn't that nice?"

"It certainly is," Julian said easily, and after the three of us had bid Boris good night, we started to make our way out of the club—until we were stopped in our tracks.

Five — Irma

A pair of blonde women and a man in his late twenties descended on Violet in the main hallway, along with young Ryeleigh, who looked vaguely shellshocked, the poor dear.

The two other ladies looked to be somewhere in their forties, but were probably fifty-something, a dash of cosmetic upgrades helping them maintain that façade. Their clothes were this year's fashions, same with their shoes. The handsome young man with them was Asian, with a compact build, and I was not fond of the jaded look lurking in the corners of his eyes.

"This is Norman Tsang," one of the women squealed. "Maura's fiancé. He's an investment banker."

Norman stuck his hand out to shake Violet's. As soon as they finished, the woman threw herself at Violet, kissing each cheek.

"Hey, Stassi," Violet murmured. To Norman, "Nice to meet you. And congrats."

The second woman, not to be outdone, kissed Violet's cheeks four times. Once Violet had recovered somewhat, she completed the introductions. Stassi Kent was Ryeleigh's mother, the second woman was Stassi's best friend, Quinn, and Norman was marrying Ryeleigh's half-sister, Maura, who used to work for Violet. Well, that was nice.

"What happened to Snookie's documentary?" Violet asked Ryeleigh.

Ryeleigh blinked a few times. "I seriously...I have no idea. All the normal footage, I edited that, put it together. The stuff at the end, like, what the...?"

"Who did you give the footage to after it was done?" Violet asked.

I had to admit I was curious to know who had knitted the final version of that movie together, myself, although all I really wanted right now was a stiff drink and to put my feet up.

"I gave it back to the filmmakers after Snookie signed off on it. They brought it here. But..." She took in a wheezing breath. "I don't know what went wrong."

"There, there," I said, patting her on the arm. "It's not your fault, dear."

"Of course not," Stassi said, a practiced smile in place. "We don't want to keep you, Violet, but when Ryeleigh told us you were here tonight, we couldn't believe the coincidence. Maura will be so happy to see you."

"Yeah," Violet said. She seemed a touch more awkward than usual, but perhaps tonight's commotion had been a bit much for her.

"Nice to meet you all," Norman said, although his phone was already out and in his hand. They excused themselves, and our little caucus dispersed. Violet, Julian, and I made our way to the parking lot, eschewing a valet since we all needed to stretch our legs.

Julian was driving one of his father's favourite cars this evening: an older model Jeep, similar to the one I had tucked away in my very own carport. After we settled ourselves inside and no stray sets of ears were listening, I asked Violet if she'd been the one to do it.

"Do what?"

I gave her a look.

She rolled her window down. "No, I did not do anything with that Snookie Smith footage." She even sounded like she meant it.

"Hrm." I sat back in my seat. Violet was a dreadful liar, so if she said she wasn't the responsible party, she most likely wasn't.

"Are you saying it wasn't you?" Violet asked.

I put my hand on my décolleté, meeting her eyes in the rear-view mirror. "I am saying exactly that, dear."

"I dunno…" Violet said. "You looked like you had a plan of some sort before we left tonight."

"Oh, I did," I said with a smile. "My plan was to not throttle Snookie in the ladies' room. And I didn't, so mission accomplished and all that."

Violet threw me a grin.

"What about Viggo?" Julian asked, starting the car and inching us out of the spot. Both he and Violet drove like they were night-blind marmosets, further evidence that they were perfect together.

"What's his motive?" Violet asked. "Or Ryeleigh's?"

"Snookie probably drove Ryeleigh completely mad," I said.

"She looked pretty upset," Violet said.

"That's true. And I'm wondering how someone was able to collect those night vision shots. That was the most impressive, really," I said, wondering if Perrie Kowalczyk had had anything to do with it. She'd been the one to stand up and accuse Snookie of stealing her *Crocus sativus*, plus, everyone knew that Perrie had gone through an extended vindictive phase as a child. But then I remembered the look on Agnes O'Muffin's face when that footage was airing.

"Or maybe Snookie annoyed her film crew so much, they decided it was worth their reputation to show everyone the truth." Violet threw her wavy chestnut hair over one shoulder, then turned to look at me. She had amber eyes, a lovely heart-shaped face, and a beautiful smile when she actually used it. "Oh!" She snapped her fingers. "What about Agnes?

She looked pretty happy when everything was going down."

"Quite true, dear," I said, impressed that Violet had picked up on that particular detail.

"I don't know if I've ever actually seen her smile before."

"She's a very pleasant woman—in her own way," I said, lowering my window as Julian drove us out the club's gated service road instead of out the front. It was a beautiful night, and we all needed some fresh air after being locked inside like sardines for so long.

The winding road meant for the club's vendors and service providers offered more privacy for those of us who used it, and it was a beautiful section of land: a thick birch forest on both sides, the sound of the lake in your ears, the wind in your hair. It never failed to put me in a good mood.

Mother and Dad had always driven fast down this particular section of road, especially when it was time for Sunday brunch or regatta races—my favourite events when I was a child. This stretch of road always felt to me like a summer that would never end.

Julian took the road like he was ninety years old and in need of an oil change. But it didn't bother me. It was unlikely that assassins would be lying in the ditches on either side of us, and it was a beautiful night for a drive.

"What's that?" Violet said after a bit, an undertone in her voice that I did not care for. I did not want to see her upset by anything on this particular road. Or the island, really. We'd become acquainted while serving on the board of the Beaver Island Ballet Academy over the past few years, and when she'd expressed a desire to take some time off this summer, I'd been thrilled to host her for a visit. But it was fair to say that things hadn't gone *quite* according to plan.

In my defence, the island had always been relatively quiet and crime-free, at least of the type of crime that would draw the attention of the local constabulary. And moneyed summer inhabitants were always loath to involve public officials in their private matters.

"Stop the car, Julian," I said, my voice urgent.

The brakes squealed.

The back of my neck turned cold. The winding service road leading out of the club had an S-curve at this particular spot. And at the top of that *S* sat a baby blue ten-year-old Ford on the side of the road, its lights pointed at the paved shoulder, the driver's door yawning open. It was a four-door sedan, in pretty good shape, with Newfoundland plates.

I already had my seat belt off and was out the door. After a little squat that warmed up my Achilles, I retrieved the package I'd stowed under Julian's car earlier in the evening, a .22 with a pearl handle.

Sadly, my favourite handgun, Vera, had gone overboard after Violet and I had been ever so slightly shipwrecked recently. But Tallulah was almost as good. She was small and quiet, and we'd been through a lot together. Handguns were quite restricted in many parts of the country, but that only meant it was important not to get caught with one.

"Stay here," I said, hearing a tone of authority make its way into my voice. I'd had many specialities during my long career, but my favourite had always been risk prevention. Making sure nothing bad happened to civilians. Bringing everyone on my team home alive. And helping punish the guilty when needed, of course.

After snapping on a pair of latex gloves, I fished a little telescoping mirror out of my handbag, took hold of my gun, and let the bag fall to the ground. The mirror was on a slender metal stick, a tiny flashlight at the other end. I clicked the light on over Tallulah, so I could be sure of what I was looking at.

"Irma—"

I put a hand up for silence.

The Ford's trunk was slightly ajar, and I flung it open quickly, pointing Tallulah at its interior.

There were no dead bodies in it, and no live ones either. A quick scan of the trunk showed that the jack was missing. A perfectly normal state of events, if one was changing a tire. So…where was the person who'd been changing tires?

The road and shoulder near the car were clear, but I did not care for the shadows reaching for me from the woods on the passenger side. I circled the car slowly, my gun at the ready. There was no driver anywhere.

I took another look at what was lit up with the Ford's lights. Fresh tire tracks marked the shoulder, leading off the road, then back onto it. Most likely another car had been parked there. Had the driver of the Ford left in someone else's vehicle?

I took another look at the stretch of grass between the shoulder and the woods, sweeping my torch across the grasses.

There. A large lump lay in a depression.

And a gush of adrenaline hit my system.

If there had been an attempted carjacking or something similar—unlikely, considering the types of cars clustered behind the club's gates versus the Ford in front of me—the driver could be injured.

I took a few steps closer, then directed my flashlight toward that log-looking thing in the ditch. A car jack rested on the grass beside it.

Sadness briefly bloomed in my core. The dead man was in his late fifties, a baseball cap obscuring part of his face, wearing jeans and a white t-shirt, blood staining the back of it. Even so, he reminded me of the gentleman Boris and I had noticed at the club.

After Julian had snapped on some gloves and confirmed that the man was no longer among the living—most likely because of the two close-range, small-calibre gunshots to the base of his skull—we called 911. Julian, of course, felt terrible for contaminating a crime scene, although as a medical professional, he'd really had no choice.

While we waited for the police, I liberated a go-bag from behind a trunk compartment I'd had installed in Julian's jeep the last time he had it detailed, exchanging it for Tallulah. Best not to give the local constabulary anything to get in a snit about.

Behind us, an ambulance and two police cars zoomed down the road, lights flashing, sirens blaring. They came to a halt twenty feet away. Doors opened, and a police officer emerged from each vehicle.

Both were a surprise to see. One was Walter Rudinsky, the station's desk sergeant, a man who didn't go more than five minutes without his eyes on a wall clock and his keister in a chair.

The second was Mavis Pickle, the island's police chief.

"Yoo-hoo, Mavis!" I waved, delighted to see her. The chief had been suspended from duty after Igor Ivanovitch, one of the island jail's inhabitants, had decided that captivity just wasn't for him. I still had a bone of my own to pick with young Igor, whom I suspected was still on the island. In my defence, it had been a very busy summer.

"Irma," Mavis said drily, slipping booties on her feet then tossing the box to Walter, who missed the throw completely. Then she moved toward us, a determined look on her face.

Six — Violet

Officer Rudenko slowly approached the Ford, a spool of yellow crime scene tape in one hand. Behind him stood Chief Pickle. She was a little older than me, probably, with a tanned complexion and a trim figure. Her shoulders were thrust back, and either she was really angry or she'd spent a lot of time outside lately.

"I do believe she got some sun on her vacation," Irma said cheerily.

"Let's all walk toward me now, please," Chief Pickle said, her voice crisply authoritative.

I moved, Julian with his hand hovering at my waist. Irma marched past us, her hand thrust out toward the chief, and the two of them shook hands before Irma and I were ushered into the back of one of the squad cars. Julian stayed at the scene, switching into doctor mode.

"Hi, Violet," Officer Matthew Jones said from the front seat. He was ten or fifteen years older than me, with short black hair and an average-sized frame.

"Hey," I said.

"How was your vacation, dear?" Irma asked.

Jones started a rambling monologue about his fishing trip while whisking the two of us back through the club's side gate, then out the front entrance.

At the station, I was settled into the "nice" interrogation room, while Irma was shuttled down the hallway to the one with the flickering light bulb that always made me feel like I was about to have a seizure.

Officer Jones told me he'd be back soon to take my statement. Was it bad that I knew exactly how all this was going to go? Was it wrong that the unease I usually felt when confronted by people in uniform had dimmed somewhat over this crazy summer? Maybe I was actually getting better at all this Irma stuff.

I rummaged through my bag and grabbed my phone so I could entertain myself while I was waiting. I had recently become addicted to a Match-3 game that was essentially ruining my life. But as I lifted the phone up, a note slipped onto the floor. Frowning, I picked it up. In incredibly neat penmanship, the note said: KNOCK IT OFF, VIOLET.

I tried not to giggle. Not appropriate, given the circumstances. But last week I'd tried to give Irma some rent money and failed completely, so I'd had to spin up a mission to get the money to her somehow. First, I'd shoved an envelope under the front door of her flat while she was asleep. I was a night owl; the only time I was alert and Irma wasn't was about three in the morning, so I'd gotten away clean on that one.

In response, she'd crossed out the IRMA I'd written on the envelope and written: YOU'RE STAYING HERE AS A FAVOUR, VIOLET. Then she'd stuck the envelope inside my microwave, where I'd found it in my deadbolted apartment the next morning while heating up a pizza pocket for breakfast.

It had taken me a while to figure out how Irma had made her way into my apartment, but eventually I remembered the suction-cup shoes she'd used earlier in the summer to scale an Airstream in the world's fanciest trailer park.

That, or she'd walked right through a wall to do it.

"You doing okay?" Officer Jones stood at the entrance to the room, smiling. He held a glass of water in one hand, a computer tablet in the other.

"Yeah, thanks."

"Seems like you and Irma got up to some stuff while I was on vacay," he said, taking a seat.

"Mostly Irma."

"I hear that." Then he launched into his we're-going-to-need-a-statement spiel. "So, what did you see tonight?"

I folded my hands in my lap. "Not much, honestly. Julian was driving me and Irma home, and we saw the car on the side of the road."

"Abandoned."

"Yeah. It was in this loopy part of the road, so we could see it from pretty far away. All the lights were on, and the door was open, so it was obvious that something weird was going on."

"And what did Irma do?"

"Um…she just walked around and took a look at everything." Which was the truth, if you forgot about the gun and Irma's decades-long spy career. Irma was fond of the local police, but I didn't know this guy. And I didn't want to say the wrong thing.

Officer Jones smiled, then crossed his arms. He sort of reminded me of one of those small-town police officers from the '50s you could see on reruns, simple and squeaky clean. It was a bit of a mystery how he got along so well with Irma. "Anyone else there?"

"No, not that I could see. It was pretty dark out, though."

"Could someone have been hiding in the trees?"

I tried not to shiver. "I…I can't say. I don't think Irma saw anyone."

"What did you do when she went to check things out?"

I shook my head. "Nothing. I didn't even get out of the car."

"You sure about that?"

"When Irma tells me to stay in the car, I stay in the car."

He grinned, then tapped the tablet a few times. "So," he drawled, "I heard about that brouhaha at the club tonight."

"Right."

There was a moment of silence I didn't quite know how to break.

"Snookie Smith got exposed for all her gardening shenanigans, I heard."

"From who?" I asked.

"People," he said vaguely. "There was some sort of video played?"

"Yes."

His facial expression was hard to read.

"Yes, Officer Jones."

He held up a hand. "You can just call me Matty. Everyone does." Then he threw me a smile that he probably thought was charming.

"Okay."

He cleared his throat. "So, I hear you're a big-time tech guru."

"Not really."

Some more throat clearing happened. I pointed at his glass, and he took a sip of water.

"Who would you call a tech guru?" he asked.

"I dunno. Steve Jobs? Linus Torvalds? Shigeru Miyamoto?" I said.

"I know that Jobs guy, but the rest…"

"I just have a small local company. Those guys changed the world."

"Solar power could change the world," Officer Jones said.

I tried not to get excited. Renewable energy was one of my special interests, and I could talk about it for hours. And I do mean hours.

"It could," I finally said, voice careful.

"I was at the deli recently. You know Epstein's?"

"Yeah, they have those amazing smoked meat sandwiches." Irma had taken me there for lunch soon after I'd rolled into town: a lean smoked meat sandwich on rye with a hint of mustard for her, fatty with a slather of yellow for me. "And their coleslaw is amazing."

"It is, I agree," he said with a smile. "I was in there the other day, and some guy from Sisu Solar was yapping about the build they're doing here on the island."

I had a moment where my heart stopped completely. Sisu Solar was a Scandinavian tech firm that built wind and solar farms, many of them offshore and aquatic. I'd heard recently that they'd been surveying the waters near Beaver Island.

"I'll have to start following them on social media," I said.

"Prob'ly makes sense," Officer Matty said with a lopsided grin. "Especially since he was talking about you."

I made a small wheezing noise.

"You invented some solar thing? I dunno, but he was talking about it to some lady."

Sisu Solar had a set of siblings at the helm, Finnish twins so pale they reminded me of Mrs. Sepp, Irma's quirky Estonian expat neighbour.

"Wow, that's amazing."

"It is. But you don't want them to hear you did something bad to Snookie Smith."

I jerked my head up to meet his eyes. "Uh, what?"

"Snookie Smith is saying she wants to file harassment charges against you and Irma."

"Can she even *do* that?"

"She can try," he said, "and sometimes that's all it takes. So, just between the two of us, did you fudge some footage in Snookie's video and—"

"No!"

"And—"

"Nope."

"But the—"

"No, seriously, no. I had no clue she was even working on a video project."

"Well, you were at the club tonight."

"Irma told me to come along because we were going to have a nice dinner and there was going to be a tribute to her mom. That's it."

"I see." He tented his fingers. "Well, who *would* know how to do that kind of thing?"

I gulped. Should I tell him about Ryeleigh? I came from a world where nobody squealed on anybody. Ever. "Can I have some water, please?"

"Sure," he said with a smile, then ducked out of the room.

Unease fluttered in my chest. I couldn't get Maura's sister in trouble, could I? And if Snookie was as mad as the officer was saying, she'd narc on everyone who'd been involved in her mini-movie and the officer would find out who'd worked on it anyway.

Officer Jones came back in the room and handed me a mug full of water. I drank it down in one go and placed the empty mug carefully on the table in front of me. I was still parched.

Finally, I took a deep inhale. "It's not hard to combine data streams, which is really all film editing is. Almost anyone could do it. The real question would be who shot that extra footage. And that I can't help you with."

He scrawled something in his pad, and we went through a few more details about the town's most recent murder scene. After he'd written up my statement, I signed it. Trying not to think about what Irma was up to.

Seven — Irma

I do believe I'm being sweated. It was a strange
thought, since I had never been in law enforcement
and didn't know much of the lingo. It was just a term
I'd heard when I was watching a police drama.
NYPD Blue? Murdoch Mysteries? Something like
that. Looked like it was high time I checked out a
few books about police procedure from the island
library. Agnes O'Muffin would be thrilled to lend a
hand.

I sighed, then took a minute to assess my
situation. I was very lucky I'd had time to grab the
little go-bag I kept in Julian's trunk before Violet and
I were shuttled inside the police station in the dead
of night. Well, not quite, but the sun was going down
earlier and earlier these days, so it was fairly dark
outside now.

I rustled inside the go-bag and pulled out a bottle
of water. Then I wondered if I'd been put into this
specific interview room on purpose. I must admit I
smirked at the thought. Unless Mavis planned on
shooting at me while the lights flickered and the fans

rattled, I was probably going to survive her interrogation.

I popped an electrolyte pill in my mouth and swallowed. It wasn't a perfect fix, but it just wasn't possible to keep my beloved protein muffins in Julian's car, for obvious reasons. But the electrolytes would keep me peppy for a bit, anyway. Luckily, Violet, Julian, and the rest of us had been stuffed with the most divine dinner. I could last for quite a while on that.

I also had a novel in the bag for situations just like this, so I pulled it out and started reading. I normally enjoyed pulpy bestsellers, things with a lot of action, but Violet had nudged me toward a Toronto sci-fi writer, and I was digging into her latest. If the Pickle was going to leave me here to dangle in the breeze, I was at least going to absorb some culture while I waited.

Seventeen minutes later, Mavis Pickle strode into the room. She looked good. Rested, even. It was lovely to see she'd leveraged her recent suspension from duty into a vacation.

"You look very nice, dear," I said to the forty-something chief. "Have you gotten some sun?"

Mavis's hair was pulled back into a feature-tightening bun, just like usual. Her olive skin was deeper today, a splash of red on her cheeks that might be the result of outdoorsy pursuits, or perhaps a bit of irritation at someone in the station.

Surely…she couldn't be irritated with me? I'd done nothing but help Mavis ever since she'd come to town. Although the two of us were wary with each other, she was a solid officer who cared about the people in the community. I respected that.

"I'm quite irritated with you," she said, as if she had been reading my mind.

"Dear?"

A long, meaningful sigh left her body. I took another sip of water—not so much that I would need to go to the bathroom any time soon, a need that could easily be denied if Mavis got cranky with me.

She placed a file folder between her hands, lining it up against a grid I couldn't quite see. "Would you like to tell me how you've been found standing over yet another dead body?"

I pursed my lips. Would I? Not particularly. To be honest, I'd prefer to collect Violet and Julian and go home and have a nice big drink. Plus, then Julian would be able to spend some more time with Violet—unless he'd been tapped to autopsy tonight's victim.

"It's not a multiple-choice question, Irma," Mavis said quietly.

"I'm trying to think of a nice way to say that I don't, really. We left the banquet to get some peace and quiet, and—"

Mavis held up a hand. "What did you do to Snookie this time?"

"Nothing. She was the one who pulled the tablecloth off my table, soiling our belongings and whatnot."

Mavis leaned forward and splayed her fingers on the table. "I'll bet you a hundred dollars that you saw Snookie coming and got out of the way in time."

"I don't know if that's the nicest thing to say, dear." Briefly, I wondered if Mavis and I needed to do some sort of therapy together. She might just benefit from it. "And you do seem unhappy with me. Perhaps you could tell me why that is, so we can deal with it."

She crossed her arms. "I don't understand how you got mixed up in another murder while I was on vacation, and how you ended up standing over yet *another* dead person tonight, someone who died violently." She saw the look on my face, then held up her hand again. "Especially considering your history."

Briefly, my jaw clenched. It was just my luck that the Pickle had an uncle in MI6 who'd decided to spill the beans about the fact that I'd been an intelligence asset during my government career, not a supply chain manager like I—and that very same government—claimed.

"Snookie had a memorial to my mother scrubbed from tonight's program," I said crossly. "So I decided to go home and consume an adult beverage. Is that all right with you, dear?"

I kneaded my forehead for a moment. I didn't
want to get annoyed at Mavis. It wouldn't help
anything, and would most likely make things much
worse. Plus, I really was getting tired.

"I'm sorry about your mother's memorial," Mavis
said. And then she let a silence grow between us.

If I had been twenty-three and green, I might
have broken that silence. But there was no way I
would do any such thing now. So it was a not-short,
not-pleasant moment.

Eventually, Mavis cleared her throat. "I
appreciate that you were able to help root out a
problem on my team—"

The problem she was referring to was the fact
that one of her officers had developed a penchant for
bumping off islanders.

"—and help prove that Igor Ivanovitch's jailbreak
in June was successful due to a criminal act from
someone on the inside of the force. My force."

"Well, you're very welcome, dear. Are we all done
now?" I made as if to rise. I knew she'd tell me to sit
back down, but perhaps she'd get a move-on with
regards to her interrogation. The left side of my
bottom was falling asleep.

"Sit."

I hovered.

"Please."

After raising my shoulders in a conciliatory
manner, I sat.

"I *am* grateful for all that, Irma. But how is it that we have a brand-new murder on our hands?"

"I can't imagine, dear. Such things are not even close to being in my wheelhouse."

"Don't you think it's odd?"

"Not particularly."

She put her head in her hands. Really, she seemed most unhappy. "Well, it is odd, Mrs. Abercrombie, it surely is."

"Please call me Irma, dear. I do find it somewhat odd, I suppose, but I'm no stranger to dead people. Although I *was* a stranger to the gentleman who lost his life tonight."

"Never met him before?"

I shook my head.

"Never saw him before?"

There was a beat.

"I believe he was at the banquet," I said carefully, "but I can't say for certain. I only saw him briefly, from far away. He had a similar build as the victim and the same sort of hair, but he was wearing a suit at the party, and the man we found was in jeans and a t-shirt. Plus, John Doe had a baseball cap covering most of his face, so…"

"You didn't move the hat?"

"Most certainly not." And it was even the truth.

She thrummed her fingers on the table.

"So, who was the victim?" I asked. "What was his name? Where was he from—"

She held up a hand.

I squared my shoulders. "Well, as a private citizen, surely you can understand how worried I am about these sorts of things."

"This is an active investigation, so I can't share any information with you at this point."

No matter. I'd have any details I needed about five minutes after I left Mavis's interrogation room, which was why I might have looked a little smug when I sat back in my chair.

"And neither can Dr. Julian Harper."

"Of course, dear." Perhaps I was a bad person, because it did not bother me that Julian sometimes spilled the beans about the recently deceased. Medical privilege was all well and good, but Mr. Dead Gentleman was in no danger from me knowing a few tidbits about his demise.

I had no intention of pulling Violet into a non-nerdy investigation, but I did have a bit of spare time on my hands these days to ask a few questions, especially when the safety of the islanders was at stake. Plus, I'd always been a curious sort.

"What did you notice about the man at the banquet?" Mavis asked.

"I couldn't tell who he was the guest of. He seemed to be on his own."

"And what did you make of that?"

I raised my shoulders a fraction of an inch.

"Did he set off any alarm bells for you?" she asked, a faux-casual note in her voice. Her eyes were intense. More so than usual.

Perhaps that was why I decided to answer honestly: "Yes."

Mavis, who always had excellent posture, straightened her shoulders even further.

"Who was he, dear?" I asked.

"No ID on the body. Someone took his wallet."

"It's not in the car anywhere?"

A head shake.

"Huh. Any other valuables missing?"

"He had a fairly cheap watch, but there was some cash tucked in a little compartment under the driver's seat."

"Hard to find?" I asked.

"Not particularly."

"How much?"

"Ten thousand dollars." She tilted her head.

"Good heavens!"

"Exactly."

"Well, that certainly does seem like a pickle for you, dear," I said cheerily. "I'll leave you to it."

"Aren't you concerned about a killer running around on the island?"

"I have faith in you, Mavis, and you do look very refreshed from your time off."

"Uh-huh." She let those crossed arms loosen a titch. "So, I'm not going to bump into you at any point during my investigation?"

I held my hands up and smiled. "Of course not."

Her eyes narrowed.

"Oh, Violet will absolutely murder me in my sleep—or at least she'll try—if we get hooked into another investigation. She's quite retired from crime investigation. And so am I."

"You sure about that?"

"She threatened me quite profusely after our last adventure."

"I see." She cleared her throat. "While I've got you here, did anything else that was strange happen at the banquet?"

I took a minute. "They're having some problems with the announcement system. Imogene almost went out of her mind."

"I see. Nothing else?"

"Not that I can think of."

"I hear that some…unfortunate footage ended up in Snookie's presentation. Do you know anything about that?"

I burst out laughing. Honestly. It took me a minute to stop, and every time I looked at Mavis's face—and let's just say she was not amused—I'd start up again.

Eventually, I composed myself. "I can barely program my alarm clock, dear. I most certainly did not tamper with Snookie's video, which was professionally produced, you know. Perhaps you should speak to the directors of her little docudrama if you feel like a crime has been committed. Although I do wish you could tell me what crime that might be."

"Snookie is saying that it's libel. And criminal harassment."

I snorted. I couldn't help it. "I have never been more innocent of anything in my entire life, dear." Then another laugh escaped me—in snort form, I had to admit.

"What about your roommate, Violet?"

I pressed my lips together to keep from smiling. "She's really more of a houseguest, dear."

"She's an engineer with a master's degree. Which she had by the time she was, what, twenty?"

"Something like that. But she didn't do it, dear."

"It seems to me that Violet would do quite a bit for you."

"How nice of you to say. I'd do the same for her," I said, somewhat surprised to realise it was true. When Violet had originally agreed to come for a visit, I was thrilled. We'd always been friendly during our Beaver Island Ballet Academy board meetings, but the way she talked…mostly about work. So many things I mentioned she wasn't aware of, mostly fun things—*outdoor* things.

She was well read and kept up with the news but never seemed to have time for any fun. Which was what I'd planned to show her during her visit. What I hadn't realised was how brave she was, or how reliable. And she also had an excellent sense of humour, which could not be discounted in these troubling times.

Mavis continued: "If she had plans like that and told you about them..."

I slammed my hand on the table. Mostly for dramatic effect, but there was a little heat gathering at the back of my neck, I had to admit. "Poppycock. You are not going to sit here and try to blame me for things we all know I didn't do. I'm surprised at you, Mavis."

That surprise was mirrored in her features. "Because you think I owe you?"

"Pardon *me*?"

She crossed her arms and sat back in her chair. Her eyes were hard. "For ferreting out a bad seed on my force. For clearing my name."

Ah. I crossed my arms to mirror her and leaned back in my seat before giving up and folding myself forward again. Really, it was not a comfortable chair. "Let me tell you something, young lady," I said softly. "You don't owe me a bloody thing. There was a very convincing fraud on your force. The only thing that person did all day long was lie to people, with a bit of murder thrown in during their off hours. I did the right thing, and it needed doing. If you don't feel indebted to me as a result, that's just fine with me. And now the island is safer for all of us."

"Except for the dead man you just found."

"Exactly. Except for him, it's safer for everyone. You really can't win them all, dear."

"I don't think I'll ever understand you, Irma."

I smiled at her use of my name. It was a tiny crack. A minuscule breach in her defences. "Most people don't understand me, dear. I've never really found it to be a problem."

The Pickle's arms uncrossed and her hands went back on the table. "So, you aren't going to be meddling in my investigation?"

"Of course not," I said, sliding the strap for my handbag over my shoulder. And I most certainly meant it.

At the time.

EIGHT — VIOLET

We took a cab home from the police station since
Julian was heading to the clinic to help Dr.
Angelique Beaulieu with the autopsy. I tried a few
times to strike up a conversation with Irma, but she
kept shooting meaningful looks at the cab driver.
After she mimed strangling me if I kept talking, I
decided to zip it.

It was after eleven when we got home, and a chill
was in the air. It was two weeks before Labour Day,
but the nights were already starting to get colder.
Summer was almost over.

"Let's have a fire," Irma said cheerfully.

"You read my mind."

She shuttled us both into her cozy main-floor flat,
where all the framed snapshots and artwork
competed for attention. Her furniture was older but
in impeccable shape and very comfortable. Good
leather, nice club chairs, a treasure trove of
handmade blankets, and a metric ton of doilies.

Irma's flat took up a corner of her house's main
floor, the rest of which held a formal parlour along
with a dining room and kitchen, and a few other

rooms. Some of the furniture was ancient and expensive-looking, things I would know nothing about. Milk crates had been a staple of my decor for much longer than I liked to admit.

I plopped onto Irma's couch and listened for the clink of her good highball glasses, and she did not disappoint. Once she'd set us—and a little fire—up, she raised her glass in a salute, then took a sip after sitting down in her favourite chair. "I do hope Julian doesn't have to stay up late tonight."

"He doesn't seem to need sleep like normal people," I said, then blushed. It sounded like I'd seen him sleep, which I had not.

"Doctors are like that," she said, looking into the fire, which smelled like heaven and was crackling away. There really was something about gathering around a fire that eased something inside me. Max had always said it was because I was a pyromaniac at heart, but I'd always found the different ways humanity had heated themselves over the ages to be fascinating.

Two hundred years ago, North America would have looked just like this: little fires everywhere. Then energy production became centralised. Now, some of us were generating heat for our own homes again, only now with renewables. I was itching to convert Irma's roof to solar. She had a huge house and a ton of good locations for the new panels my company was about to start beta testing.

The scotch was Monkey Shoulder, and it went down like a symphony. When I got back home, I definitely needed to up my scotch game. I rested the glass in both my hands. It had a weight to it, a sense of tradition and timelessness, something passed down through the generations. The only thing I'd been given as an heirloom had been a long and drunken how-to lecture on how to kite cheques, courtesy of my mother, Phyllis. It was a niche crime that the kids at school hadn't exactly understood.

"Violet?"

"Huh?" I whipped my head around. Somehow Irma had ended up sitting beside me on the couch. I had enough alcohol swirling around inside me that I didn't even scream. "You're creepy when you do that, you know."

"Thank you, dear."

"Not a compliment, Irma."

She lifted her shoulders in that effortlessly elegant way of hers, and I laughed.

"I just wanted you to know," she said, looking into my eyes, "that you and I will not be investigating anything to do with that poor unfortunate man who was gunned down probably while trying to help a stranger in distress."

"Uh-huh." I did not believe a single word out of her mouth when it came to this type of thing, sort of how you'd never believe your best friend who always ate all your Oreos—thanks, Max—even though they promised not to, right before you came home and found them surrounded by crumbs and giggling from a sugar high.

But in this particular case, there was absolutely nothing nerdy or technical about this poor dude's death. What had happened to him was terrible, but terrible things happened to people all the time. And this guy had been a stranger. Just passing through. So Irma's hyperactive over-protectiveness might not actually kick in this time.

At least I hoped so.

"I wonder who it was," I said.

She smiled sadly. "There was a stranger at the club. Someone I've never seen before."

"And?"

"And I do believe he was our victim, dear."

"You aren't sure?" Like I'd told the police, I'd seen nothing, exactly the way I preferred it.

She shook her head. "I didn't want to roll him over in case there was evidence on the body that might get dislodged. Plus, his baseball cap was obscuring his face. Although, if it was that gentleman, he'd changed his clothing before leaving. The John Doe I found was wearing a baseball cap, jeans, t-shirt, sneakers, all very generic. But I do believe it was the same man."

"The Pickle didn't tell you?"

"It's an active investigation, dear. They don't release names unless the family has been notified. Plus, his wallet was missing, so…" A shrug.

"That officer didn't even really ask me about the murder."

"I had a quick word with Matty before you made your statement, dear. He knew you stayed in the car."

"That's nice, but honestly? He seemed more focused on Snookie."

Irma took a sip and nodded, looking at the fire. "Sometimes people need to focus on smaller, easier things." She met my eyes. "When tragedy strikes. Don't forget, Beaver Island has always been a safe place. Matty has barely seen any action at all."

"I guess that makes sense."

My purse vibrated on the couch, and I reached forward to turn my phone off. I needed some peace and quiet. But a smile hit my face after I saw who the text was from.

Vi, can you come out and play tomorrow night? We can grab dinner at my place. —Maura

I laughed, then replied: *You got it.*

YAAAAAY! Three unicorn and seven rainbow emojis followed.

"Who is that?" Irma asked.

"Maura Wong-Kent, the one who used to work for me. Ryeleigh is her sister. She's here on the island, too."

"How wonderful."

"Yeah, except..."

Irma quirked an eyebrow.

"Her ex was at the club tonight."

"Maura's? Is this a bad thing?"

"I don't think so, but I hadn't realized they'd broken up—and she's engaged to someone else now. I just hope everything is okay."

"I'm sure it is." Her expression lightened. "I almost forgot, I have a surprise for you." She rummaged through a box on one of her side tables and let out a noise when she found what she was looking for. "Here you go."

I looked at the strange little tool. It was small enough to hold in the palm of my hand, with a flat plastic circle at one end. "Uh, thanks."

"Well, you're very welcome, dear."

"What is it?"

"A car escape tool. You can use it to shatter your window."

"Like, if you're driving me to the gym and I want to escape, I can just use this?"

She grinned.

"Looks pretty small, though."

"Just put your back into it, dear. The blade on the side can be used to cut your seatbelt."

"And it isn't even my birthday."

"I got a few on sale," she said, smiling. "Another drink?"

"I've had enough, I think. I have to be up early."

"Early for Violet early, or normal-people early?"

"I'm normal."

There was a delicate pause while Irma took a deep sip of her own drink. I had no clue where her tiny body put all the cocktails she imbibed, and there was no point in asking. Probably her liver was as hyperactive as the rest of her.

"Why do you need to be up early tomorrow?" she asked.

I took a minute before answering. Irma had given me some rudimentary lessons about resisting interrogation efforts, along with a stack of literature on the subject, shortly after I'd arrived. I'd been working through it slowly this summer, when I wasn't reading manuals about sailing and new developments in solar energy.

"Maura wants to have dinner tomorrow night, but I have to get a bunch of work finished before I go."

After another sip, Irma set her tumbler down on the coffee table, a chocolate brown boxy thing that looked like it had been a shipping container in another life. An old-fashioned lock dangled off of its front. "The good weather isn't going to last for that long, Violet."

"I know."

"Just don't work too hard."

"Okay."

Now that all that was settled, I just needed to wait until she went to the bathroom or something similar so I could work on my project of giving her some rent money. After such a crazy night, I wanted something positive to happen. I'd originally come to Irma's for a month-long visit that I'd way overstayed. Time to make it right.

It would be easy for me to shove the money under a couch cushion, but I'd already tried that, and it had not gone well. In fact, Irma had written a mildly threatening reply on the envelope and left it in my shower. Then I'd put some cash in her entranceway Ficus, tucked just under the telescoping baton she kept there in case of unfriendly visitors. That, she'd left in my fridge with a smiley-faced sticky note that showed all of the face's teeth.

But tonight I was simply going to slide an envelope into her mail. I'd written a fake letter claiming she'd won some money in a contest. It was hard to think of Irma actually entering a contest, but I was running out of ideas. Now, all I needed to do was distract her a bit.

"What kind of wood are you burning in the fireplace?" I asked, sliding the letter out of my clutch.

"What?"

"It smells so great."

Irma turned her gaze to the logs neatly aflame in the fireplace, and I popped the letter into the pile of mail on her side table.

"It's birch. A little cedar, too," she said.

"It's awesome." I let out a deep sigh, satisfied. I'd finally fooled her.

Nine — Irma

After a nice long run late the next afternoon I made a big pot of tea for myself to enjoy on the back deck. Violet was working, or else I would have offered her some.

I let the tea steep, then poured a cup that I doctored with lemon. While it cooled, I thought about the task in front of me, trying not to be irked. I loved that stretch of road outside the club. Not only had the killer put a pall over the little S-curve, they had snuffed out the life of a young-ish man.

Luckily, there was no technology component to this particular crime, so I would not need to involve Violet whatsoever. And I wasn't really going to get involved myself. Just ask a few questions. I couldn't have a killer romping around the island, could I?

But where to start? The victim had been a stranger, and I did not yet have his name or know anything about him. Well, drat.

"Yoo-hoo!"

My next-door neighbour, Mrs. Sepp, was trundling her canine charge, Mr. Pugglesworth, over to my yard in her good wheelbarrow. Mr. P was zipped into a lifejacket, his tongue hanging out of his mouth, his head adorably tilted.

"Good afternoon," I said cheerily.

Mrs. Sepp was wearing her favourite housedress, a pale cornflower blue with daisies, along with orthopedic shoes so sturdy you could easily use one as a deadly weapon. She wrung her hands briefly. "I am sorry for intruding, Irma. It's just that we were going to use your dock—"

"Don't be ridiculous, Mrs. Sepp. I've told you a million times to make yourself at home here."

"Well, thank you. It's just that I don't see a reason to build a dock of my own. Or perhaps I'm just too lazy."

"Tea?"

Her left side twitched briefly. I hoped she wasn't having any health challenges, although I had no intention of inquiring about it. Mrs. Sepp was a proud, private woman. "No, thank you, Irma."

Well, her loss. I deposited the teapot on my table, then walked down to my dock with them, teacup in hand. Mr. P blinked at me a few times and made that whining noise that meant he wanted to be petted. After Mrs. Sepp eased him into the water, he floated, all four legs limp.

"Swimming lesson?" I asked.

Mrs. Sepp settled herself into one of the Adirondack chairs on the dock. "I have received some terrible news."

Adrenaline jolted through me. I sat down and put a hand on her arm for comfort.

"The vet says that Mr. P needs more exercise!"

One of Mr. P's eyebrows raised, then lowered. Then the second one went for a ride. He knew he was the subject of our little chat, and he knew whatever we were talking about was bad news for him, poor little thing.

"Well, that does make a certain amount of sense," I said gently. I'd tried many times to get Mr. P to actually *walk* on our walks. His reluctance was why I'd acquired a doggie knapsack so he could at least get some fresh air while I jogged. And my attempts to train him as a guard dog had all ended in disaster.

"I know," Mrs. Sepp wailed. "I have failed my poor Mr. P!" Some Estonian ramblings followed this pronouncement.

"It's not your fault," I said. "I've also failed."

"Even when he was very little, he refused to go on walks. He preferred it when one of my boys put him in a wagon and pulled him."

"Sounds like Violet," I said, and we both laughed.

"He does not like to swim, either," she said. Currently, Mr. P was slowly twirling in the water. And doing nothing to stop it.

"No," I said. "No, he does not."

"The cats won't stop moving! But Mr. P..."

Mr. P yipped, turning his head around to try to see us. And twenty feet away, a swan was preening itself. I was keeping an eye on it and the little pug.

Swans could be vicious little things—if that really was a swan and not an aquatic drone.

"I have purchased a tiny treadmill for him," she continued.

"Well, that might work." Or probably not.

"And she wants him to eat this new diet food. She says he is allergic to gluten. But…" She put her head in her hands. With her short white curls and rosy cheeks, she'd always reminded me a little of Mrs. Claus. "He does not like it!"

"Er, no. I don't suppose he does."

Mr. P finally came around. His mouth was hanging open, his tongue lolling to the side. For a minute, he reminded me of my third husband.

"I give him too many treats," she continued. If this didn't let up, she was going to confess every bad thing she'd ever done.

"I do too," I admitted, and the two of us started tittering.

"The vet said I should get a pool and an aquatic exercise instructor," she said mournfully.

"Good heavens, what's wrong with the lake?"

"Sometimes Mr. Pugglesworth feels like it is too cold."

"I see."

She nodded. "And on top of all that, I have a new client who is driving me out of my mind. And Mr. P is always sad when I'm…not as happy as usual."

"Are you sure you don't want any tea?" Tea could be such a comfort for people.

"Thank you, Irma darling. I do not."

"What's wrong with the client?"

"I do not enjoy people who bark instructions at me and change things because they do not know what they want." She held up a hand. "Changing your mind, this does not bother me. But asking for an avant-garde modern design with Victorian details and arid zone flowers…oy," she said, blowing out a sigh.

Mr. P was floating close to the dock, and Mrs. Sepp seemed to feel like that was enough bobbing around for one day. She plucked him out of the water, removed his little life jacket, then rubbed him dry with a beach towel so thoroughly that I briefly worried he was going to be bald when she was done.

"Who's the client?" I asked.

"Norman Tsang," she said, sitting back down. "Nobody you know. They are here just for August. He's just gotten engaged to a lovely young lady, and the flowers are for the party to celebrate this. Or they will be if he stops changing his mind."

"Norman Tsang?" I said, my ears perking up. That was the name of Violet's friend's fiancé. "Is he some sort of floral expert?"

"He's an investment banker or some such. And no, he really knows nothing about flowers or presentation or design or green initiatives, or anything of the sort." In a quieter voice, she added, "Although he believes he does."

"Many people out there think the same."

"This is true," she said, clipping Mr. P's lifejacket together. "And Maura's sister—oy. She is spoiled. So is the mother."

I held my breath. Mrs. Sepp almost never made negative comments about others. "I actually met the sister last night. Ryeleigh, correct?"

Mrs. Sepp nodded.

"She seemed quite nice. Timid, almost."

My neighbour cleared her throat. "Sometimes, Irma, I have noticed that people's true selves only really come out in the privacy of their own homes." Mr. P jumped into her lap. She stroked his head gently. "Who's a good boy? Is it you? Is it?"

I was quite certain that Mr. P was a very good boy—and that Mrs. Sepp had an excellent point about people hiding their true natures when not at home. I, too, had seen this phenomenon. Who knew that intelligence work and floral design had so much in common?

She continued: "Also, I am so busy with this project that I haven't had time to take Mr. P for a good long walk. I've just been putting him outside so he can run around. But he is only sitting, not running."

"I can take him out tomorrow."

"Would you?" She sighed in relief. Mr. P looked from her to me, then launched himself at my lap. He didn't quite make it, but he tried, and that was what was important. I patted his silky fur. "Mr. Tsang does not like dogs at all. I asked him if I could bring Mr. P to one of our meetings."

I raised an eyebrow.

"They are allowing dogs at their engagement party. I believe his fiancée loves dogs. So I assumed that the house—and the rest of the family—would be dog friendly. Alas, it is not."

"That might mean he and his betrothed are incompatible." I took a deep sip of tea. I could tell that Violet thought quite highly of her friend Maura. How unfortunate, if an unsuitable beau had latched on to her.

"True, Irma. Quite true. He seems to behave as if Maura is a…what is the word…possession, I suppose."

I thought back to my discussion with Violet the previous evening while Mrs. Sepp smoothed out the front of her dress. "Is it true that someone was murdered outside the club last night?" she asked.

I nodded, cradling my teacup.

"How terrible. Who was it?"

"I believe it was someone from the party, but I didn't know him."

"What a strange evening you must have had. I wonder who he was."

"Me too." I was focused on my tea, so it took me a moment to connect all my thoughts together.

And then I realized who could help me put a name to the island's latest victim.

TEN — VIOLET

Harbour House was basically insane: Set on a tiny island and attached to the rest of Beaver Island by a little wooden causeway, the huge, fancy-looking house was bursting with enormous windows and balconies—three that I could see so far.

"Wow," I said.

"Yeah, you can see why Norman wanted to host the engagement party here." My former director of HR, Maura Wong-Kent, grinned as she pulled us into a roundabout parking lot back on the mainland, her smile taking up her entire face. It was impossible not to be in a good mood around her. She was much smaller than her half-sister, Ryeleigh, but an enormous personality was trapped in that tiny body. Her hair was dark brown and fell to the middle of her back. Today she was wearing jean shorts and a pink t-shirt that had YAY stamped across the chest, with pink sandals. She was in her late twenties but looked much younger.

Without Maura hitting a switch of any kind, one of the garage's four doors started to lift as we approached. She drove inside and parked, the rolling garage door shutting automatically behind us.

After parking her beloved, mint condition 1977 Austin Mini, candy apple red with pink racing stripes, she threw me another smile. "C'mon," she said, walking us toward the garage's side door. A digital panel mounted on the wall beside it turned from red to green, and the door opened automatically as we approached.

"Fancy, schmancy," I said.

"You ain't seen nothin' yet," she quipped as we stepped through. The door closed itself behind us. "The entire estate is ultra secure, with a high-tech security system. It's pretty groovy."

"Groovy," I echoed, even though "ultra secure" systems always made me a little nervous. First of all, the only systems that really were secure were turned off and in a locked room. And when people depended on technology that wasn't reliable, bad things could happen. I tried to brush those thoughts away. Irma was definitely making me paranoid.

Outside the garage sat two golf carts, a pink two-seater and what looked like a six-seater.

"What are these for?" I asked.

"Whipping around the estate," she said, gesturing at the turning circle in front of the garage and the different driveways spinning off it, toward a tennis court, a pool, and probably an underground bunker of some kind. "Or to get to the actual house," she said with a grin, walking toward the pink golf cart.

I laughed. "I've always been a fan of not using my legs."

"I hear ya." She motioned for me to stay where I was, then slid into the two-seater and backed up, doing a three-point turn and coming to a stop right beside me. Then she started giggling. Soon I was giggling and she was giggling and I didn't even know what we were laughing at.

After we were mostly done, she said, "Hop in."

So I hopped. This was no standard golf cart. The seats were upholstered in leather that was smooth and comforting against the backs of my legs, and there was a roof and slats at the side that could be closed up tight.

"In case it's raining," Maura said cheerfully. "Or snowing. Although the owners normally don't spend the winter here."

So they were summer people. No real surprise there. Even Irma used to be a summer person. The island was packed with them, jetsetters who popped up at one of their homesteads here for a few weeks, then moved on to another five-star abode.

I smoothed down my t-shirt, which had started flapping in the breeze as soon as Maura hit the little causeway connecting the estate to land.

"Wheeeeee!" she squealed as we drove, and the two of us started laughing again.

The house got even more fancy the closer we got. Like it was built to impress, which meant that Maura's fiancé was probably new money, unlike

Irma, whose fortune had been safeguarded by tiny little Abercrombies over the centuries.

As a general statement, I didn't love all the money on the island. It led to an awful lot of bad behaviour: hacked tractors, shipwrecked houseboats, wonky medical equipment, rampaging drones. On the other hand, I wasn't averse to money itself. I'd grown up with almost nothing, escaping my mother Phyllis's home at sixteen and thrusting myself into engineering classes at the University of Toronto.

But now I had a bit of money in my pocket, a few zeros of my own. I owned a small condo in Toronto, a place where real estate was worshipped like it was a religion. I liked good food and wine and excellent company, and…ease. Perhaps some day I'd figure out how to enjoy myself like Irma did. To live well.

"Dinner tonight is gonna be awe*some*! I've cooked some of that chicken molé you like so much," Maura said conspiratorially, leaning her head toward mine. She'd always given me the impression that we were the very best of friends every single time we'd ever talked. It had always made me feel special, and when I'd seen her behave the same with practically everybody else, it never bothered me. It felt petty to be jealous that other people liked being in her sunshine, too.

The trip from dry land to the estate took longer than I'd thought it would—probably because the little cart had the same amount of horsepower as a windup toy—but we eventually arrived. A gorgeous vegetable garden hugged the shoreline, and a small private beach was visible just around the corner. The front of the house pointed east, which meant that the side facing out to the lake would get spectacular sunsets.

"And don't forget about my engagement party this Saturday! You *are* coming, right?" Maura said cheerily.

I made sure not to sigh. Irma and I had been dragged into some wedding shenanigans back in June that I'd barely recovered from. But for Maura, I'd do it. "Absolutely."

We disembarked from the little pink cart. The courtyard we found ourselves in was paved in interlocking stone and looked like it had been recently swept. Come to think of it, the parking area beside the garage had looked the same. This island really was a whole new world: a place where they cleaned the outdoors.

We made our way inside. Almost immediately, she said, "Oooh, this is for you. I forgot to give it to you earlier." She handed me a small pink gift bag from her enormous purse, a fancy designer bag almost as big as that four-car garage. I peered into it: three different kinds of candy hearts. My favourite. Along with two little stuffed beavers who were smooching each other. They wore t-shirts that said *Maura + Norman forever.*

And then Maura was hugging me.

I went limp and patted her back. We could be here a while.

"Ms. Wong-Kent." A staid older gentleman was standing in front of the grand staircase, his hands folded behind his back, the marble floor blindingly polished around his feet. He had an English accent much stronger than Irma's and was a little taller than me, wiry like an athlete. He wore a casual but pressed pair of khakis and a dress shirt, his hair neatly ringed the edges of his head, and he had a nose just big enough to look down on us over. He looked refined and cultured and he was not smiling.

"Hey, Jerrod," Maura said, a grin bursting over her face again. "Howzit hanging?"

Jerrod's stern manner collapsed. First, amusement splashed into his eyes. Then the ghost of a smile took over his mouth. "Quite well, ma'am," he said.

"Stellar!" she said cheerily. "Violet, this is Jerrod, our major-domo for the month. This is Violet Blackheart. She's a genius."

"Uh," I said, raising a hand. "No."

She bumped my hip with hers. "And she has an awesome solar storage device she invented that's going to make her a millionaire."

On paper, I was already a millionaire. Most people who owned real estate in Toronto were. Problem was, none of us could eat our houses.

"Ms. Blackheart," Jerrod said, his voice warm. "I've heard so much about you."

I laughed uneasily. "Yeah, everyone on the island seems to know everything about everybody else."

He nodded formally. "Actually, it is Ms. Wong-Kent who has spoken about you."

"Sure have," Maura said, grinning. "What can I do for ya, Jerry?"

"It's the flowers for the engagement party, ma'am. There is an issue. Mister Norman says..." He trailed off, then flicked his eyes toward me before looking back at Maura.

"But I have molé for Violet..." She exhaled like she was getting rid of every breath she'd ever taken, then nodded. "I'll just be a sec, Vi. Sorry about this. Jerrod, can you scare up a drink for Violet, something that'll go with the molé, and show her to the main balcony, pretty please?" She patted me on the shoulder, then disappeared around one of the house's many corners.

"Of course. Ma'am, what may I bring you?"

"Just Violet, please. How about some white wine?"

"Right away." He walked with me to a balcony on the other side of the house, and made so sure I was seated with the view I wanted that I felt like I was being tucked in.

I took in that spectacular view after he left. The balcony hung over the lake, which was calmly sending its waves to the shore. The deck was covered in upscale, gorgeous lounging furniture, couches that looked like they could be re-arranged in many different configurations, like a full-scale game of Tetris.

All the furniture was plump white cushions over rattan frames. An array of side tables for setting down drinks was gracefully scattered over the space. In one corner stood a huge stone barbecue along with a mini-kitchen.

The decking was done in a deep brown herringbone pattern and the railing around the deck was made of a see-through material so the view wasn't interrupted.

"Ma'am." Jerrod stood slightly leaning over me with a glass of wine on a tray. This was no normal wine glass; enormous and delicate, it could have easily hosted a goldfish.

"Oh, thanks so much." I took it from him, the wineglass's bowl jittering from that tiny amount of movement.

"And thank you for coming to dinner this evening."

I looked up. It had been a pretty normal sentence. What had been odd was his tone of voice. "Uh, of course," I said.

He nodded stiffly, but nicely, at me before withdrawing.

I took a moment to try the wine—excellent, no big surprise—and contemplate Jerrod's tone. *Oh, Irma.* He'd sounded worried. And I didn't think I would have noticed it before Irma had gotten me in her teeny tiny clutches.

Why would Maura's fiancé's butler be worried? Not enough starch for the sheets? Not enough pigs-in-a-blanket for cocktail hour?

I had another sip while my thoughts bounced around inside me and took another look at the patio. It was a luxe hideaway, that was true. But then I spotted the cameras, at least three of them. One was perched on the house and directed at the BBQ area. Another was pointed at me and my chair.

I got up and moved one spot over to the right. The camera followed. *Blech.* I hated being filmed like this.

My next sip went down nicely. And then the wine was gone. I would have just sat here and waited for Maura to come back, but I also needed the ladies' room.

I set the glass down on a side table, hoping it wouldn't get carried away by the wind. I had a strong suspicion that it had cost more than my mortgage payments had, back when I'd had a mortgage.

The small panel mounted beside the sliding doors—the same sort of unit I'd seen in the garage—was a solid red that didn't change to green when I approached.

A tug at the door handle didn't get me anywhere, either.

I was locked out on the balcony.

Eleven — Irma

After Mrs. Sepp and our mutual friend had taken their leave, I made a call, then hopped into my vintage power boat, *Vitamin Sea,* so I could pick up dinner in town, and perhaps run a few little errands while I was there. Mandy McGuire was testing out a new hot sauce at her pub that I knew Violet would appreciate, so the plan was to have Mandy make up a batch for her to eat for lunch tomorrow, as Violet was at her friend's house for dinner tonight.

For myself, I'd have Mandy's island-famous tilapia with roasted summer squash—tossed in a little brown sugar and Farmer Ezekiel butter—along with a crisp summer salad. I'd throw in a few snap peas from my garden and be all set for tonight's supper.

And if I happened to schedule my little trip at the same time as Officer Matty Jones's weekly ice cream run, could I really be blamed? I think not.

The trip into town was rougher than usual. Waves slapped the bow of the boat so hard, I had to sit down at one point. After docking, I wandered down Main Street, taking in all the restaurant patios that spilled onto the sidewalk, the neatly outfitted stores, the overstuffed hanging baskets of flowers in blues and purples and splashes of orange. The shop owners would switch all of them out after Labour Day, which was fast approaching, so I tried to enjoy the last of the summer blooms.

"Hey, Irma!" Officer Matty Jones stood in front of the Brain Freeze Ice Cream Parlour, hands on hips. He was in his late fifties, with a full head of black hair that was greying handsomely at the temples, a cheerful smile and kind eyes. He was a lovely boy.

"Hello, dear. How are you doing?"

"Good," he said, patting his stomach, flat as ever. Matty was a runner like me. "I'm trying to talk myself out of ice cream."

"I was just thinking about having a cone," I lied.

"Really?" he said. "But you don't like sweets. You're the only person I know who's accidentally doing Keto. And enjoying it."

"Well, an interesting life is sometimes about taking risks, Matty. Might I buy you a treat?"

"Sure," he said easily, and we walked in together.

The counter was manned by a local teenager with electric blue hair and an abundance of both freckles and enthusiasm. Matty ordered a Rocky Road mega sundae instead of his usual smaller fare, and I got a single scoop vanilla cone. After selecting a table on the empty back deck with a perfect view—of

ingress/egress points, and also of our beautiful lake—
I raised an eyebrow at Matty.

"What?" he said with a lopsided grin. "I know
that look. You're just buttering me up with ice cream
so you can grill me on our John Doe."

"I can dress it up a bit more if you'd like, dear." I
took a happy lick of my cone. Vanilla, done right like
they did here, was always an exquisite treat.

Matty's spoon was poised over a mound of
chocolate, whip cream, and sauce. After a pointed
look at me, he dove in.

"Any ID on the victim as yet?" I asked.

He shook his head.

"Who owned the Ford Mr. Doe was driving?" I
asked.

Another head shake. "Plates were from
Newfoundland, but they don't match the car. The
VIN's been scratched off, so we're trying to raise the
numbers right now."

"Stolen?"

"Those plates were."

Interesting... "When?"

He pointed his spoon at me. "That, we don't
know. They were taken off a car sitting in a junkyard,
no cameras anywhere, so who knows when that
happened."

"Do you think someone was banking them for
future use?"

"That's the theory."

"Speaking of theories, what does Mavis say about all this? And how is she doing these days?"

"Mavis seems fine. Why do you ask?"

Oh, that was a neat trick. "Just wondering, my dear."

He let out a heavy sigh before attacking a fudge-covered fjord at the edge of his bowl. After that was in hand, he said, "She might be a little on edge."

"Well, I'm sorry to hear that," I said. Mavis had seemed back to her old self during our most recent conversation, but if she was jittery, she might not be at the top of her game, and to deal with the island's latest murder, she would have to be. Lives depended on it.

"What's your theory on John Doe?" I asked.

"I think he was a PI in town on a case, you know, something for one of the richies—"

I cleared my throat.

"Not you, Irma."

"How sweet," I said, the comment about the victim being a private investigator percolating in my thoughts.

"You know, someone trying to find out if their spouse is having an affair, or to prove that one of the step kids has sticky fingers so they can disinherit them, that kind of thing."

"So, whoever the private detective was investigating knocked him off before he could bring their dirty deeds to light?"

"Could be." A shrug. "Or what happened to John Doe might just be an opportunistic crime."

"But there was a considerable amount of money left behind in the car," I said. I'd perhaps watched a few too many A&E crime documentaries earlier in the day, which accounted for some of my suspicions. But it was always a challenge to contort my brain to backtrack and try to figure these sorts of things out.

I'd always had intel dropped in my lap. Had always been more of a do-er than an investigator. Plus, I'd always been more focused on harm prevention. Picking through clues to recreate what had happened and who was at fault was not in my wheelhouse, I had to say.

"Might be," he conceded, "but we can't seem to find a connection between him and anyone on the island."

"How very interesting."

Another shrug.

"Why do you think he was a private investigator?" I asked.

"Because a PI who matches his description has just been reported missing."

"In what jurisdiction?"

"Newfoundland. It was reported by a neighbour. He and the missing PI have a weekly date for online poker. He apparently never misses a game, but he didn't show up last night."

"Does he have an assistant or something of that nature, someone who could shed a bit of light on his current cases?"

"Nope. This guy was analog and old-school and kept his mouth shut."

"What's his name?"

"Like I said, we don't know."

I raised a suspicious eyebrow.

"I can't tell you, Irma."

I tried not to grind my teeth. Without that intel, I was sunk before I even started. "Of course not. Well, our John Doe is quite far from Newfoundland."

"It's only a four-hour flight. Not that long."

"I suppose." I sat back in my chair and contemplated all this information while Matty launched a frontal assault on the last of his ice cream. "Tell me, Matty, what kind of injuries did the body have?"

"Two point-blank shots to the back of the head, small calibre handgun, we think." *Slurp.* "The bullets are being examined."

"Contact burn on the entry points?"

"Yup."

"Any defensive wounds?"

"Nope."

"So, someone was standing right behind him when they did it?" I mused.

"Yup."

"Any other details you'd like to share, dear?"

"No, and I shouldn't be telling you any of this in the first place."

"Matty, darling, do I need to remind you—"

He glanced around the still-empty patio. "You're not going to bring up that time you changed my diaper when I was a kid again, are you?"

"Well…" I raised my shoulders.

"Because Mom swears you were just in the room the one time."

"I was providing her with some much-needed emotional assistance, dear. The situation was worse than a crime scene, I'm quite certain."

"Uh-huh." He eyeballed me warily. "Well, there is one more thing. The car was wiped clean of prints."

I raised an eyebrow. "Someone wiped the car down, but left a large amount of cash behind? More concerned about being identified than money?" It was perhaps saying all that out loud that galvanized my desire to poke around a little more regarding Mr. Doe. Between Igor Ivanovitch—our resident jailbird—possibly still flouncing around the island, and whoever had knocked off our most recent murder victim, I was feeling an ever-growing anxiety for the safety of the island's residents.

"Okay, so it probably *wasn't* a crime of opportunity." Matty dropped his spoon into the bowl. "I guess we were doing some wishful thinking there."

"Don't blame yourself, dear."

"You guys want something else?" The perky teen's head popped out the door, curly blue locks bouncing in the breeze.

"Tea would be lovely, please," I said.

"I gotta go back to work, Irma," Matty said. "But thanks for the ice cream."

"You're very welcome, and may I please see some pictures of the body?"

He coughed, the back of one hand against his mouth. "No."

I tried not to pull a face.

"No chance," he said firmly. "Chief Pickle has, uh, reinforced the importance of not sharing intel with you. But I sure did enjoy that ice cream." With a wink, he left me to my tea.

It was a blow, to be sure. Without access to additional crime scene information, it would be difficult to proceed with my mini mission.

That said, Matty was certainly not my only resource. I finished my tea, then made a few phone calls.

Time to get cracking.

Twelve — Violet

It was a beautiful day, but if a storm had been brewing, being locked out on the balcony definitely wouldn't have been fun. I stuck my face against the patio door, trying to see if anyone was inside and could help, but all I saw were plush lounging chairs, abstract art that made no sense to me, and sky-high ceilings.

I palmed my cellphone and started to dial, but a NO SIGNAL message blinked from the screen. After sighing, I started lightly tapping on the door. I was pretty sure that banging would be gauche. Eventually I knocked, getting a little louder as time went on.

Jerrod eventually passed by, an expression of horror in his eyes. As soon as he walked toward me, the doors sprang open.

"Ms. Blackheart," he said, a worried frown wrinkling his forehead. "I am so terribly sorry!"

"It's okay," I said, feeling relief seep into me. "I just need to use the ladies' room."

"Of course, of course," he said, ushering me in. "Again, please accept my apologies. We are supposed to give a temporary access card to visitors who need it, but I completely forgot about the balcony access."

"An RFID card?" I had a few in my own wallet; the small RFID swipe cards were used at my office and for entry into my condo building.

He tapped a pin on his lapel. "Yes."

"Makes sense. But what are you going to do about all the people coming to the engagement party this Saturday?"

"Mr. Norman is in charge of all that, but we'll make sure to disable any balcony locks, that is certain. My goodness, how awful," he said, throwing me another apologetic look. "Please let me show you to the facilities."

"Thanks."

Jerrod led me down the main hallway, which was dotted with a collection of colourfully mottled art, before stopping so abruptly in front of a panelled door that he had to briefly touch the wall to regain his balance. He was obviously still upset about a guest being marooned outside, even though it really wasn't that big of a deal. "Here you are, Ms. Blackheart."

"Thanks very much." I wondered, briefly, if I was supposed to tip him. But then he took his leave, and I ambled into the bathroom.

It was just a powder room, but it had artfully angled ceilings and a skylight over an enormous palm tree set in one corner. The rest of the room was outfitted with a toilet, a bidet, and a sink I probably could have taken a bath in.

I greatly enjoyed my visit to the facilities, in part because it didn't feature someone jumping out from behind a tree with towels. After I was done, I started making my way back to the balcony. The air-conditioned interior of the house was gorgeous: high ceilings, lush but understated modern furnishings. Lots of room to breathe.

I'd grown up in a series of dingy Toronto apartments, many of them over restaurants or other noisy establishments, before settling in a rooming house near Cabbagetown in Toronto's east end at sixteen.

That was where I'd met my business partner, Max, and we'd scrounged up a living by renting out solar panels and other supplies to rooming houses in the neighbourhood. Freezing in winter and boiling in summer, the attics of those ancient houses were a miserable place to live until we came along. And you could have fit all of the places I'd ever lived—including my condo—into one floor of this house.

I didn't let it bother me. I had more than enough to get by in life, especially since Irma was refusing to accept my rent money, although she hadn't returned my latest offering in a terrifying way yet, so that was hopeful.

But I often had to be cajoled by Max and my other friends to actually spend any of my coin, which was probably a holdover from not knowing where my next meal was coming from when I was a kid. Some habits died hard, and I tried not to get mad at myself for still being afraid to make big-ticket purchases. Some of this stuff was going to stay with me for the rest of my life, I could tell. No reason to let it make me miserable.

Eventually I found myself in a sitting room full of overstuffed white Montauk sofas, with an enormous, artfully distressed coffee table and a bar snugged into one corner. The floors looked like polished oak. I could almost see my reflection in them.

And then I noticed the little orb sitting on top of the bar like a piece of art. A piece of art that was listening to everything everyone in the room ever said, à la Siri or Alexa. I wondered if it was recorded and stored in the house's fancy-pants security system.

A—slightly—older version of both Ryeleigh and Maura approached from the hallway. Stassi. Blonde and socialite-thin, she was wearing a maxi dress that looked casual and careless but had likely cost a fortune. I'd seen a lot of her Instagram pictures when Maura was working for me.

Maura's mom held her arms out. "Violet, darling, how are you?" She air-kissed me once, then twice. Thinking she was done, I moved a little to the left. Unfortunately, Stassi was coming in for a third round and I ended up bonking her in the nose.

"Oops, sorry," I said with a giggle that I had to struggle to stop. Stassi Kent had always made me feel like I was a country bumpkin.

"You look…well, it's nice to see you again," she said, her lips plumped in a smile that generated no actual smile lines. "I'm so sorry I didn't get to chat with you longer at the club last night."

"It was pretty busy." I made an awkward hairball-cough noise.

"Where's Maura?"

"Dealing with some kind of problem with the flowers for the engagement party."

"I see," she said, her mouth briefly twisting into an unhappy expression. "Let's have a seat and catch up a bit."

"I wouldn't want to impose."

"Jerrod!" Stassi bellowed. "Some vodka tonics, please." To me, she said, "You still drink those, don't you?"

"Uh, I—"

"It'll have to be a quick drink, though," Stassi continued ruefully, or at least I thought that was the emotion she was going with. It was hard to know what was really happening when people's faces didn't actually move.

Jerrod appeared in the room, made his way to the bar, and started prepping some hand-coddled cocktails.

"Is Maura's fiancé here?" I asked.

"Yes, but he's tied up right now," Stassi said, making it sound like he was literally tied up.

"Um…okay."

Stassi seemed to be enjoying my confusion, which made something old and junior high-ish bubble to the surface inside me. I could tell we were playing some kind of game, but like always, I didn't really know all the rules. Max had once told me he thought Stassi was just a middle-aged mean girl after he'd gotten too deeply into the schnapps at a Christmas party.

"Helloooo!" a woman's voice trilled. It was Quinn Carter, Stassi's BFF, both arms bogged down by shopping bags. She was wearing a short summer dress over stick-figure limbs, her hair artfully done in mermaid waves.

"Where have you been?" Stassi said, her voice clipped.

Quinn's smile faltered, then righted itself, like a ship lost at night. "I went to get my nails done at Spa Lala."

Stassi's head slowly tilted. Not the way Irma's did. More like she was trying to be as dramatic as humanly possible. "That's the same polish you had on this morning."

A few rooms over, someone started shouting. It was a man, although I couldn't make out who it was. Norman? Probably.

Jerrod leaned over me, tidy cocktails lining his tray. He flinched when the yelling got louder. I took a drink gratefully, and he put the others down on a side table before retreating.

"Hmmh?" Quinn looked up from her phone.

"Your nails," Stassi said. "They're exactly the same as they were this morning."

"It turned out that they couldn't take me," Quinn said. "It was ridiculous, honestly."

"Hmph," Stassi said.

"How's Ryeleigh doing?" I asked.

"She's out on a date with a young man. Viggo something? He's talking to her about getting a computer science degree."

"Oh, nice," I said faintly. Hadn't Ryeleigh asked me for the very same advice? I guessed she'd gotten an upgrade.

In the distance, a door slammed loudly enough to rattle the house.

"There you are," Maura said, emerging from a hallway. The sun took that exact moment to peek out from behind a cloud, backlighting her. Were her eyes red?

"We're just catching up with Violet, darling," Stassi said airily.

"Well, Mom, you know what a busy woman Violet is. And she's got a meeting to go to. We shouldn't keep her."

I tried not to squint at Maura. *What meeting?* She threw me an Irma-style we'll-talk-about-it-later look, so I decided to keep my lips zipped.

"It's been so lovely to catch up with you," Stassi said. "I was sad when Maura had to resign from your company—she enjoyed it so. But she would have had to leave after getting married anyway."

"She would have?" I blurted.

"She and Norman have had a whirlwind romance," Stassi said, like she was narrating a CBC radio docudrama. "But, of course, it's such a good match."

"It certainly is," Quinn said smoothly. "And she won't have time to work after the wedding, of course."

Maura's eyes were the size of flying saucers, but her smile was still firmly in place. "Well, so long, everyone. I'm going to take Violet home now."

Was that chicken molé I could smell, somewhere in the distance? I tried not to feel sad about missing out on Maura's awesome cooking. Something was obviously going on with her and Norman.

I hadn't been overly impressed with him when we met the day before, not with his head in his phone like that, but I'd been hoping I was just being overly critical.

"Nice to see you," I said, and Maura steered me out of the room.

Once we were out of earshot, she said, "I'm sorry about dinner, Violet, but there's a problem with the centrepieces and a whole bunch of party-related stuff, and Norman's all..." She made a gargoyle-ish face, then grinned. "Anyway, I have to go deal with it. I'm sorry about tonight, but after the engagement party is over, we can spend some time together," she said, smiling. But that smile wavered briefly, and I wondered what exactly was so wrong. The petunias weren't co-operating? The vases were on strike? And why would Norman *yell* about something like that?

"It's okay. You know, I was wondering about you and Brandon—"

She waved off my question cheerfully. "Plus, I didn't want Mom to get her clutches into you. Remember how she tried to convince you to get Botox when we did our Bring Your Mom to Work Day?"

"Yes," I said flatly, and Maura smiled. "What did Quinn mean, you won't have time to work after the wedding?"

"Norman wants us to try for kids right away. I want to stay home for the first few years, so…" She started down the stairs.

"Oh." It was a perfectly normal thing to want, so why was the hair on the back of my neck suddenly standing on end?

Thirteen — Irma

Stuart screamed quite loudly when I tapped him on the shoulder. In my defence, I'd let him put down the little saw he'd been holding before laying a hand on him.

He twirled, yanked off his ear protectors, and fixed me with an icy glare.

It didn't last long. Stu was perennially good-natured, plus he knew that if I was really trying to frighten him, he'd be sobbing into his hand tools right about now.

"Sorry, Stuart," I said, settling myself on one of the battered club chairs in the little nook beside his workshop. It was paired with two others huddled around an old industrial spool that now served as a coffee table.

Fishing magazines were stacked neatly in a corner, and all the tools were either arranged on a pegboard—outlined in marker to make sure that each tool was exactly where it was supposed to be—or neatly in drawers. Either Stu's organisation of his workshop was brilliant, or the sign of a personality disorder. I didn't particularly care which one it was. Understanding friends were hard to find.

"Irmie," he said threateningly.

I held out some live bait that I'd picked up from Pieter Degeyter, who was merrily selling the little suckers from his garage a few streets over. Julian had been out of office when I called on him, and I'd needed to stretch my legs, so it had all worked out perfectly.

Stu's face burst into a grin. His Moses-length beard was braided into four—no, five—plaits today, likely courtesy of his grand-niece Annie, a tyrant-tot of the first order.

"Well," he said gruffly, "thanks. I guess."

"You're so very welcome, Stuart." I had taken a "traveller" tea along with me, and I sipped at it. Stu plopped down into the chair opposite me.

"Where's Violet? Working?"

"At Harbour House for dinner with a friend."

"Huh," he said, then added, "I hear ya found another dead body."

I hoisted my shoulders in a *Who, me?* shrug, then waved him off. "I'm not here about that."

He raised an eyebrow.

"I have good news, I promise."

The other one joined it.

"I've been thinking about inviting Edward for a visit." Edward Longbottom was an old work colleague who visited me on the island as often as he could. He and Stu got on like a house on fire.

Now Stu's bushy brows headed for his hairline. "Something wrong?"

"How silly! Why would something be wrong? Would you able to do any fishing with him when he comes? Can you get someone to mind the store?"

Stu's hardware store was a Beaver Island staple. Not only did he provide the residents with all the gardening supplies they could possibly need, he repaired small appliances in his spare time, hence the workshop and all those tools. He had various islanders staff the register when he wanted to faff around with his fishing poles.

"Maybe," he said gruffly, then took a swig from a pink water bottle that had a unicorn horn/straw erupting from its lid, another treat courtesy of his niece.

"Why is Edward coming to town?"

I swallowed my latest sip, then smiled at Stu. After giving Violet that little car escape tool last night, I'd ruminated on getting a few new tools of the trade for myself. Edward was a maestro of intelligence doodads, and with Igor Ivanovitch possibly still on the island, I was feeling the need for a bit of reinforcement these days.

"That smile isn't makin' me feel any happier about all this. Especially since you just tripped over another dead body."

"Well, I certainly didn't kill him."

"And what's all this with the Snookie uproar last night?"

"If you ever came to my club events instead of fishing off the ninth hole instead, you'd already know what happened."

"Ties make me feel like I'm being strangled. You, out of all people, should know how bad that might be."

Well, I couldn't argue with that. "I had nothing to do with Snookie's problems."

"They're calling it Snookie-gate," he said with a chuckle.

"Makes sense," I said, "since it was Tractor-gate that really revved things up between us. Can't I just kill her? Pretty please?"

"If you were still a spook, would you have killed her? Would she deserve it?"

Good heavens, yes, based on my irritation levels alone.

"Hard to know," I said instead.

His eyes narrowed. "So, Violet didn't change the presentation somehow?"

"She says not. And as such a terrible liar..."

"I don't think she'd deny it," he said finally, then took another sip from that unicorn horn.

"No. What would be the point? Violet is irritated that Snookie had me served with Tractor-gate papers, but I daresay she finds the whole conflict somewhat amusing." I finished off the tea.

"You didn't shoot all that extra Snookie footage, did you?"

I snorted. "Hardly. But I have a theory."

He smirked, waiting.

"I think Agnes did it."

"Agnes O'Muffin? Eighty-somethin'-years-old Agnes O'Muffin? Why?"

"She was smiling when that footage was being shown."

He ran a hand through his hair. "A smile? That's it?"

"I have most certainly been wrong before, so who's to know?" I fiddled with my paper teacup. "What do you say, you old sod? Dinner and fishing with Edward? To be honest…"

"What?"

"I think he needs some time away. His niece has run into some difficulty in the past year or so. Opioids, I believe. She was fired from her job and had to run a fundraiser to help get first and last months' rent on a cheaper apartment."

"Well, I'm sure sorry to hear that."

"It's been quite trying for Edward, as I understand it. His mother also had some addiction issues. Died at a young age."

"Father?"

A shrug. "Who knows where he might be."

"Just like Violet," Stu said, eyes hard. Stu, who'd lived a monkish single life but doted on his nieces and nephews, was no fan of men who ignored their responsibilities.

"It is perhaps for the best when men who don't want to be fathers take their leave," I said quietly.

He waved me off. "Yeah, I'd loveta do some fishing with Edward. Summer's almost over, might as well get in as much as I can. Hey, Perrie," he hollered to the front room. "Can you come here for a minute?"

"Be right there," Perrie Kowalczyk sing-songed back to him. She soon appeared at the doorway to the workshop. In her late twenties, she was half a foot taller than I, her dark hair shorn close to her scalp and tinted red, tattoos criss-crossing her arms, a plethora of shiny things poked into her face. Today she had some jewellery running from her nose to one of her ears. "Hey, Mrs. A."

"Perrie, dear. I hope you don't get that piercing caught on any of the machinery in here."

She plopped into a seat beside Stu. A paperclip heiress, she could have easily not worked at all. Instead, she was an up-and-coming industrial artist who dabbled in gardening in her spare time. Stu had taught Perrie how to weld, and she liked to staff the register at the store periodically. Said that the customers helped inspire her work. I didn't quite understand her sculptures, myself, especially the one that looked like a cat grooming its…everything…but it was nice that she was keeping herself busy instead of just raking in trust fund monies.

It had been *her* flowering shrub that Snookie had stolen under the cover of moonlight, but I hadn't yet added Perrie to the list of suspects who'd been involved in Snookie-gate. If Perrie had known who had stolen her shrub, she would not have stayed quiet about it. She'd always had a strong personality, even as a young child.

"You able to watch the store for a few days?" Stu asked gruffly.

A crafty, scheming look took over Perrie's face. I knew I'd always liked her.

"Can I use your new blowtorch while you're gone?" she asked. "I have a piece I'm working on that's...resisting me."

"Of course," Stu said. "Just remember the safety checklist, and make sure all your gear is in good shape."

"You got it," she said, cracking some gum that must have been squirreled away in her cheek. "When are you taking off? I'm doing a Women on Wheels ride tomorrow."

"It won't be for a few days, dear. You have a nice time on your ride."

Women on Wheels, or WOW, as some referred to it, was a collection of local ladies who liked motorbikes and the open road. I found them a little slow going, but even so, I'd joined a few rides over the years and had great fun.

The sound of that sport bike's engine purring outside Imogene's window the night before flitted through my memory. Perhaps it was time for me to get back on my little Vespa.

"You should come on a ride with us, Mrs. A."

"Next time, dear."

"I'll hold you to it. It's no problem, Stu. What sort of adventure are you going on, anyway?"

Stu threw a glance at me. "Just fishing with a friend."

"Well, you have fun with that. And can I do those social media updates for the website we talked about? There'll be a lot of people in town for Labour Day."

"What, now?" Stu asked.

"Why don't I just do the updates, and if anyone comes after you with pitchforks, you'll know it probably wasn't such a great idea after all."

It was a strange business negotiation, but I'd seen odder ones, especially that prisoner exchange back in '83. In my defence, how was I supposed to know that the prisoner we were exchanging for was actually two little people squished together? Circus folk really did have an edge in these sorts of situations.

"Sounds fair," Stu said, and that was that.

Now, all I needed to do was get my hands on those crime scene photos and see if I could get a name for our recently deceased friend. I made a quick call to verify that my next stop was all set up, then was on my way again.

Fourteen — Violet

"It was so great to see you," Maura said, her smile taking over most of her face. "Sorry I didn't actually feed you any dinner. You wouldn't believe how hard it is just to figure centrepieces out."

"Well, at least all the wedding prep will be done soon."

She burst into laughter. "All this is just for the engagement party. I haven't even started on the wedding stuff yet. It's gonna be nuts."

"I never thought you were one of those big white wedding people."

She rolled her eyes. "Norman is. And he says that life is about compromise."

I didn't voice my thoughts that Norman's idea of compromise seemed to dovetail with him getting a hundred percent of what he wanted, and Maura not so much. Instead I said, "Wedding bells might be in the air for your sister, too."

"Oh?"

"She was flirting with the club's IT guy last night. And now they're out on a date."

Maura made an exasperated noise. "Ryeleigh is always flirting with someone."

I slapped my forehead. "I forgot all about that. Didn't she end up dating one of your exes in university?"

"Uh-huh. Ryeleigh's always been in love with love. I try to ignore it, honestly."

"Uh…this probably isn't any of my business, but why did you break up with Brandon?"

She hopped into the little pink golf cart, staring straight forward. Then she said, "Did I show you my engagement ring? It's an heirloom from Norman's family."

I guessed that the Brandon conversation was a no-go, so I took a look at the ring she thrust towards me. It was surprisingly understated, with a small diamond in the centre and a few baguettes on the gold band.

"Norman has this huge thing he wants me to wear," she said ruefully. "But I like this one better. It belonged to his grandmother."

"It's lovely."

She smiled at me, I jumped in, and we zoomed toward shore, Maura chattering happily about Norman as she drove. The wind had kicked up while we were inside and water was lapping at the causeway in front of us, although we still had good clearance. I felt oddly protective of Maura as she drove, which seemed to be manifesting as a tugging in my chest. Norman, if he'd been the one yelling at Maura about flowers, seemed like a complete and

total jerk. And I wanted her to be happy. She
deserved it.

The rest of the ride zipped along. The enormous
four-car garage—and all the neatly swept pavement
around it—awaited us on the other side.

And so did Maura's ex, Brandon.

Maura shrieked. Then locked on to him, pointing
the golf cart right at him.

"Maura!" I said, my heart suddenly thumping in
my ears. "Maura, slow down."

She made a gurgling noise deep in her throat, her
eyes laser-focused on Brandon.

"Maura!" I reached over and tried to steer, my
breath coming fast. When Maura wouldn't take her
hands off the wheel, I pinched an Irma-approved
pressure point between her forefinger and thumb.
She released the wheel just enough for me to jerk the
cart away from Brandon.

Maura got hold of herself and grabbed my arm as
she hit the brakes. I decided to complain about the
whiplash later.

"Sorry," she whispered. "I got tunnel vision."

Brandon was wearing a polo shirt and dress pants
His brown hair was neatly trimmed, and his normally
animated—and handsome—face was quiet, even
though Maura had just tried to run him over. He was
leaning on a nondescript grey sedan and didn't look
mad at all.

"Look," he said. "I know you're angry with me,
Maura. I understand that." He held up his hands in a

gesture of contrition. "But you can't marry this Norman guy. He's no good. He's the one who sent all those emails! He's the one who's been stalking you. Not me."

Cold gripped my throat. *Stalking* her?

"This is private property," Maura said somewhat primly, but anger underpinned her voice.

He held his hands up again. "Look, I'm not going to come any closer. But I wanted you to know that the private investigator I hired to find you has gone missing."

Uh-oh...

"You hired a detective to find me?" she shrieked. For a minute, I worried she was going to back up and run over him with the little cart after all.

"I understand that doesn't sound great," he said, gesturing for calm. "I was going to leave you alone, I was, but—"

Maura's hands were on her hips. "I told you to stay away from me."

He shook his head firmly. "I know. That's why I hired the detective—so I could honour your wishes and still get some information to you about Norman. But when my PI disappeared, I knew I had to contact you, to warn you. But you've blocked me on all your social media. That's why I'm here. I'm worried about your safety."

"Don't you worry about me," she said. "I'm staying in the most secure building on the whole island. The *safest*. So, all you need to do is get in that car and drive away. Right now."

"I understand," he said, opening his car door. "But my PI left me a voicemail yesterday that he'd found out something important. Please don't—"

"Get. Out." Maura had her arms crossed now.

The two of us watched, wordless, as Brandon finally got into his car, did a three-point turn, and drove away.

"I wasted a whole *year* of my life with that jerk," Maura said. *Jerk* was officially the strongest insult in her arsenal, so I could tell she was really upset.

Something in my stomach turned over. "Maura, this is serious. How long has someone been stalking you?"

"Oh, that someone is Brandon. I'm sure of it."

I put my hand on her arm. "Why?"

She let out a breath. "When we first got together, he was great. Picked me up at work, made gourmet dinners, took me to the ballet. We had fun together. He listened to me. Everything was perfect. It was only later that I realized it was *too* perfect."

I slapped my forehead. "I forgot to tell you I bumped into him at the club last night. This sucks. I really liked him."

"Oh, everyone always likes him. But then I accidently opened one of his credit card bills. It was maxed! He tried to tell me it was just a mistake, but there were other envelopes like that one, with red stamps. *Ninety days* overdue, collection notices, all that kind of stuff."

"I didn't even know people still got bills mailed to them," I blurted.

She smiled briefly. "He's always been a bit of a Luddite."

"So he didn't have any money?"

"It's not that. I don't care about that. It's that he made it seem like he was someone he wasn't. He totally lied and said he hadn't spent any of that money. That someone was trying to ruin his credit."

"Did you see any of the charges?"

She shook her head. "He snatched the bills right out of my hand. Told me he was taking care of it, that I shouldn't worry. And..." She sighed again and ran her hand through her hair. "After finding those bills, I started pulling back. I just didn't trust him anymore. A few weeks later, someone started stalking me, taking pictures of me going into the gym, waiting until I came out. Pictures of me at the grocery store, jogging, that kind of thing. And the emails all said that we were meant to be *together, forever.* That's what Brandon used to tell me all the time. It was creepy."

"Do you still have the pictures? Or the emails?"

She shook her head. "I couldn't stand them. I deleted everything."

"You should have called me. I could have taken a look at them and tried to help."

"I know how busy you are."

"I'm just...what if it isn't Brandon? What if it's someone else?"

She sighed. "I don't know, Violet. I get along with pretty much everyone. And I have a hard time thinking a stranger would want to scare the pants off me like that. Plus, Brandon's the only one who knows my schedule, when I'm at the gym and all that."

I gave her a hug. "I'm so sorry, Maura. This sucks."

She straightened her shoulders. "It super *duper* sucks. But then I met Norman. Well, I'd already met him, but just socially. And I was in a bit of funk with all the stalking stuff—Ryeleigh practically dragged me to the restaurant we were at the night Norman and I reconnected. And voila! Now we're engaged." Her smile re-emerged while my gray matter chugged away, thinking about the timing of Maura's romantic escapades and her tendency to think the best of people. If she was fixated on her belief that Brandon was stalking her, she might not be thinking about other options. "Anyway, let's get you home. I'm so sorry about all this."

She motioned for me to follow her to the garage's side door. The sensor mounted on the wall flicked from red to green as we approached, and the door sprang open for us. Maura must have an RFID card somewhere on her, too.

When she crossed the threshold, all the lights flickered on, alerted by motion detectors embedded somewhere in the room. The side door gently closed itself behind us.

Once inside, I took another look around. The garage's floor was made of an artfully polished concrete, and the walls were a calming blue that reminded me of the sky around Beaver Island on a nice summer day. A wall of cupboards at this end of the garage had stylish birdseye maple doors. It was nicer than some of the apartments I'd lived in.

Suddenly, Maura's vintage Mini sprang to life, its engine purring.

"Neat," I said. "Do you have one of those remote starters?"

"I do. There's just one problem."

"What?"

"I'm not the one who turned my car on," she said, frowning.

FIFTEEN — IRMA

I had another errand to run after leaving the hardware store, one that would help shed some more light on the island's most recent murder victim. Naturally, I took the long way around, a borrowed baseball cap from Stu swimming on my head.

On the way, I popped into Luna's Café, where I acquired some of my beloved protein-fibre muffins and a Death by Chocolate cupcake for Violet to have after dinner. Her cupcake consumption had decreased over the past month, but during her first few weeks on the island, she'd spent most of her time face-down in a tray of buttercream.

My transaction with Luna was as pleasant and breezy as usual, and I had a bit of a skip in my step when I left. It was another lovely day. And even though a chill had started to sneak into the air when the sun went down, summer was not over. Not yet.

Main Street was still the same old riot of colours, carefully curated flower baskets, stylish storefronts, and neighbours greeting each other. It was a perfect small-town day.

So why was the back of my neck tingling?

I kept up my pace, glancing into all those chic storefront windows to see if I could spy a glimpse of someone following me. I greeted Lorraine Santos, the island postmistress, as well as Kendelle Chang, the clinic's receptionist. I gave them a little wave as I passed, taking the opportunity to slide my telescoping mirror out of my handbag and cup it in my hand.

Now I had an excellent view of the sidewalk behind me, but all I could see were islanders going about their day. There were a few tourists scattered around the street, but none set off any alarms. Of course, if they were any good, they wouldn't. That was part of the reason I'd worked for so long. Older women were invisible, and that was exactly the way I liked it.

But there were no little old ladies on my tail today, at least none I didn't already know.

I seated myself on the bench outside Raymundo Epstein's deli. I was sitting in this exact spot when I saw the accident that had bounced Violet's brain around her head and injured my dear friend Camille Beaulieu. I made a mental note to call Cami when I got home. I had really wanted her to convalesce on the island. But if Igor, the man responsible for that attack, was still lurking about, I wanted her as far away from here as possible.

Was that Ryeleigh and Viggo having lunch across the street on one of the town's many restaurant patios? It certainly looked like it. Maura's sister had her hair pulled back in a messy bun and was wearing a white two-piece ensemble that showed off a lot of midriff. She was touching Viggo's arm as he talked and looked enraptured. Viggo was a lovely boy, but it was hard to feel happy for them. Mrs. Sepp's comments about Ryeleigh being spoiled were still bobbing around my brain. Maura's sister had seemed almost timid at the club, but had been unpleasant around Mrs. Sepp. Idly, I wondered which one was the real Ryeleigh.

I pulled my eyes away from them and tried to focus on my current predicament. The people who'd been on the sidewalk behind me had all passed by now. I realized then what a help one's cellular telephone could be, and I felt proud that I'd actually remembered to bring mine today. I peered at my phone. Violet had pinned the Beaver Island daily forecast to the main screen, so I launched that. Oh, goodie, it would be beautiful weather tomorrow!

Focus, Irma.

Right. What had set off all that raw, tingly energy, now gathered at the back of my neck? It was a very specific feeling, the sense that one was being followed. It just felt abnormal for it to happen *here*. Nobody had ever surveilled me on the island, except for Snookie when she was trying to best me somehow. I almost felt sorry for her now. Whoever had edited that video file to show what she'd really been up to in her spare time—quickstep and flora thievery—either had known she'd be shunned for

her lies, or had no clue. I was quite curious to see if
Agnes had masterminded the big reveal, but perhaps
it was best not to unmask her if she had. It was never
a good idea to irk a librarian. They knew things.

More passers-by ambled past me. No one looked
suspicious; no ankles were bulging, no one was
taking surreptitious pictures, no one was talking into
their sleeve. The street was clean.

So why was I so twitterpated?

I gave it another five minutes or so, taking in the
other side of the street as I tried to analyze the traffic
and see if anyone had been lurking in the shadows or
following me.

The buildings on Main were two or three stories
high, some with lovely apartments over main-floor
retail space, although some stores took up the entire
three floors. Perhaps there was a shut-in with a pair of
binoculars who was watching everybody, not just me.

But if it was someone up to no good, the islanders
on the street might be in danger.

I huffed out a breath, then got to my feet and
continued down the road, listening for footsteps at
the same pace I was walking. I knelt down to re-tie
my left shoe, sweeping the street behind me to see if
anyone was there. But it was just a bunch of
islanders.

Drat.

I walked back down Main, pretending that I
needed more muffins, which, to be frank, I probably
did. But none of my machinations bore any fruit. It

was most vexing. I almost wanted to call Boris to come and help me flush them out, then discarded the notion. I was probably being paranoid.

Eventually, I went north, into the town's residential area. I was able to approach Bianca Westcott's property from the rear entrance, as neither one of us wanted anyone to see us together. She must have forgotten to leave the back door unlocked, so I had to slip into her granny's garage through a window that, admittedly, was getting harder to squeeze through as I aged.

It wasn't that I'd put on weight; the issue was that I was growing ever more concerned about the healthy state of my hips. Plus, my knee had been bothering me all summer, and the cortisone injection Julian had given me a few months ago seemed to have worn off somewhat. I was reluctant to ask for another, lest he lecture me more about slowing down a bit. I'd have plenty of time for slowing down when I was dead.

I jimmied the back door and slipped off my shoes, as Bianca's granny hated outdoor footwear in the house. Bianca was sitting in the living room, a pot of tea at the ready. She knew I liked it strong. Her own cup was full, steam wafting into the air.

"I poured mine already," she said with a wry grin. "Coward."

She threw her head back and laughed. Bianca was a police support worker and had been off on vacation for most of the summer. It looked like she'd had some work done while she was gone. Her eyes had that "refreshed" look so many islanders had, and I briefly wondered if she'd financed that work with some of the lucre I'd bribed her with over the years, a scenario that had benefited us both. I didn't avail myself of her services often, but in emergency situations like the one I currently found myself in, I was happy that she and I were sympatico.

Bianca was a stout five-five, with hazel eyes and excellent hearing. She favoured no-nonsense flannels paired with cutesy shoes that would most certainly not help her flee were a terrorist to attack her, but I'd mentioned it once and then let it go. Bianca was a woman unafraid of bluntness, a quality I very much appreciated.

"Here," she said, pointing at the file folder resting on the coffee table beside us. "I made a copy for you."

"Thank you, dear." I let the tea continue to steep, then picked the folder up.

"I thought you might like to take a look at the crime scene photos. You know, from the latest dead body you've found. Quite a summer you've had, I hear."

"Quite," I echoed. "Muffin?"

"I'd rather not, thanks. Those things don't agree with me."

"Fibre is an essential part of one's diet, dear."

"That's a no from me, Irma."

"Understood."

The crime scene photos were stacked at the end of the file. There were a few written reports, along with our statements. Thankfully, Bianca just thought I was a nosy old lady. Or I paid her enough that she didn't ruminate on it too much. Either way worked for me.

"You can take it with you," she said, fairly cheerfully for someone who'd skirted the law to give me this intel. Of course, when Chief Klein was in charge, he'd been willing to look the other way when I procured information from his department. The Pickle might actually pickle Bianca if she found out about it.

"Thank you, dear."

She blew on her tea. "Welcome. Are you ever going to pour yours?"

"Not ready yet."

"It's ready."

I looked up from the pictures with a smile that didn't reflect the grim images in front of me. The deceased had most certainly been the same man Boris and I had noticed at the banquet. "Both the tea and the drinker have to be ready, dear."

"I'm not even gonna ask what that means," she said with a barking laugh. Then, slyly, she added, "You the one who mucked with Snookie Smith's video footage?"

I flipped over another photograph. John Doe had no look of surprise on his face. *It was a woman*, my senses thrummed in my ears. *Someone non-*

threatening. But those weren't always the same thing, were they?

I looked up. "No. Not me."

"What about that computer chick who's living with you? She your niece?"

"I'm an only child," I said, my gaze back on those pictures. "Any highlights you want to tell me?"

"Doe was in pretty good shape for his age. Some callusing on the hands and feet. The clothes could have been bought anywhere in North America. He was wearing off-market sneakers. No debris under his fingernails."

"It's odd he'd allow a stranger to stand behind him like that if he was a seasoned investigator."

"Maybe it wasn't a stranger."

"Perhaps." I crossed my arms. "Do you have an ID on the victim yet, dear?"

Bianca grinned broadly, and I could see dollar signs in her eyes. "We sure do."

If my lovely Camille had been in fighting shape, I would have simply gone to her for the name. I could, perhaps, engage Camille's fiancée, Françoise, to do some digging on my behalf, but the poor dear had enough on her hands with Camille's recovery, and they had a full roster of clients to deal with at their security company on top of that.

"So, Irma," Bianca said cheerily, "what's his name worth to you?"

Sixteen — Violet

Maura frowned as she swiped at her phone's screen. "I'm trying to turn my car off, but it won't stop. Can you try? You're the computer expert."

"I'm more of an expert at sitting in meetings these days," I said. "But sure." She handed her phone over, and I navigated around the remote starter software. After finding the *Power Off* button, I pressed it. "There you go."

"So, why isn't it stopping?"

I frowned. "Try again."

She tapped the button a few times, then shook her head.

"Can't you just turn the car off with the key?" I asked.

"No. The key mechanism was removed when the automatic starter was put in a few years ago." She shrugged sheepishly. "It's this complicated fancy thing. Ryeleigh got it for me for Christmas. And you know how much I hate getting in a cold car in the winter."

"I hear ya. Okay, let's open the side door and get some fresh air in here," I said. "Cars from the seventies probably pump a ton of garbage into the air when they idle, and I have no plans to die of carbon monoxide poisoning today."

"Yeah," she said, laughing nervously. "Me neither."

I reached the side door first, Maura hot on my heels. The digital lock mounted on the wall beside it was still a cheerful green, showing that it was unlocked. But it hadn't popped open when we'd approached, which felt a little rude after the white-glove service we'd received before. When I turned the knob, it moved easily in my hand—but nothing happened when I pulled.

Heat started to sizzle in my veins.

"What's wrong?" Maura asked.

"The door isn't opening." I rattled the handle again.

"You're kidding, right?" she asked.

"Can you take out your RFID card and put it in front of the sensor?"

She took off a bracelet and moved it around the front of the sensor before tapping it against the flat surface.

After looking at Maura's phone for a minute, I realized why shutting off her car via the app hadn't worked. Her cell wasn't on the network. NO SIGNAL was blinking at the top of the screen.

"Does the estate's security system work via Bluetooth?" I mumbled. I tried pairing the digital lock on the door to my phone, but it failed.

Behind us, the red Mini pumped carbon monoxide into the air—and it didn't look like it was planning on stopping.

"Any way your car is super low on gas?" I asked. Maura shook her head.

I looked out the side door's window to see if anyone was around. Nope. "Is there anything we can use to break this window?"

She rubbed her forehead. "I hope so. I know all the windows in the house are reinforced because they get a lot of wind here sometimes. But maybe they aren't in the garage."

Was she starting to turn red? Four cars was a lot of cars, and the garage had enough room to accommodate them, but it wasn't *that* big. If we couldn't get that car to turn off soon, or figure out how to open a window, we were going to be in trouble.

I swallowed hard. "Okay, we gotta get out of here. Any chance there's another door somewhere?"

"I mean, there's four garage doors."

"Good point." I checked each one, trying to rattle them loose from their locks. No dice.

"I'm going to call the main house," Maura said. "Someone will come and help." She took her phone back and started to dial.

I tried to text Irma with mine. There was no way she hadn't gone through something similar in her past. She'd know how to get us out of here.

"I can't get a signal," Maura said.

"Can you try 911? We should still have access to emergency services." I restarted my phone to see if it would pick up a network on the boot, while Maura peered out the door's window, the only window in the building. My phone was a prototype I was testing for a buddy of mine, and it had the capacity to amplify weak cell signals. If I couldn't get online after the restart, then we had a real problem.

"No, 911 won't connect."

And when my phone came up, I couldn't connect to emergency services either. My stomach clenched. "Maura, can you see if there's anything in those cupboards we can use to break the window, please?"

A look of horror flitted over her face. "No problem." She started to rustle through shelves while my phone came back up. I tried to connect to the cell network again, but got nothing. I should be able to dial 911 even without cell service. It didn't make sense. The only thing that would...

...was if the signal was being jammed. But that would mean someone was doing this on purpose. And that someone might have even worse plans in store for us.

Adrenaline jolted through me. "Maura, anything? What about tools? A crowbar, something?"

"Most of these shelves are empty," she said, showing me. "But there's a stool!" Her voice sounded suddenly upbeat. There was the Maura I knew.

The stool was metal and functional and before I knew it, I was whacking away at the window with it.

It was surprisingly hard work. *Whack whack whack.* After a few minutes, I was already out of breath, with nothing to show for it.

"Can you see if any of the garage doors will open for you?" I asked Maura, my heart clanging in my ears.

She straightened her shoulders and tried to raise the garage door behind the Mini. It rattled but stayed locked in place. Then she started banging at it with her purse. It was a fancy designer bag and pretty resilient, but it didn't make a dent. And then the purse got hooked on something. When Maura yanked, the bottom seam split open, spilling its contents on the floor.

"What the heck?" she panted, breathing hard. Her items were all in a jumble. Wallet, keys, makeup, a small rubber unicorn that had made a squeaky noise when it landed, and a flat white disc with the Apple logo stamped on it.

"Any of those keys work for any of these doors?" I asked, cold pressing down on my lungs.

"What's that?" she asked, looking at the little circle.

"That's an AirTag."

"Which is…?"

"It's a tracker."

Her eyes met mine. For a minute I thought we were both going to barf. If she didn't know what it was, that meant someone had slipped it into her purse.

"Brandon's been *tracking* me?" she said, her voice hitting an odd note.

I tried to smash the door handle off with the stool, but it didn't budge. My heart was rattling in my ears.

We were definitely in trouble.

Maura took a turn with the stool and that window, and I sat in the car and tried to figure out how to disable the engine. The only problem was that I knew a lot about computers, but almost nothing about cars. And this garage held no actual tools!

"Anything?" Maura called. She was coughing.

"Not yet," I said grimly, then tried to text one character per line to Irma. Small messages might work better with weak network signals.

9

1

1

"Maura, I hate to ask this, but can you drive your car into one of the garage doors? I mean, just tap it a little so we can get some fresh air in here."

She looked horrified, briefly, then nodded before climbing into the car, but when she tried to put the Mini into reverse, nothing happened. It didn't turn off, it didn't back up.

"Has it ever done this before?"

She pushed some hair back from her forehead. "No."

In desperation, I took my knapsack and emptied it on the polished concrete floor. Keys, phone, wallet, a power bar, a note from Irma threatening me if I tried to give her rent money again, and then…Irma's car escape tool. Energy zinged through my veins. I'd bet my butt it would work on that window.

My heart was beating a drum in my ears. *Window window window.*

"It's okay," I said.

All I could see was that window.

It took ten years to reach it. Outside, a bird was perched on a fence, its head cocked as if it were wondering what was going on.

I slapped the escape tool against the window, but I couldn't activate it. What had Irma said?

Oh yeah: *Put your back into it, dear.*

I tried again. Not even a scratch.

And behind me, the Mini's engine roared merrily along.

Seventeen — Irma

I negotiated for the victim's name with Bianca, our
starting point being a truly obscene amount of
money. Eventually I got her down to a spot where we
were both somewhat dissatisfied—the hallmark of
any good negotiation.

"Spill," I said after passing her an envelope of
cash.

She slid it under a cushion, then cracked her
knuckles. "His name was Harvey Allen. Fifty-seven
years old, no middle name. And guess what?" She
tittered. I'd be in a good mood, too, if I'd just
squeezed a little old lady out of that many zeros.
"He's a private detective."

Aha! "Where from?"

"Newfoundland, looks like. It's in the file."

My handbag vibrated furiously. "Excuse me," I
said, reaching for my cellular telephone. After I saw
the reason for all the buzzing, I jumped to my feet
and shoved the folder under my arm, an icy cold
descending on the back of my neck. "I have so
enjoyed our little chat, dear, and I do thank you for
your services. Must run." The tea remained

unpoured, which was no big loss. It was never going to be strong enough anyway.

"You're very welcome," Bianca said grandly.

Outside, I stuffed the papers into my handbag and ran down the street, glad I was wearing plimsolls. The text from Violet had been brief and to the point: 911.

I considered popping into the police station to get help, but it was possible Violet was playing some sort of practical joke, although it really wasn't like her. But nothing good would come from me dragging the local constabulary to someone's house for no good reason. Plus, I'd be at Harbour House in a flash.

I hopped into my boat, pointed it in the right direction, and hit the gas. Once I was a few hundred feet offshore, I activated the turbo action that the island airport owner, Luis Camacho, had so nicely installed for me. Whatever Violet was up to, I had to get there fast.

The waves were deep and rolling, and I slapped into their peaks over and over. So much so that I was starting to feel seasick—a condition that I did not appreciate. Nor did I enjoy the adrenaline that had flooded my senses.

But *Vitamin Sea* was built for speed, and I reached Harbour House quickly, my heart tapping a beat against my ribcage. I docked my boat in the little harbour that had given the estate its name.

Once on land, I didn't know which way to go—to the enormous main house, or the gargantuan garage?

The problem solved itself. Violet and her friend were propped up on the ground outside the garage. I ran toward them. Violet was the closest to me, and I took the pulse from her wrist.

"I'm not dead," she said crankily.

Beyond her was a side door with a window that had been shattered. If I knew my implements like I thought I did, she'd used her car escape tool on it. But why?

The answer came with the purr of a vintage automobile. The two of them had been stuck in the garage with a car running. A sudden, sickening fear knifed through me.

"Well done, my dear," I said, voice quiet.

Violet's eyes were bloodshot. And angry.

"What happened?" I asked.

"Doors locked, car turned on, used your creepy little car escape tool, yay."

The young lady sitting beside her gave me a little wave. She was clothed entirely in pink and had a gorgeous smile. "You must be Irma."

"How are you doing, dear?"

"We're fine. We just need to lie down for about ten hours."

Someone on a little blue golf cart was zooming towards us on the flimsy causeway that connected the mainland to the estate.

"Who's that?" I asked, voice sharp.

Maura's eyelids fluttered, and then she turned to look. "Jerrod. Our butler."

The cart skidded to a halt. A man in his sixties with a compact build, Roman nose and natty khakis, climbed out and ran toward us, then stumbled over his own feet and fell, both arms out.

"Aw, man," Violet said.

I put the back of my hand on Maura's forehead. It felt clammy, but not terrible. "How long were you two locked in the garage?"

"Longer than was enjoyable," Violet said wearily.

I fast-walked to Jerrod, who had propped himself up in a seated position. He'd skinned the palms of both hands. "Do you think you broke anything?" I asked him.

"Are the girls okay?" he asked, brushing me off and standing. He was a little wobbly on his feet after that spill, but he seemed to manage. "What happened?"

"They got locked in the garage with a car running." To Violet, I said, "We need to get you both checked out at the clinic."

Maura tried to wave me off. "We probably weren't in there that long. And the garage is huge, so I don't think—I mean, it looks worse than it was."

"Irma's right," Violet said gently. "If something happened to you, I'd never forgive myself. And neither would Max."

"I'll take the both of you," I said. "It'll be faster on my boat."

"Faster than what?" Maura asked, her nose wrinkled.

153

"No speed limits on the water, dear." I smiled at her. "Let's go, please. Jerrod, do you need your hands looked at?"

"I believe so, ma'am," he said. "I'll text the main house and let them know what's happened."

Maura practically jumped into *Vitamin Sea*, showing me she wasn't a boat person. Well, Mother had always told me life was full of challenges. Jerrod gently lowered himself in, trying not to get the blood from his hands on the woodwork, the sign of a true gentleman. After Violet climbed aboard, we were off.

When we were a few hundred feet away from Harbour House, Jerrod and Maura started to fiddle with their phones, probably texting the people back at Harbour House. I had Jerrod call the island clinic to apprise them of our situation so they'd be waiting for us.

Once inside the clinic, Dr. Angelique Beaulieu met us, along with a physician I'd never seen before. He was thirty-something, short and balding, with a plump figure and eyes that didn't look like they missed much. I briefly had an urge to knock him off his feet and go through his pockets to see if he had any weapons, but I tamped down on it.

The new doctor took over care for Maura, whisking her away. Jerrod was assisted by a nurse practitioner, while Julian, Violet, and I went to another exam room. Angelique looped an oxygen cannula over Violet's ears and directed her to lie back on the examining table.

"Any confusion?" Julian asked her.

"No more than usual."

He patted her on the shoulder, then snuck a glance at me.

"It'll be all right, dear," I said, squeezing his arm.

"We need to run a few blood tests," Julian said to Angelique. "And please make sure we check for cardiac ischemia."

She elbowed me out of the way, which I didn't even take personally, she was such a lovely girl. I took a seat in the corner while they worked, tucking my feet under my chair, crossing and re-crossing my arms.

I didn't know what to do with my hands.

A thought flitted through my head: *I should call Boris.*

But just as quickly, a memory overtook it. The other day, the two of us had enjoyed a lovely sail on Stu's boat, then retired to my bedroom for a wee nap. Boris had curled up behind me, and then we—old rusty spies, the pair of us—had spooned while the afternoon sun flitted away. He wrapped an arm around me, tucking his hand into mine. My feet found his. It was a miracle that we were still here, that we were still alive. It was warm and safe and lovely.

It was terrifying.

And so my cellular telephone stayed in my handbag.

Julian stepped away from Violet, snapping his gloves off. I caught another glimpse of his eyes. He was worried.

But I wasn't.

I was angry. And anger, I'd found, was the very best fuel for the work I had to do next.

Eighteen — Violet

As soon as they were done running a bunch of tests on me, Irma suddenly appeared, as was her incredibly creepy way.

"Hello, dear," she said sweetly.

"Hi," I said, then wiggled my nose. The oxygen tubing was still stuffed right up there. Sexy. "How's Maura?" I asked.

"Both of you seem just fine," she replied.

"They're too tough to get taken out by all this mess," Dr. Angelique said with a cheerful smile. She was wearing purple scrubs with bunny rabbits on them, her warm brown skin glowing against the fabric. She asked me a few more questions about how I was doing and seemed satisfied with my answers. "Although I wouldn't have wanted you to be in that garage for much longer, young lady."

"I'm, like, ten years older than you."

"It's just something my granny used to say," she said with a grin. "It calms people down when they've had some excitement."

"When can I leave?" I asked.

Dr. Angelique crossed her arms. "About that…"

Irma patted my arm.

I looked from her to the doctor. "What's wrong?"

"What's wrong is that it's almost nine o'clock at night," Dr. Angelique told me. "Our lab is closed for the day. We sent your bloodwork to the mainland to get tested, but we won't get the results back until tomorrow."

"That doesn't seem so bad. And I feel okay."

"Julian and I have decided that you two should stay here overnight. Just for observation," Dr. Angelique said. "If you want to see your friend, she's resting next door."

Irma smiled at her all the way out of the room, then sprang to her feet and closed the door behind her.

I looked at her suspiciously.

"Nothing's wrong. I just wanted a little chat."

I sighed, then caught Irma up on what had happened in the garage, throwing in the fact that I was less than thrilled that Maura was planning on spending the rest of her life with a jerk like Norman.

"Do you think Norman is trying to isolate her?" Irma asked. "He did bring her all the way out to an island, after all."

My breath came out in a puff. "Look, you know I'm not much of a people person, but I've always liked Brandon. And the stalking started a month after Maura found out about his financial issues, not right away. Plus, that was around the time that Norman popped up and made a move. It *is* possible that someone set Brandon up, and that that someone was Norman. Maura thought the stalker was Brandon because he knows her schedule. But someone sewed an AirTag, a tracker"—I stopped here and explained what an AirTag was to Irma—"into the lining of a very expensive purse of hers. That takes a certain amount of planning and foresight."

"And access."

"Exactly. And once it was done, they could have tracked her anywhere."

"How long has she had that purse? If it's new…"

"Great question."

"Thank you," Irma said modestly. "But I really don't like those sorts of trackers in civilian hands. Or security systems that don't work."

"You don't need to convince me of any of that." I sighed. "The problem is that Maura always thinks the best of everyone. She's the kind of person who makes three new friends when she's standing in line at the post office—friends that she'll send Christmas cards to for the rest of her life! She loves people, and they all love her. I know that probably makes her a little naïve, but it's also why I kind of believe her that Brandon isn't a good guy after all. It must have been a bad situation between them for her to think he was even capable of stalking her."

"I wonder how much Norman tried to convince her of that, though."

"Another excellent point."

"I'm blushing," Irma said cheekily. "Tell me, how hard would it be for someone to hack into the security system at Harbour House and lock you two in there?"

"Security infrastructure isn't my area of expertise, but if any system isn't properly locked down, then anyone can get in. But, I mean, it's possible that what happened was a system glitch and not intentional at all. It's just..."

"What?"

"I think you're rubbing off on me."

"Thank you, dear. I'd tend to think that a single point of failure could be a glitch of some kind, but a car that won't turn off along with a garage you can't get out of? That feels like a bit much."

"Yeah, you're right. Plus, I'm concerned that the cell signal problems we had might have been a bit more..."

"Nefarious?" Irma suggested helpfully.

"I hate to encourage you, but yes," I said with a little smile. "I could barely get a signal when we were in there. Same with Maura. And no 911 service."

"That part of the island has always had issues with cellular signals," Irma said.

"But what if someone planted a cellphone jammer somewhere?" I asked. "I don't know much about them, though. Like, whether or not any signals can get out if a jammer is in use, or if it's a complete blackout."

"Your text messages got to me."

"You're right. Well, the best thing to do would be for me to get access to the security system at the estate and poke around a bit. Then I'll take a look at how cellphone jammers work."

"Good, let's do that." Then Irma sighed, which was unlike her. "In other developments, I have a name for the dead gentleman we found the other night. Harvey Allen, a private detective from Newfoundland."

"And guess who hired him?"

She'd been patting my arm in a soothing manner, but tensed at my words.

"Ouch."

"Sorry, dear."

"It was Brandon."

Irma's tiny arms crossed themselves over her chest. "Pardon me?"

"Brandon hired the detective to find Maura so he could warn her about Norman."

"Oh, my." Irma's head slid into a tilt. "Mrs. Sepp doesn't like him, you know."

"Who?"

"Norman."

I swallowed. "That isn't good. She likes pretty much everyone."

"She wasn't overly fond of Maura's mother or her sister, either."

I frowned. "Stassi I can see, but I thought Ryeleigh was okay."

"Mrs. Sepp said she seemed spoiled."

"Huh."

"I'm going to get background checks run on both those young men. And perhaps the rest of the family, too."

"Sounds good. I'll dig into the tech stuff."

Irma put her hand on my arm again. "Your friend is going to be all right, Violet. I promise we won't let anything bad happen to her, or let her engagement party be ruined."

"Thank you, Irma."

We exchanged a look that I couldn't quite attach an emotion to. We were an odd sort of team, but I knew Irma would put her life on the line for my friend if needed. When I teared up, she looked away, but her hand found mine and she gave it a little squeeze. "*Courage, ma fille*," she said softly. *Courage, my girl.*

A tap at the door. "Excuse me, please, ladies," Jerrod said. His formerly pristine ensemble now had dirt on the knees, and both of his hands were bandaged. He looked exhausted, too.

"How are you doing?" Irma asked warmly after introducing herself.

"I'm a bit embarrassed to have wasted the clinic staff's time, to be frank. I just have some scrapes. It's my own fault for not being more careful. Are you all right, Miss Blackheart?"

"Violet, please. And I'm fine. They're just keeping us here because they're overprotective."

"I'm very glad to hear it, and that you'll be able to keep Miss Maura company." He shrugged apologetically. "No one from the house is able to come see her right now, but someone will come fetch her tomorrow."

"Oh?" Irma said, head on a tiny tilt.

Jerrod nodded. "I'm going to take my leave now, but please know that I am thinking good thoughts for you."

"Ditto." I smiled and waved. After he was gone, I said, "Nice guy. A bit poncy for my taste, but nice."

"He's quite lovely, apparently. I don't know him, but he's been on the island for a decade or so. He's a moonlighter."

"Huh?"

"He'll provide major-domo services for a family or couple or what have you for a limited period of time, then move on to another estate." She crossed her arms again.

"Speaking of estates, Maura and Norman had an argument before we left Harbour House. In fact, Maura cancelled our dinner because something came up with the engagement party planning."

"Doesn't sound like anyone is getting along all that well over there," Irma said.

That reminded me of all the unhappy families I'd already seen on the island this summer. And a lot of times, all their cash really didn't seem to cheer them up that much, although I'd also seen that money come with a lot of strings attached.

"Why don't you go visit with Maura, dear? I'm going to chat with Angelique for a bit. Her mother wants to have us over for dinner sometime soon."

"Sure, sounds good."

I didn't have far to go to see Maura, but I still didn't quite get there. Someone was in her room.

"I'm going to look at it tomorrow, Rye," Maura was saying. Her voice was calm in the way it was when she was dealing with something or someone difficult. I'd seen her like this only a few times at work, and never in her personal life. So maybe that was why I found myself lurking in the hallway outside her door.

"Norman wants all the arrangements for the party decided today, Maura. You know that."

"I've already agreed with everything he wants, Rye. There's nothing else I can do but agree. And I've agreed, agreed, agreed."

"But I sent you some new ideas for appetizers—"

"Ryleigh, the menu has been set for weeks. The caterer is already working on some of it. It's too late to make a change."

"But if you look at this Instagram account I just started following, you can see that the style right now is—"

"Ryleigh, if you bring up something from the Kardashians again, I'm going to ship you back home."

"Mom would never let you," Ryeleigh said. "And neither would Norman. It's important that the engagement party is an elite event. How else do you think I'm going to find a halfway decent husband?"

What tone of voice was Ryeleigh using? Was it...taunting? Or conniving, maybe? Definitely unpleasant. The nice, timid girl from the club the other night seemed to have disappeared completely.

Maura sighed. "I have no interest in having an elite event, or whatever, Ryeleigh. I just want my friends and family—"

"*Our* friends and family."

Suddenly, a hand was clapped over my mouth and I was pulled backwards and around a corner. Amazingly, I managed not to scream, probably because I could smell Irma's Chanel Number 5.

"What's the situation?" she asked quietly, after making sure we were far enough away from Maura's room that nobody could hear us.

"I'm...well, I was eavesdropping."

"Oh my goodness, I'm so sorry."

"Huh?"

"I thought there was a threat of some kind and you were making a plan."

"I think I'm all planned out for today, Irma."

"Yes, of course," she said apologetically. "What were you listening to?"

"Ryeleigh's being a jerk about wedding stuff."

"Let's put an end to that, shall we?" Irma said. "I believe that Maura's had enough to deal with for one day." Then she marched herself right into Maura's room, me behind her.

"Hey, kiddo," I said, checking to see if Ryeleigh was lurking in the shadows somewhere, but she must have flounced off in the brief time we'd been gone.

"Hey, yourself," Maura said with a wan smile. She looked small in the bed. Childlike, almost.

"Well, you can't say we don't go to interesting places together."

"You're in excellent hands here, dear," Irma said.

"Oh, I know." Maura smiled sadly. "But I just want to go home. I think I'm at that point where I can't deal with one more thing going wrong, you know what I mean? I just want Brandon to leave. He's going to ruin everything!"

Irma smiled sympathetically. "We should call the police."

"No police," Maura said.

"Why not?" I asked.

"I can't…" Maura swallowed. "If we have any bad press before the wedding, if anyone finds out that Norman's fiancée is running around breaking windows and destroying property for no reason—"

"We had an excellent reason," I said, "and *you* didn't break anything. Just tell them your friend is nuts."

Irma lifted her shoulders in a *that'll probably work* shrug.

"Stassi will kill me if this gets out, and Norman is not fond of the police. Plus, their family is, like, a big deal in Toronto, and they don't want to have negative press, or social media, or anything like that.

I just need to survive the party on Saturday, and then everything will get better."

"Have you considered cancelling your event, Maura?" Irma asked.

Maura shook her head. "I can't even think about that. Everything is going to be fine. It has to be."

"One thing that will help with that is you checking for other trackers around the house and in your belongings, dear," Irma said.

"Why don't I try figuring out where that AirTag came from in the first place?" I asked. "Can I have it?"

Maura rummaged in one of her pockets and handed it over.

"Who would have had access to your purse?" Irma asked.

"I've been staying with Stassi lately, who always has people over or something going on. Plus, Ryeleigh is back living with her these days, and has friends in and out all the time. I don't use that bag often, so someone could have done it a while ago." Her eyes widened. "But..."

"What?"

"I just remembered—I bought that purse after Brandon and I broke up."

"Huh," I said.

"Maura," Irma said gently, "why do you think Brandon is behind all this?"

Her eyes flashed with anger. "The emails said that we belonged together. Together forever. That's what Brandon always used to tell me. And if it *isn't* him doing all this, I still don't want him anywhere near me. He came on private property today to get at me, even though I told him to leave me alone. I stopped posting where I was on social media after everything started, and I asked all my friends not to post anything about me. Someone tagged me at a birthday party, and I stopped going out at all. I'm not going to live like that anymore. And I can only do that if he's gone."

"It's okay, Maurie," I said, although I was thinking about how *together forever* was pretty generic stalker-talk. It didn't necessarily mean that Brandon was the bad guy. Even the little beaver buddies with the matching t-shirts that Maura had given me earlier said *Maura and Norman forever.* Forever was a big deal for people in relationships.

"Perhaps someone should speak to Brandon," Irma said sweetly. "Make sure he goes home."

"That would be great, but who?" Maura asked.

Irma leaned forward. "I can have a word, dear."

Maura's sun-eclipsing smile burst over her face. "Thanks, Irma. I appreciate it."

"No, really," I said, putting a hand on Maura's arm. "She'll make sure he never bothers you again."

Maura narrowed her eyes.

"Seriously."

"Uh…Violet, you've never steered me wrong before, but…"

"Trust me."

"Yes," Irma said toothily. "Trust us, dear. We'll take care of it if you don't want the police to step in."

"O-okay. Thank you," Maura breathed.

"And I think you need to stay out of that garage for the foreseeable future, dear."

Maura held up a hand. "Oh, I will. And I spoke to Norman earlier. He told me that nothing looks weird in the security system."

"Does Norman know anything about computers?" I asked.

"And does Brandon?" Irma interjected.

Maura shook her head. "Norman is okay, but not great, with tech. And Brandon can barely set the time on the microwave."

"I can relate," Irma muttered.

"But Norman called the security company. Someone's coming out in a few days to take a look at the garage in person."

"I wouldn't mind nosing around that system a bit," I said. "When is Norman coming to see you? I'd like to get my hands on the login info."

"He's working late tonight," Maura said with a shake of her head, and for a minute she looked incredibly young again. "He's got a big deal to close before the party. I'm sorry to bother you guys with all this."

"Oh, it's all right," I said almost cheerfully. "Irma's not bothered at all."

Irma threw me a smirk.

At my request, Maura typed out Brandon's information and emailed it to us. And like I said, Irma didn't look even remotely bothered.

She looked like a woman on a mission. A mission I was definitely joining her on.

Nineteen — Irma

The young man was sitting on the patio at Fleur
Bleue, a fussy fine-dining restaurant that was
purposely small to ensure that getting a reservation
was always a bloody nightmare, especially since the
owner and I weren't on the best terms. He didn't
recycle and had once dinged my car in the parking lot
of the club before driving off. It was only the keen
eye of one of the valets that had uncovered him as
the culprit.

But how did a twenty-something stalker afford a
table at Serge Laframboise's poncy restaurant? I tried
not to be irritated that the contact I'd reached out to
hadn't yet gotten back to me about the background
checks I'd requested for young Brandon and all the
rest. I'd promised myself that I wouldn't bother
Camille and Françoise; they had enough on their
plates.

A sip of tea warmed my innards. I unwrapped my
protein muffin, wishing that it wouldn't seem odd if I
pulled out a pair of binoculars and took a closer look
at Maura's ex. And that I'd been able to suss out
where Brandon was staying while he was in town. A

three a.m. incursion would be so much easier than all this.

I was annoyed it had taken me so long to track him down, but at least I knew that Violet and Maura were still at the clinic. They'd both had a lovely sleep, from what I'd been told, but their bloodwork had taken longer than expected to process. I wasn't bothered. They were safe there, and I had eyes on Mr. Brandon.

Maura's ex was slender and perhaps six feet tall, with narrow shoulders and a face that held excellent cheekbones. He was a handsome boy, dressed in a preppy black polo shirt over dark khakis, with sandy brown hair and an easy smile.

My protein muffin had a bit more heft than usual today, which was nice. I could use all the fibre I could get with whippersnappers like these flouncing around my town. I did not care for men who scared young ladies. Violet might have been fond of Brandon in the past, but if yesterday's shenanigans in the garage had been deliberate, it was time to seriously reconsider those assumptions.

The waiter poured more sparkling water in Brandon's glass, the two of them engaging in idle chitchat. And I had to say, young Brandon looked pretty cheerful for someone who might have tried to kill his ex-girlfriend yesterday.

I remained in my seat. It was a bit odd that my feet weren't jiggling impatiently and that I wasn't itching to jog over there and wallop the little twerp.

But when I was surveilling a target, I often entered a concentration zone that made everything else fall away.

Perhaps that was why it took me so long to realise that a second man, sitting on the patio of the bistro next door, was also setting off alarm bells. Good heavens, that was a lot on one's plate.

I squinted at the newcomer, keeping watch out of the corner of my eye for Brandon, who looked like he was finally finishing his extravagantly late lunch.

Was the second man Igor Ivanovitch?

Young Igor might have had an unusual job as hired muscle, but his looks were fairly run-of-the-mill. I'd noted his height and weight when I first encountered him. But this gentleman, from the back, had bigger shoulders. And his neck looked like a tree trunk.

Igor had been leaner. I was sure of it.

Maybe.

My attentions returned to Brandon, who was signing the cheque with a flourish. Once finished, he dropped his napkin on the table and stood. On the next patio over, so did the young man whose meaty neck had drawn my attention. Was it a new foe? Or was it Igor, pumped up on steroids? Some mercenaries did exactly that when they were on a job. It helped them maintain the simmering rage that helped fuel their dirty work.

Man number two laid down his napkin and exited the patio. I could see that he had a full beard, while

Igor had been clean-shaven. He turned right and
started walking down the sidewalk. I knew that walk.

...or something close to it. It wasn't *exactly* right,
but it was familiar.

Or was I just being paranoid?

Brandon ambled down the sidewalk to the left.

Which one to follow?

I had an unpleasant moment after that. Really, it
was critical to get Brandon off the island. Violet's
friend had put up a brave face last night, but under
all that she must be half demented with worry that
her ex was going to ruin her engagement party. And
if Igor was still in town, I wasn't going to be able to
manage two angry young men intent on island
mayhem. I simply didn't have the time.

So I followed Maura's ex, rolling the collapsible
bicycle that I liked to keep at the island clinic beside
me. Brandon was still sauntering along, which could
mean anything: he thought he was home free, he felt
like the world was his oyster, he simply liked to
saunter...

He turned toward a more residential part of town,
although a smattering of businesses still dotted the
road, including Aunt Paddy's perfect fish and chips,
which I patronized every now and again.

The young man picked up speed. I kept pace,
along with the focus that a long career in intelligence
work had gifted me. Cold had blanketed my
shoulders, a frosty counterbalance to the warm
summer day.

Another left turn from young Mr. Brandon. He was several streets north of Main now, deeper into the town's residential area. The houses here were smaller than many of the island homesteads, some of which seemed more like castles than homes. More show than family. I'd always wondered if people bought enormous houses like that so they could get as far away from their relations as humanly possible.

Brandon stopped in front of a charming Cape Cod style cottage, cornflower blue trimmed with white, set off with a tidy front yard.

I paused on the other side of the street, putting the bicycle on its kickstand and kneeling to tie my shoelaces, making certain to ignore the twinge in my knee when I did so. I was going to have to get Julian to look at it again, bloody hell.

The picket fence gate squeaked open; Brandon let himself into the cottage with a key. In the driveway was a clunky sedan with tinted windows that looked like it came from an upmarket brand.

And then the back of my neck started buzzing again. Like I was being watched. I pulled in a breath, making a surreptitious survey of the block that didn't produce any potential stalkers of my own, and the sensation passed, although it had ratcheted up my anxiety somewhat.

I tried to shake it off, then walked around the block to burn some time so it wouldn't seem like I'd followed Maura's ex, keeping an eye out for anyone wandering around behind me, and eventually marched up to the very same door that Brandon had entered.

There was no doorbell, but a charming beaver-shaped doorknocker whose clanger hung right under a delightful little set of buckteeth. After admiring it for a moment, I rapped it against the metal.

"Hello?" Brandon was at the door in a flash. Up close, he looked more twitchy and unhappy than he had while supping on Serge's patio. There were puffy circles under his eyes and some strain in his jawline. Interesting.

"Hello there," I said chirpily, deciding to go with *lost little old lady.* "Is this Hogton Street?"

"No," he said, smiling politely.

"Oh dear," I said. "I do believe I've gotten turned around." I clutched at my handbag. "Do you think I could have a glass of water, by any chance? I'm sorry to impose, but it's hot out there."

"Of course," he said, opening the door and ushering me in.

Honestly, I felt somewhat bad. Especially when I closed and locked the door behind me while Brandon filled a glass for me from the kitchen tap. It was a darling little cottage, with bright white trim and coastal knickknacks scattered throughout the living and dining areas.

The overly large windows promised a lovely view of the other houses in the neighbourhood, or they would have if the blinds weren't all drawn, a surprisingly convenient state of affairs.

Maura's ex handed me the glass with an encouraging smile. I laid a hand on my chest and said, "Do you mind if I sit down, dear? I'm a little dizzy."

"Of course," Brandon said. "Is there anyone I can call for you?"

I drained the glass. Honestly, I really had been thirsty. After setting it down on the side table, I returned his smile.

"No, thank you, Brandon," I said, before leaning forward and gracing him with a conspiratorial smile.

His expression faltered.

"Why don't we have a little chat, Mr. Ott?"

A frown formed on his forehead. "Who are you?"

"I'm a friend of Violet Blackheart, dear. And as they say, a friend of hers is a friend of mine."

"Maura," he said slowly.

"Yes, quite."

"It's not what it looks like."

"What isn't? You following her to a remote island?"

"I don't really think it's that remote," he said, a smirk tugging at his mouth. It wasn't bothersome. In the end, they were always sorry for underestimating me.

"It can only be reached by boat or ferry," I said pointedly. "Or air."

"I suppose submarines would do the trick too."

"They would indeed, dear." I uncrossed my legs.

"So, look," he said, holding both hands in the air. "I know I shouldn't have rocked up on Maurie yesterday, but I had to let her know something urgent."

"And what's that, dear?"

He hesitated. "I mean, I don't even know you. You could be anyone."

I grinned wolfishly. "I certainly could be."

A less self-assured expression overtook his features. "I haven't done anything wrong."

"No?"

He plopped a cushion into his lap and squeezed like it was a good accordion.

When he didn't speak, I said, "I hear you've been stalking your ex-girlfriend, dear. That doesn't feel like nothing to me."

He held his hands up in a gesture of contrition. Or capitulation. "I'm not the one who's been stalking her," he said. "Hey, do you want a beer?"

"No, thank you, Mr. Ott. And you don't want one either."

He flinched but tried to rally. "No?"

"No."

"Well, I sure didn't stalk Maura."

"You didn't show up at her summer rental yesterday?"

The hands went back up. "No, I did."

"I'm curious. How did you know she was on the island?"

He looked at his lap. "That's private," he mumbled.

"As in, the private investigator you hired found her? The one who met a messy end outside my private club the other night?"

His head jerked up. "Okay, okay. Yes. He found out she was on the island."

"Why did the two of you decide to go to the club the other night?"

"We didn't. Harvey'd left me a voicemail earlier in the day about Maura being at the club that night, and that he had something big to tell me about my case. I went to talk to him first and find out what that was. But I never saw him, and when I realized Maura wasn't there, I left. Thought I'd just catch up with Harvey the next day."

"So the two of you didn't leave together?"

He shook his head. "Never saw him, like I said. Look, I know all this sounds bad, but someone is setting me up."

"And who would do a thing like that?"

The lips disappeared again. "I think it was her fiancé. I introduced them a few months before all this started."

I tried not to flinch. "And?"

"And he told me he was going to take Maura away from me, no matter what."

Twenty — Violet

After a good night's sleep, both Maura and I seemed to be feeling a whole bunch better. I wanted to start researching some of the stuff Irma and I had talked about, but I'd ended up crashing early the previous night, and had spent the morning in work meetings, playing catch-up with a new project my team was dealing with.

Maura spent the morning napping—the poor kid must have been exhausted. She perked right up after I ordered in lunch for us from Mandy McGuire's: hot wings and a summer salad full of sweet baby lettuce, bell peppers, and fresh cucumbers with a zingy dressing. Now we were just chatting until Norman came to pick her up.

"Speak of the devil," Maura said, her smile getting even bigger.

In the doorway, Norman held flowers in one hand and a designer briefcase in the other. His suit was quietly expensive, his shoes shiny. He seemed like a man who enjoyed projecting a certain kind of image. Maybe that was why he'd chosen such an impressive-looking house for his engagement party. I wondered briefly who he was trying to impress. The same people that Ryeleigh was following on Instagram? And why were Ryeleigh and Norman co-ordinating stuff for Maura's engagement party, anyway?

"Nice to see you again," I said.

"Hey there." He flashed me a quick smile before passing the flowers to Maura. They looked like he'd picked them up at a gas station sometime last week, but Maura grinned, smelling them. It didn't surprise me that Maura would be happy with $4.99 stems. It *did* surprise me that Norman didn't seem to feel like Maura was the one he should be impressing. "I'm so sorry about all this nonsense, you guys. The security company is coming out to take a look at the system first thing on Monday. We've disabled the garage software."

"I think you should take the security system down completely," I said. "Turn it off so nothing else like this can happen until they figure out what the problem was."

"They have figured out what the problem was," Norman said before kissing Maura on the top of her head.

"And what's that?" My stomach tightened.

"The logs show that the system responsible for securing the garage froze. A few features might have still been working, but ultimately it was in a crashed state. That's why the door sensor showed that it was unlocked, but it really wasn't. It was just a little snafu."

"I'm sorry," I said bluntly, "but what happened yesterday was no snafu."

"Alright then, a freak accident. A product failure." Norman flashed the kind of smile that suggested that the people in his circle were in the habit of agreeing with him. And that I was overreacting.

Maybe I was just being paranoid. But no reputable tech company would complete an investigation so quickly after an incident when so much was at stake. If their customers started dropping dead because none of their clients could actually unlock their locks, they were going to be in huge trouble.

So either Norman was lying, or they were.

"This wouldn't have been a big deal if there had been another exit in that garage. They really should put one in," Maura said.

"It's a rental, babe. Not much we can do about it."

"If you say so," she said quietly.

"I can take a look at the system if you like," I said. "Just to make sure. All I need is the login info."

Norman waved me off. "I'm sure you'll void the warranty or whatever if you log in. We have a big party to get ready for and all that jazz, so we're going to let the experts take care of it."

"Maura could have been hurt," I said. "*Really* hurt."

"Are security systems your specialty, Violet?" Norman asked.

"No," I said slowly. "But the review I need to do is fairly basic."

"There's nothing basic about these advanced kinds of systems," Norman said, speaking even more slowly than I had. "And their product experts are going to take a look. They've admitted that the system froze, and they're going to fix it. They also think that a...confused signal from their system is what impacted Maura's car and made it start."

"I really doubt that. And 'confused signal' is not a technical term."

"I'm sure he was just dumbing his explanation down for me."

"Norman," I said, trying to be patient. "Someone has sewn an AirTag into the lining of Maura's purse. Think that's an accident, too?"

He let out an exasperated noise. "I told you to stop buying designer brands second-hand," he said to Maura, who looked sheepish. To me, he said, "Thank you, seriously. Maybe I can finally get her to stop doing that."

I struggled to keep my face from moving into a glower, another trick Irma had tried to teach me. I just wished she'd taught me how to punch someone while being invisible, because that would seriously come in handy right about now.

"Maura has a stalker. Do we all agree on that point?" I asked.

He gave me a shallow nod.

"But the stalker isn't the one who sewed an AirTag into her purse? It came like that from Wisconsin, or wherever?"

Norman sat down heavily, and in the improved light, I could see the strain under his eyes. "You're right," he said. "We'll give the Toronto police a call when we get home."

"Thanks, sweetheart," Maura said with an exhale and a beautiful smile. "Thanks for all your help with this, Violet. I know how scary all this has been. But if the security company knows what happened, everything should be fine."

"What about the island police?" I said to Norman.

Maura's fiancé waved me off. "I've spoken to a friend of a friend who's on the Toronto force. If Maura's stalker hasn't done anything violent or destructive, there's very little they can do. And if her stalker did access the bag somehow and stick that thing in, it would have happened in Toronto, not here, so there's no reason to bother the Beaver Island police. All they'd tell me is that there's nothing they can do."

He wasn't wrong, which was probably why I was now so completely annoyed.

Maura tugged at his sleeve. "We should drive Violet home when we go."

If you weren't looking for it, you would have missed the irritation that flashed over his features. "It's not really on the way, babe," he said.

"It's a small island," she replied, a pleasant tone in her voice.

"I'm fine," I said, lifting a hand. "I'll take a taxi." Or maybe Stu could give me a lift.

"I'm sorry, Violet," Norman said, pinching the bridge of his nose. "I'm not thinking clearly. I'm just so worried about my Maura and everything that's been going on with this stalker."

Was it wrong that all I could think was: What if her stalker had come with her?

"Maurie!"

The three of us turned. Stassi Kent stood in the doorway, an array of upscale shopping bags hanging from one hand, a designer set of sunglasses swept off her face and held in the other. She dropped everything but the glasses, then crossed the room and threw herself at Maura.

Watching it, something reminded me of Phyllis. She'd always put on a good show when other people were watching.

I tried not to shudder. I adored Maura, but she was an adult and her family dynamics were private. Norman was never going to give me that login information, so it was time for me to take off.

"Violet?" Julian was, mercifully, at the door. "Can I speak to you for a minute?"

I got to my feet, glad that he'd come to save me. And hoping that nothing new was wrong.

185

TWENTY-ONE — IRMA

"So, Norman told you he was going to take Maura away from you? That doesn't seem particularly nice," I said. "Was he a friend of yours?"

Brandon put down the mug he'd been holding in his left hand and tousled his hair with his right. "An acquaintance. Right after he says that, all this weird credit card sh—stuff—starts happening, and Maura gets more and more distant. Then all the stalker-type stuff happens. Maura broke up with me, and Norman made his move. He's bad news, and I don't want her to get hurt."

I crossed my arms. "Because you're the one who wants to do all the hurting?"

"What are you talking about? I'd never hurt Maura. Ever."

"She seems to think you would. And that you were the one who locked her in a garage yesterday and turned on a car that just happened to be in there with her."

"*What?* Is she okay?"

"No thanks to you."

He let out a relieved-sounding breath. "I have to go see her."

"On the contrary, dear, I'm here to ensure that you leave the island. Although I would like you to answer a question for me before you go."

"Oh?" he said, eyebrow raised.

"What do you think your private investigator found?"

Brandon let out a frustrated exhale. "It could only have been one of two things. He figured out who hacked my credit, or he could prove who was stalking Maura. But whoever Harvey fingered must have knocked him off before he could tell me."

"And you think all this was done by Norman?"

"Who else could it be? I'm a nurse, not a divorce attorney or something. I don't have any enemies or conflict at my workplace. I don't deal with terminally ill patients, so no one's mad at me for accidently killing their great-aunt Lulu or whatever."

"I'm assuming that you've spoken to the Beaver Island police about all this."

A nod. "Harvey never answered any of my calls yesterday, so I went in to report him missing last night and they told me what happened to him. The police asked me a bunch of questions."

"Did they ask you if you'd recently given him some cash?"

"How much?"

"I couldn't say."

"No. I had to read Harvey my credit card number on the phone so he could run it remotely before he did any work. Like it was the 80's."

That definitely dovetailed with what Matty had told me about Harvey Allen being old-fashioned. "And do the police think you're a suspect?"

"For killing the man who was going to help me turn my life around? Not really, no."

"How was Harvey going to do that?"

Brandon let out a huge sigh. "He was going to clear my name."

"Perhaps, but that doesn't mean that Maura was going to take you back."

"No, I get that. But she would at least know the truth. I thought we were going to be married. Her opinion matters to me."

I started warming up my ankles. "Did the police tell you not to leave town?"

He shook his head. "They have all my personal contact info and they've notified the police back home in Toronto, so…no."

I let out a breath of my own. "Wonderful. Would you like me to help you pack?"

"I'm not going anywhere."

Outside, I could hear the rumbling of classic motorbikes, probably Women on Wheels heading out for their ride.

Focus.

"Let's get started, shall we?" I said cheerily.

That smirk finally bubbled to the surface. "I mean, I don't think I will, ma'am." After a pause: "And I don't think you can make me."

There was a beat.

"I do see your point, dear. Could you please help me up? My knee has been bothering me lately, and this is a very squishy couch."

"Sure," he said reluctantly, then crossed the small room to hold a hand out to me.

I took it, and as I rose, I nudged the back of his knees so they bent suddenly, an old trick of mine. One of its great benefits was that it enabled one to neutralize a threat without much effort. As Brandon fell to his knees, I tapped him on the forehead with my own to disorient him, then rolled him onto the floor, face-down. Once there, things got quite a bit easier. I snugged an arm behind his back at an angle that would be fairly painful while not leaving any marks that might incriminate me.

"How did you do that?" he squealed. "You didn't even *move!*"

"It's all in the wrist, dear," I said cheerily. "Look, Maura doesn't want you here, so it's really for the best if you go on home. And lucky for you, I'm here to help. How long will it take for you to pack?"

"I don't have much," he mumbled into the shag rug.

"Lovely," I said. "Let's get cracking, shall we?"

"Okay," he said quietly. But there was an undertone in his voice I'd heard before. It was him underestimating me. He thought that once I let him up, he'd be in control. I tried not to sigh as I slowly released him.

He rolled, quick as a bunny, onto his back, and kicked at me. I grabbed his foot, pinched a nerve near his Achilles, and he moaned in pain.

"Had some martial arts training, dear?" I asked pleasantly.

He nodded, cradling his ankle in one hand after I let go of it.

"It's quite important to make time for sparring practice as often as you're able," I said. "Or else you really don't have a sense of how fights unfurl in the real world."

He made a whimpering noise.

"Unfortunately, my schedule is quite full these days. So if we could move this along, that would be lovely."

Then the air seemed to go out of him. "This is what Maurie wants?"

"It is indeed."

Brandon muttered a few complaints that I decided to ignore before making his way to the bedroom, where he threw some clothes into a small suitcase, mumbling the entire time. I didn't take it personally.

When he was done, he stomped into the living room, glowering at everything in sight, including me, which I also didn't take to heart.

"Where do you need to leave the keys?" I asked.

"On the kitchen table. The front door will lock behind us."

"Fabulous. Shall we?"

He tried to convince me to go out first, but since I was quite certain he'd slam the front door behind me as soon as I did, I demurred. After a heavy sigh from Brandon, we made our exit, the door lock clicking merrily behind us.

"You're going to be sorry about this," he said. But his voice was flat, vanquished.

"I certainly shan't."

Brandon had the good manners to hand me the car keys when I asked for them, then took a few minutes to type angrily into his phone while I stowed my bicycle and his suitcase in the back seat of his car.

Once he was done with his tiny tantrum, I unlocked the car doors and took a seat. Brandon did the same, and after I gave him the keys back, he nosed his car onto the road. I changed the radio station to something less annoying, and we were off.

It felt good that I'd been able to accomplish this one small thing. Maura's fiancé might not be the nicest young man, and perhaps he'd had a hand in yesterday's unpleasant events, but I wouldn't be able to focus on that until young Mr. Brandon had been ousted from the island.

Happily, my charge was not a slow driver, and he opened the car up on the highway. It was an older model with terrible suspension, but it was a beautiful day and the sun was shining, so I tried to focus on the positive.

When we reached the ferry crossing, two cars were already lined up and waiting, but I did not recognize them. Tourists, perhaps. Behind us, a blur came into focus. It was the Women on Wheels ride, always an odd collection of motorbikes—some classic cruisers along with a handful of Vespas and other scooters. Sometimes Perrie Kowalczyk, paperclip heiress and artist, drove Agnes O'Muffin in a sidecar attached to her Triumph, although I didn't see them today.

Simone Summers, a local wedding planner, pulled her 1969 Harley Sportster beside my window and leaned forward with a smile. "Hey, Irma. You going to the mainland?"

"Just having a little ferry ride," I said with a smile.

"Nice day for it!"

More of the motorbikes reached the landing, the noise of their engines filling the air.

"You should join us sometime," Simone added with a grin.

"I think you're probably right about that, dear."

The two of us chatted for a bit—Brandon staring forward, typing on his phone again—while the ferry barrelled toward us. The ship was compact, and carried a determined ferry master. Plus, it had some lovely CCTV cameras that sometimes offered up juicy tidbits about the comings and goings of island inhabitants.

A few minutes later the ferry master, Asif Ahmadi, docked the ferry, and its passengers disgorged themselves before the two cars in front of us drove onwards. The ship was a roll-on, roll-off design, with an open parking area that reminded me of the flatbed of a truck.

We followed, a muscle jumping in Brandon's jaw as he parked the car and turned off its engine. After the automobiles were aboard, the Women on Wheels followed, tucking themselves in between the cars.

"Shall I trust you to keep your word, or will I be travelling further with you, dear?"

That muscle swelled, then deflated. Brandon turned slowly to look at me. "I didn't do it."

"Do what?"

"Any of it!" he snapped. "I'm a nurse. I don't hurt people." He ruffled his hair and seemed to calm himself. "But, fine. If Maurie wants me gone, I'll leave. Okay?"

"Thank you, dear," I said.

"But can you do something for me?"

I raised an eyebrow.

"Can you watch out for her? I mean, you have a pretty mean right hook."

"I didn't even hit you!"

He smiled, and then I saw how handsome he might be in the right light. "True. But I'm pretty sure you pack a mean punch."

"That's very kind of you to say. And I will certainly watch out for Maura. Stay out of trouble, young man."

Asif pumped the ferry whistle and I decided to remain onboard so I could make sure Brandon didn't get any big ideas about staying around. After retrieving my bicycle from the back seat and shutting the car door, I went to locate a good spot to secure my little two-wheeler, else I'd end up walking home. I'd once dropped an ice cream over the side of the ferry, so I knew how the lake sometimes reached for its treasures.

We left shore and I relaxed somewhat, hearing the ferry's enormous motors clang into action, so loud it could be hard to hear the person beside you at times. Then someone started blaring pop music from their car.

I so loved the island's ferry. Similar to the service road that led to and from the club, the ferry had been a tremendous source of happiness for me ever since I was young. When I was a child and we were coming home from somewhere, Dad and I would always get out of the car and stand at the railing while we crossed. Back in England, we'd moved around a lot. Stepping on the Beaver Island ferry always felt like coming home.

One of the WOW women on a grey sport bike—a Ducati?—wearing a full-face helmet and a black motorcycle jacket, leaned forward and gestured at Brandon. He said something to her in reply.

There was some chop on the water, and the breeze was perfect at keeping the worst of the heat off us. I lifted my head to the gorgeous sun shining down on me.

"Howzit going, Irma?" Asif, the ferry master, had left his station and cozied up to me at the rail. I'd picked a spot that was relatively quiet, so we didn't have to holler at each other over the engines.

I turned to smile at him. "I certainly hope you put the autopilot on before leaving your cabin."

Asif laughed. He was mid-fifties, from a long line of businessmen. He'd come to Canada to make his fortune in his twenties but had been pulled onto the water almost immediately. He had some sort of online radio show in his spare time that was apparently quite popular, and he was more than willing to share intel with me without asking many questions. He'd once told me he enjoyed the thrill of it, but really he thought I was nothing but a nosy old lady, which suited me just fine.

Today he was wearing his usual: worn blue jeans and a beige uniform shirt with his name embossed on the left breast. "Haven't seen you in a while."

"I've been using other modes of transportation," I said, my thoughts turning sombre when I remembered how I'd recently flown to Toronto after Camille had been injured by Igor Ivanovitch.

"It's my loss," Asif said, grinning broadly. "Where are you going now?"

"Just escorting someone off the island, dear," I said. "I'm going to be returning home directly. But please do let me know if that vehicle comes back." I motioned at Brandon's car. His elbow hung out of the window as he exchanged pleasantries with the Woman on Wheels rider beside his car, although it was hard to see for sure what was happening because of his car's tinted windows. Most of the other riders had parked their motorbikes and made their way to the rail.

The pop song changed to something even more screechy and full of boom-boom-boom.

Asif tried to look casual while he palmed his cellular telephone, then took a picture of Brandon's car and plates.

"By the way, did you happen to notice a blue Ford sedan coming to the island recently?" I asked.

He shook his head. "I've been doing overnights this week. Haven't seen anything strange, though."

"Thank you, dear."

He smiled slyly. "I heard about that Snookie Smith implosion. The ambulance came through here too."

"Do tell."

"Snookie didn't want to go to the hospital on the mainland," Asif drawled, grinning. "She wanted to be taken to the island clinic. She argued with that poor EMT about it. He finally had to get out and walk around for a bit to let off some steam."

"Oh dear."

"Gotta go." He touched me on the shoulder, then strode toward his post.

The shore approached and the motorbike club started to assemble themselves. I always enjoyed the moment when the ferry touched the opposite shore. It had seemed dramatic and exciting when I was a child, and I supposed I'd never really lost that feeling.

The car engines, all shut down for the brief trip, sparked back to life.

Except for Brandon's.

His left arm was now dangling outside his window. Despondently? I'd once had to pry a stalker off a head of state right before she was about to get inaugurated, and I had no great patience for them. I simply wanted the young man to be gone. Then I was going to have a nice long jog and work some of the ants out of my pants.

The ferry's gate lowered and the first few cars slowly rolled off. The motorcyclists all swarmed to shore like a school of fish. When Brandon's car didn't ease forward, the car behind him pulled around and drove off the ferry.

Asif hit the ferry's ear-shattering klaxon to hurry Maura's ex up, mouthing a *Sorry* at me.

Still, Brandon's car did not move.

I made certain that my bicycle was secured, then walked toward him, the back of my neck slowly turning cold.

Twenty-Two — Violet

"Oh, I know!" Maura said, a smile breaking over her face. "Jerrod can drive Violet home."

"He needed some time off this afternoon," Norman said, and he sounded irritated about it. Like, how dare his elderly butler take a minute or two to regroup after falling and hurting himself while trying to help Norman's fiancée?

I gave Maura a little wave goodbye, then let Julian lead me to his office, his hair standing on end the way it did after he'd run his hands through it a few times. Helped him think, he'd told me. After shutting the door, he said, "I thought you could use an out."

I let out a relieved breath. At least nothing new was wrong. "Thank you. What an absolute wiener that guy is. Hey, can I go home yet?"

Julian gave me a kiss, then hugged me. "Yes, but carbon monoxide can be serious stuff, Vi. And you've just recovered from your concussion."

"I've got a hard head."

He gave me a look. "You're starting to sound like Irma."

"Take it back!"

His eyes twinkled.

"I need to do some work," I said. "And then I have to do some digging about the security system they're running over at Harbour House." I caught Julian up on how we'd gotten locked in the garage, the AirTag in Maura's snazzy handbag, and how Irma was currently running my ex-employee's ex-boyfriend out of town.

"So, why hasn't anyone called the police about what happened at Harbour House?" Julian asked. "The ex was there right before everything went down, right?"

"True, but if we can't prove he did anything, it's better to get him away from her, no? And Maura says he's a Luddite, so I don't see how he could have figured out how to hack into the system. Plus, over eighty percent of network or app breaches come from inside. It's much more likely that someone at the house did it."

"Someone like Norman, you mean."

"Yes, except Norman's claiming that the security company admits their system froze at the time we were in there and that what happened was just a technology glitch. And they think their system might have turned Maura's car on."

Julian's eyebrows rose. "But you don't believe them? Or is it Norman you don't believe?"

"Wireless technology isn't witchcraft, Julian. If the door lock and the car's starter were running on the same frequency and their command set was similar, that could potentially be a problem. But the security company would know that when they designed their system and would pick a higher communication band for their app to get around it. I mean, predicting that cars with automatic starter technology will be in garages that have digital locks isn't exactly rocket science."

"So you think they're lying?"

"Nope. I think Norman is. Now, all I need to do is prove it."

"Can't you just call the alarm company and grill them?" He grinned.

"I mean, I could, but they won't tell me anything about the system at Harbour House. All that type of data would be confidential." I ran my own hands through my hair and sighed. "All I know is, if something like that happened to someone I cared about, I'd want to know what went wrong. But Norman seems to have no curiosity about it at all."

"Maybe that's because he already knows what happened."

I shivered. "I know, right? Maura is an awesome person, but she really seems to have terrible taste in men."

"Well, you're not seeing Norman in the best light, right?"

"True."

"So your money's on Norman for locking you guys in remotely? And he knew Maura was in there because he sewed that AirTag into the lining of her purse, and he can sew well enough for her not to notice that the bag had been tampered with?"

"That's a good point." I sighed. "The purse is second-hand, so it *might* have showed up that way. And Norman looks too spoiled to sew."

"How does someone—"

"Let's just say I know it when I see it. But, yeah, Norman didn't need a tag for what happened yesterday. He could have just watched us from the house."

"Is it possible Norman's a jerk, but he's not the one behind any of this? Who else might have had access to that security system?"

"Her sister, her mother, and her mom's BFF, probably. And…"

"What?"

I shook myself. "I know that Maura's sister Ryeleigh dated one of Maura's exes in university. Ryeleigh is single, and she's a few years older than Maura. What if she's jealous that Maura's getting married before her? Plus, Ryeleigh talked me up at the club the other night, saying she was thinking about doing a computer science degree, but she could have easily talked to someone back home about that. Toronto's packed with nerds."

"So, why would she cozy up to you?"

"Maybe she wanted to insert herself between me and Maura for some reason. And she was at the club the night the PI died. She could have killed him."

"Why?"

"What if he found out something about her?"

"That's a stretch, don't you think?"

"There is literally nothing about this island that isn't a stretch," I said with a smile.

He grinned at me before turning rueful. "It really doesn't sound like Harbour House is a very happy place right now."

"Even the butler seemed unhappy about something when I showed up there yesterday."

"The *butler*? How?"

I nodded. "Like he was anxious about something—probably having to share the same space as Norman. When you're living with someone who yells and fights all the time, it can get...well, it produces anxiety, let's just say. You have to walk on eggshells all the time because you never know what'll happen next."

He gave me a focused look, waiting for me to say more. When I didn't, he said, "Irma should shake his tree. Domestic staff often see a lot of behind-the-scenes stuff."

"Good point." I sighed. "Anyway, I want to get started on my research about that security system. There's only one problem."

"Which is?" Julian asked, an adorable smile tugging at one side of his mouth.

"I don't know which one is actually installed at Harbour House. Most companies have their logo or company name on everything they produce. But I didn't see anything like that at the estate."

"Why don't you contact Wendy Wilson?"

"Who's that?"

"She does all the arrangements for those types of rentals."

"She's a real estate agent?"

"More of a real estate doula."

"I don't even want to know what that means. Can you give me her number, please? I'm going to head back to Irma's to do some of my real work, then get started on all this."

He put his hand on mine. "I was actually hoping you'd want to have dinner together this evening. You could use my office to work this afternoon and we can try to get out of here early. Well, early-ish."

I smiled. "Sure. You still have that laptop I left here last week?"

"Yup."

"Told you it would come in handy."

He smiled. Then, after a deep breath, he blurted, "My folks are going to be in town for Labour Day."

"Huh."

"My mother has been asking about you, and...she wanted to see if you could come over for one of her famous Sunday brunches."

"She a good cook?" I asked.

He threw his head back and laughed. It went on for a while.

"Alright, Julian. What's so funny?"

"My mother hasn't cooked in her entire life. We have help."

My smile faded. No wonder Julian knew that domestic staff had an inside track on private family matters. His family had *help*. And old money. And just one son.

"Yeah, I'm actually busy basically forever," I said, my hands up in a defensive motion.

"They won't be back for a year. It would be nice just to get it over with."

"Huh?"

He closed his eyes for a minute. "I'm not doing a good job of this, and I'm sorry." His shoulders were slumped forward, and for a minute he looked like a little kid. I remembered that kind of youthful slumping, since Phyllis had often caused the same kind of hopeless feelings to stir inside me. I'd bet twenty bucks Julian's parents were nicer to him when other people were around. That was probably why he wanted me to come.

A heat kicked up somewhere under my spleen. Julian was the nicest guy I'd ever met. I liked the way his eyes looked when the sun was going down, how my head fit perfectly on his shoulder, the way we could enjoy being quiet together.

But what kind of future did we have?

You could stay, the little voice at the back of my head whispered. *Stay on the island. Meet the parents. Survive Irma.*

"Okay."

His smile was quick and delighted and surprised. "You sure?"

"Wouldn't miss it."

"I'll set it up." He sat back in his chair, still smiling. "I guess you want that laptop."

"Sure do," I said. "And I also want something delicious for dinner."

"No problemo." He rustled under his desk for a minute and grabbed the little Lenovo I'd stowed here.

I took it with a smile. Time to get to work.

Twenty-Three — Irma

I approached the car slowly, signing *problem* to Asif, who lowered the barrier against the cars straining to roll onto the boat. One of Asif's brothers was deaf, and because of all the noise onboard the ferry, Asif and I sometimes used British Sign Language with each other.

My heart thumped in my ears while my left knee pinged all my senses, distracting me. Two cars were still behind Brandon's, one a blue minivan full of children shrieking in happiness. Their frazzled mother was looking straight forward, hands on the wheel, her frizzy brown hair not even trying to stay in its bun.

Cold formed between my shoulder blades.

I had no real weapon with me, and I was alone, surrounded by civilians. Little ones.

What if Brandon was simply asleep? Perhaps stalking his ex-girlfriend and being invited to leave town had exhausted him.

"Hey, lady," the man in the car in front of the minivan called out as I passed. He was in a sporty little red car; it had been him blaring pop music the whole trip over.

When I didn't answer him, he grabbed my right arm, swallowing up my wrist in his meaty paw. I slipped out of his grasp, then put a finger over my lips in the universal sign for *Do please shut up.*

His mouth puckered, then he flipped up the sun-shield portion of his eyeglasses. His eyes were blue and pale. Watery. Weak. If something was wrong, he'd be no help at all.

I kept moving, the back of my neck tingling.

Normally, I'd be taking in the environment: the exits, the people, the escape routes.

But this was the ferry. My ferry. I knew every inch of it.

From his operator's shack, Asif blew the horn again, concern etched into his features. I held up a hand for him to wait.

Finally, I was at Brandon's door. He was wearing a black polo shirt, mouth hanging open, chin resting on his chest. I put my hand on his arm. It came away wet. Wet and *red.*

The air left my lungs.

I turned and signed *emergency.* Asif, one hand splayed against the glass window of his cubicle, snatched up a phone in the other.

My left hand reached for Brandon's jugular while I scanned his car for threats. His pulse was faint, but he was still alive.

Things needed to move very quickly now. I cut through his seat belt with my trusty car escape tool, then grabbed his cellular telephone and stuffed it in my handbag, which I slung across my body like I was a postman, before pulling Brandon out of his seat and onto the floor of the ferry. He flopped down like a good tuna, his head whacking the metal surface. Well, I'd never said I was perfect.

After balling up part of Brandon's t-shirt, I tried to stuff it into the wound just under his left armpit, catching a glance of what was there as I did. A neat, small circle, welling with blood. A bullet wound? Could it be from the same gun that had dispatched poor Harvey Allen the other night? And why was such a small hole bleeding so much?

Someone skidded to a halt beside me. "I called 911," Asif said breathlessly, first-aid kit clutched against his chest.

"Thank you, dear," I said.

He dropped the kit on the ground. It held a few squares of gauze, some nitrile gloves, a bottle of disinfectant, and a few other bits and bobs, but not enough fabric that would actually help me stop the bleeding. The Band-Aids were stamped with smiley cartoon beavers.

There was no choice.

I sterilised my hands with the disinfectant, along with Brandon's armpit, thrust my right hand into a nitrile glove, then plunged a finger into the young man's armpit to see if I could grab onto the errant bleeder. He groaned.

"It's all right, dear," I said, knowing there would be no morphine shots in a first-aid kit that had cartoon Band-Aids in it.

"What happened?" Asif asked.

The man in the car behind us cranked his door open. Asif tensed immediately. "Please stay in your car, sir."

"I have a very important meeting to get to."

"We have a medical emergency."

"Can't I just drive around them?"

I didn't turn to look at the man. I was afraid of what my face would show him, that old warzone mien: calm, purposeful, focused. It looked a lot like cold, calculated evil. Someone had once snapped a photo of me that had almost ended up in the paper. Thankfully, the editor in chief had been willing to listen to reason.

There.

I pressed against the mass of veins until the dripping slowed, then stopped. Brandon's axillary artery might be bunged up, so it was important to hold it together without squishing it.

In the distance, sirens.

"You okay, Irmie?" Asif asked.

I struggled to find a good position in which to hover over Brandon, finally settling on kneeling, even though the metal surface of the ferry deck was as hard as at least one of my former husbands' heads.

"Thank you, Asif. I've got the bleeding stopped and the ambulance is almost here, so we're home free. Can you please clear the entrance to the ferry? Tell those cars they'll need to stay here for now, but the ferry is cancelled for the rest of the day."

He turned to go, then stopped. "The whole day?"

"It's a crime scene, dear. He's been shot."

Asif turned pale, then pasted a determined look on his face before marching toward shore. In front of me was an empty ferry. All the Women on Wheels riders had scooted away as soon as we'd hit land. I kicked myself, then thought about whomever had been fraternising with Brandon. He certainly hadn't shot *himself*, so the police would definitely want to talk to the rider of that Ducati.

The man behind me bellowed again, "Lady, when are we—"

"Come here," I snapped.

He got out of his tiny sports car and approached me slowly, gasping as he got an eyeful of the scene.

"Do you have a pillow or a blanket I can put under my knees?" I asked the little twerp from the little car. My knees, I'd finally had to admit to myself, were not as bendy as they used to be. If I had to kneel for much longer, I was going to have some problems.

His footsteps slapped the deck as he ran back to his car. The giggling girls in the minivan were finally silent, perhaps sensing their mother's unease.

Then I was nudged from the side. "Here," the man said.

It was a folded-up, faded blanket, probably kept in the car for winter emergencies. I raised my right knee, then my left, and he pulled the blanket under me. I almost swooned with relief.

"What happened?"

"He was shot," I said shortly.

"Huh? What do you mean? He was shot, then drove onto the ferry?"

Since I'd driven here with Mr. Brandon and hadn't shot him myself—however much I'd wanted to—I was quite sure that hadn't happened.

But what had?

"Hold his hand, please, dear," I said quietly. Those sirens were getting louder, which was a good thing, except for the fact that these were mainland sirens. I tried not to sigh. The next few hours were not going to be pleasant.

"What?"

I pulled his hand on top of Brandon's.

"You hang in there, dear," I said to Maura's ex as the comforting klaxon of a firetruck—no, two of them—rang out.

Asif had directed the mainland cars to move over to accommodate the emergency vehicles. I hoped none of them decided to simply leave the area. They were witnesses, witnesses who must have seen something.

Because I surely hadn't.

One minute, Brandon had been speaking to one of the Women on Wheels members, then…honestly, I could have kicked myself. That woman—or whoever it was—had leaned into Brandon's window while chatting him up. I should have been more paranoid. Hadn't I heard a sport bike at the club the other night—right before Harvey Allen was murdered?

I let out a breath. My knees, briefly comforted by that blanket, were starting to throb again.

But it was going to be all right. The firemen were pounding down the ferry toward me. On shore, an ambulance rolled up, sirens wailing. I could have kissed them all. I was almost done. In minutes, I'd have my fingers back. And my bloody knees.

"Ma'am?" one of the firefighters said. I didn't recognise him, but if I'd had a gun to my head I would have guessed that he was a real fireman and not an impostor squeezed into a blue uniform. He was an enormous forty-something gentleman, Estonian-blond with a hefty moustache perched under his nose, a cleft in his chin, and shoulders the size of Texas. Obviously, I liked him immediately.

"I'm a paramedic. What's happened?" he barked. Not too loudly, more like he knew the importance of not mucking about.

"Twenty-something male with what looks like a small calibre gunshot in the left axillary area. I have my fingers inside the wound and—"

"Don't move them."

I nodded brusquely. "Of course. But I'm very happy to see you. My hand is going numb."

He placed a meaty paw on my shoulder. "Understood. Just hang on, please, ma'am." He updated the team via his walkie, then holstered it again. "Any other injuries?"

"Not that I can tell, dear, although he did hit his head fairly hard when I pulled him out of the car." I decided not to mention how I'd also headbutted Brandon earlier. The firefighter had enough to work with.

While he did a quick external exam, I took a minute to remind myself that it really would be nice if Violet took a field medicine course. This was not the first wound I'd stuck my fingers in. Because I was so small, I'd always been the one holding team members together if we ran into a little snafu with our projects, although now that I was thinking about it, I could use a refresher as well. What a nice way for Violet and I to spend some quality time together.

The paramedic pulled out a stethoscope and took some vitals. Then he examined the wound carefully. Thoughtfully. He looked like someone who was focused and paid attention to detail. If Violet hadn't already been sorted out—

Perhaps not the right time.

Mr. Fireman called out to the two EMTs, who started toward us.

"Am I ever glad to see you boys," I said when the first two reached me. "Oh, hello, Jake. Are you moonlighting?"

"Mrs. Abercrombie," Jake said with a lopsided grin, "what have you gotten yourself into this time?"

I bit back a spicy retort.

Jake did a quick exam, then consulted briefly with the rest of his team. After some spirited debate, he turned back to me. "Irma, I have something to tell you that you're not going to like."

"It's been that kind of day, dear. What is it?" I moved my weight to my right side. My left and I weren't getting along so well at the moment.

"You have to hang on for a bit longer."

"*What?*" I made sure not to shriek, even though one was bubbling up behind my sternum. I'd been in much worse situations, but I hadn't had seventy-one-year-old knees at the time. Thankfully, my hips weren't in any danger. One could really only deal with so much in a single day.

"We're going to slide a backboard under the victim and move him to a gurney. We'll need you to stand when we raise the gurney and walk beside him."

"Then I can take my hand back and you'll put a dressing on the wound while we're in the ambulance?" I asked hopefully, blinking against the sun in my eyes. It really was a scorcher out.

"We'll try," Jake said. "But we might need you to hold on—literally—until we get him into surgery."

"Good heavens."

A gurney was being wheeled toward our little crime scene. I tried not to think about the stretcher that had rolled Snookie out of my sight the other evening. If she was still at the mainland hospital, I did not want to bump into her. She'd probably fake a heart attack and sue me for *that*, even if the root cause was really her own tiny, shrivelled heart.

"We need better imaging equipment to see exactly what's going on. If his axillary artery has been damaged, he might bleed out if you let go before we get to the hospital. And I don't think we have anything small enough to clamp that artery."

"Understood."

"Ma'am?" a woman's voice called.

I looked to the shoreline, then swallowed back a sigh. A uniformed officer was standing there, most likely ready to start interrogating me.

It's fine, I told myself. She doesn't know anything about you. You're a retired supply chain manager. You garden and sail in your spare time. You like doilies—I didn't really, but Mother had been ever so fond of them. You have a houseguest who's a bit of a nutter, and your friends are slightly odd, but really, whose weren't?

Brandon was starting to turn grey.

"Irma, we're gonna need you to stand when we lift the stretcher and walk beside it," Jake warned, then gave me a few instructions about what not to do, lest Mr. Brandon bleed out all over my white shirt, which was already dappled with blood.

Perhaps I would have to call Boris to come pick me up from the hospital. If so, I'd have him bring me some fresh clothes when he came. A warm flush spread across my chest at the thought that I had someone who could be a helpmate for me. And I for him.

If I would let him.

"Ready?" Jake asked.

"I can't feel my legs, dear," I said.

"No problem," the burly paramedic—Lars—said. "I'm going to pick you up."

"You most certainly are not," I retorted.

Jake put his hand on my arm. "Irma, we gotta go."

I took in a breath, then nodded. This was going to be difficult for me, but it was going to be far worse for Brandon, whose countenance was now decidedly green.

"On my count," Lars said, then did exactly that.

Two things happened: Lars put his arm around my waist, grasping me from behind, and hoisted me up while the stretcher was raised to its full height. Then we moved together.

I let my knees slowly straighten, my lower extremities dangling under me like fresh laundry on a line. Lars was holding me about a foot and a half off the ground, so, happily, there was lots of legroom.

"You okay, ma'am?"

"Irma, please."

"Irma," he said, and I could hear a smile in his voice. "I'm Lars."

"You don't happen to have any Estonian heritage, do you?"

"Swedish, actually."

"Isn't that nice. How do you think Brandon is doing?"

We moved off the ferry and toward the embankment.

"We're going to do the best we can for your friend, Irma."

I bit back the response that Brandon was not my friend. He needed one and I was here, and so now he was.

"Can you tell me what happened?" the uniformed officer asked as we passed her.

"Not right now," Jake said evenly. "We need to get this man to the hospital."

"Surely I can interview her after you take the patient away?"

"I'm afraid that I'm going with them, dear," I said.

The officer tugged at the rim of her hat, then stepped back. I had the distinct impression that she had no plans of forgetting about me.

Bother. Attracting the attention of local law enforcement was always a big no-no for people like me.

It was bumpy, getting the lot of us into the back of that ambulance, but we managed in the end. Jake was joined by another EMT who looked like she was about twelve. She was tiny—although taller than I—with a blonde buzz cut and at least three tattoos, and was busily setting up an IV line for Brandon while Jake attached monitors that beeped and whirred in the little space. Someone banged on the back of the ambulance and we took off toward the mainland hospital, St. Rita's—patron saint of the impossible.

Twenty-Four — Violet

I grabbed a corner of Julian's desk and attended to a bunch of issues at my office while he worked. In between meetings, I tried to track down real estate doula Wendy Wilson, who seemed to have a much more active social life than I did.

I'd bet Norman's is pretty good too. So I jumped on his Instagram while attending an administrative meeting that I didn't actually have to do anything for. Like I'd suspected, Norman's Insta was full of fancy parties and snazzy suits. The most recent ones had Maura on his arm, but a lot of other women graced the older entries, and they were all taken at high-end restaurants and swanky resorts.

Eventually, my work day ended and I started digging into some research about cellphone blockers. It looked like when they were in use, they caused a complete communications blackout, sort of like a cone of silence. So maybe everyone was right that Harbour House was located in a spot with terrible cell service after all. But I wasn't wrong about Norman. I was sure of it.

Next, I decided to focus on AirTag snooping. I'd never used any tags or tiles or whatnot to find my stuff, but I had to admit they made a lot of sense for people with memory issues.

And I discovered that Apple systems now had a built-in feature to alert people that they might be being followed by someone else's AirTag. But Maura and I had always been Android users. Luckily, there was an app for that, so I immediately set it up for myself and sent a link over to Maura for her to download, telling her to do a walkaround of her stuff to check for other trackers. She answered my email with two unicorn emojis, followed by three beavers and an apple pie which, being from Maura, almost made sense.

Julian came back after his last appointment and plunked into a chair. "Hungry?"

"Starving," I said, snapping my laptop shut. I needed to recharge, and eating something delicious with Julian sounded like the perfect way to do it. "Where are we eating?"

"Somewhere very exclusive. You'll like it, I promise."

Julian turned off his desk lamp, grabbed his briefcase, and we were off. He drove a nondescript car that I'd only recently realised was a Porsche. I tried to put the thought out of my mind.

Julian pointed us at the island's west side, heading down winding roads that—unlike Irma's crazy driving—he took at a sensible speed, his hands looking strong and comforting on the wheel. I had a thing for hands, and his were especially nice.

Finally, we arrived at a gated entrance before a driveway that disappeared into a stand of trees. You couldn't even see the house from the main roadway. I shifted in my seat. I'd never been to Julian's place, but I knew he came from money. I just hadn't realised he came from *this* much money. My hands were suddenly in my lap, twisting the straps of my knapsack into corkscrews.

The driveway was so long that the terrain changed three times before we hit the main house.

Or maybe I should say *estate*.

After we rounded the last corner, I could see at least five buildings: a gargantuan main house, another huge garage—this one with room for five cars, so maybe Norman wasn't as rich as he thought he was—and a few outbuildings. It wasn't an estate. It was a compound.

I gasped. The farthest building was a barn. Beside it was a fenced paddock with three horses. Two were even wearing matching plaid jackets.

Julian drove past the main house and the garage, past the horses, around a corner and down a little jog. There stood three buildings that were probably referred to as cottages but were bigger than most houses.

He stopped in front of the one farthest away from the main house, a detail I filed away for later. If pressed, I'd have to say that Julian wanted to be as far away from his family as possible.

I could relate. If Phyllis ever got wind that I was dating a kazillionaire, she'd do everything she could to squeeze this estate out of him. One little cottage wouldn't do for her. She'd always wanted it all. Everything.

I was getting a bitter taste in my mouth, so I closed my eyes for a minute. *Go away, Phyllis.*

"You okay?" Julian asked softly.

"You betcha," I said, forcing a grin to my mouth.

Julian patted my arm, then exited the car, leaving it unlocked.

The cottage, built in a coastal style like the main house and the other buildings, was sky blue with blindingly white trim and a wraparound porch. A picket fence would not have been out of place here.

And of course the front door was unlocked.

As he entered, Julian casually dropped his car keys in a bowl beside the door, probably a priceless antique. I stood on the threshold, taking the room in. I was expecting designer furniture, crazy accent pieces, and a whole lot of weird modern art.

Instead, it was a comfortable-looking sort of rustic space with good leather couches, an unfussy coffee table in a burnished brown, and a woodburning fireplace. An upscale kitchen sparkled on the other side of the room.

Something was definitely stuck in my throat. I set my bag down on the floor, then pulled each of my shoes off with the other foot.

"You're sure your parents are out of the country, right?" I asked.

"Yup," he said over his shoulder. "And this is my place, anyway. They're not going to bust in, I promise. C'mon."

He made his way to the kitchen, where an oversized breakfast bar sat opposite the kitchen's working space. It was obviously a spot for visitors to talk to the chef while staying the heck out of the way. I got started trying to mount one of the high stools. It took some doing to get up there, but I made it eventually.

The kitchen had two sinks, a ridiculous amount of usable workspace, and a funky patterned blue and white backsplash that evoked thoughts of Greece.

Marble counters offset the pale yellow of the cupboards, and the fridge had been covered in the same doors as the rest of the kitchen, so it was impossible to know where it was without opening every single cupboard. And was that a pizza oven in the corner?

Julian started gathering supplies, and after pouring me a glass of ice water, started muttering about the stuff he'd assembled.

"Something wrong?"

"I'm out of truffles."

I giggled. "Oh no! What are we gonna doooo?"

He met my eyes—I tried not to lose myself in their blue-green depths, but it was a struggle—then smiled. "It's just that it's hard to make a mushroom-beef risotto with truffles without actual truffles."

"Yeah," I said, trying to sound sympathetic.

Julian reached under the breakfast bar and came up with a walkie-talkie. "Can someone please bring me a black truffle? I'm out."

"Right away, Dr. Harper," burst out of the radio.

"You make your staff call you Dr. Harper?" I asked.

Julian sighed, then depressed the *speak* button again. "Thanks, Sidney. Now Violet thinks I make you call me that."

A string of laughter was the only response.

"I don't," he said to me. "Honestly. Sidney has been calling me that ever since I was a kid. She gave me a doctor's kit for Christmas when I was seven, and I was hooked. So she started calling me Dr. Harper."

"And Sidney is?"

"Our estate manager."

"Oh, of course."

He started organising his culinary booty on the workspace between us. First, he washed some Boston lettuce and diced a mound of shallots. When that was done, he started prepping a salad dressing.

"Hellooooo," someone called from the porch.

"C'mon in," Julian called back, and Sidney burst into the cottage with a surprising amount of energy.

224

"I'm Sidney." She thrust a hand at me, and I shook it. "Nice to finally meet you."

"You as well."

She set a half-ounce truffle down on a plate that Julian had set out. "You staying for dinner?" he asked her.

"Can't. I'm in the middle of something," she said. "Nice to meet you, Violet. You kids have fun."

After she was gone, I asked, "Do you guys eat dinner together often?"

He was julienning carrots on a mandoline, then switched to making paper-thin slices of radish. "As often as we can. We each cook about half the time, but with my schedule being so weird and her being a night owl, we sometimes eat really late."

"Speaking of *late*, I wonder how Irma did with Brandon. I texted her a few times, but no answer yet."

"She's probably up to something."

"I'm trying not to think about it." I shifted in my chair. "So, why do you and Sidney eat dinner together?"

Julian slid the veggies into a bowl, then shook the dressing, poured some on a lettuce leaf and took a bite. He repeated the same action, this time holding the leaf out for me. "What do you think?"

It was delicious. Heavenly. Shallots, champagne vinegar, a little honey, and some fresh parsley. "That's amazing!"

"Glad you like it," he said with a grin. Then he seasoned a gorgeous-looking New York strip with kosher salt and pepper and set it to the side after rubbing it with a clove of garlic that he'd smashed open with the side of a fancy-looking knife.

I noticed Julian hadn't answered my question about Sidney and decided not to push it.

After pouring some olive oil into a Le Creuset pan, he added a handful of risotto rice, stirred to cover it with the oil, then threw some diced shallots into the pan along with a deliciously obscene amount of garlic. The pan sizzled with a vibrant kind of energy.

It reminded me of Irma, all that buzzing. If I was being honest with myself, I'd have to admit that I still hadn't quite recovered from yesterday. And I sure hoped she wasn't up to something nuts right about now, because I was beat.

Plus, I really wanted to see where my evening with Julian might go.

Twenty-Five — Irma

"You all right there, ma'am?" the twelve-year-old EMT asked as the ambulance turned a corner. The name on her uniform was *Big Shirl*.

"Yes, dear. Thank you." I closed my eyes. Brandon was unconscious, which was troubling, but his innards were still warm and the bleeding had stopped. *Focus on that.*

Big Shirl patted me on the shoulder. "Just keep doing what you're doing—you're a natural. We'll be at St. Rita's soon."

She and Jake busied themselves discussing some of the readings they'd taken. I knew a bit of field medicine, and Julian had taught me a few tricks of the trade over the years, but most of the discussion went right over my head.

I crouched beside Brandon until Big Shirl slid a small stool under my tuchus. I sat down in relief. I knew I was going to have to get Julian to look at it again, which was bothersome because I'd only been kneeling for a short amount of time. I'd once knelt for three hours while waiting for a target to finish an interlude with a local fortune teller. I never did find out exactly what she was telling him, but she certainly hadn't seen me coming.

We squealed around another corner expertly, then slowed. I didn't know who the driver was—and hopefully no one had hijacked the ambulance so they could finish the job with Mr. Brandon—but they were excellent. Perhaps I could cajole them into teaching Violet how to get her car out of third gear and start enjoying life a bit more.

Stop it, Irma. She's seeing Julian now. That's progress.

A few more calming breaths, another corner, and we came to a halt. The back doors were flung open while medical staff converged on the ambulance in a veritable rainbow of scrubs.

Instructions were shouted, Brandon's IV line was lifted into the air, and Big Shirl started directing me on the best way out of the ambulance.

I did not particularly enjoy it when strangers told me what to do, but she had a nice manner and it needed to be done, so off I went on my derrière, as per Big Shirl.

When I reached the edge of the ambulance, all I had to do was put two feet on the ground before the lot of us could walk into the hospital like adults. There was just one problem.

My left knee collapsed under me when I tried.

"Whoops," Lars said, catching me. "Looks like we're still dance partners for a bit." He curled his arm around my waist and hoisted me into the air, my legs dangling like yesterday's fish, and our little parade marched toward the ER doors.

I glanced around to see if any snipers looked like they were about to finish the job with Maura's ex, but it was a half-hearted attempt at best. The adrenaline was starting to recede. My work here was done, and it was someone else's time to be in charge. I caught a glimpse of myself in the reflection from the glass front doors and decided not to dwell on the fact that I looked like a hand puppet.

My breath started to calm, especially when I caught an eyeful of the police presence in the ER admissions area, along with the metal detector that was being wheeled into place, a straggly queue forming in front of it. Apparently, someone had called ahead about there being a gunshot victim en route. It was true that we were on the mainland, but this town was no bustling metropolis. Gunshot injuries would be extremely rare here, with exceptions for the occasional whoopsie-daisy when someone shot their own foot during hunting season.

As Lars lugged me, my brain kicked into high gear. How had Brandon's shooter known he was going to be leaving the island at that particular moment? The ferry was in constant motion during the course of the day, a seventeen-minute trip each way, back and forth, and over and over. There was no set schedule. And Brandon had had no plans to leave today.

Then I remembered my feeling of being watched while skulking around outside Brandon's little cottage. I'd brushed it off at the time, but perhaps I'd been right after all. Or maybe Brandon had unknowingly texted his would-be assassin before he'd driven us to the ferry? His thumbs certainly had been energetic before our little drive. Really, I needed to get Violet to go through his cellular telephone, still safely tucked into my handbag.

Lars trundled me down the blue hallway, around a corner and toward the operating rooms. STAFF ONLY PAST THESE DOORS, the sign screamed. We burst through them, our odd little ensemble, and into OR number thirteen. I was briefly glad I held no superstitions against the number.

The trauma surgeon looked no older than Big Shirl, which I allowed myself to believe was a comfort. There was a lot to be said for experience, but one could also make a convincing argument that youthful energy was equally valuable. And Brandon needed all the luck he could get.

The surgeon leaned forward, her mask nested under her chin. "You've done some great work, Mrs. Abercrombie. Any feeling left in your fingers?"

"I've been afraid to wiggle them." I closed my eyes and reached out to my right arm with my senses, then my wrist, the palm of my hand, and the fingers that sprouted out of it. But past my wrist, things got dicey. "I don't believe so."

"All right," she said with a decisive nod that made me like her instantly. If she was a rogue agent intent on slicing and dicing Mr. Brandon, he was done for. "This is what we're going to do."

What followed was a somewhat difficult-to-parse discussion. If I couldn't unclench my hand, we would do X. If I could, we'd do Y. There was also briefly talk of a plan Z. I very much wished Violet were here so she could explain it to me in non-nerdy terms. But I got the gist eventually: they were going to do all the work. My job was to let go and get out of the way.

"You ready?" she asked Lars, still holding on to me like I was a basket of apples.

"Sure am."

"I'm going to want you to walk Mrs. Abercrombie out of the room when we take over pressure on the wound."

"Sounds good," he said cheerfully.

"Mrs. Abercrombie?" Her eyes were a lovely hazel with vibrant flecks of green. Smart eyes. Capable eyes. "You ready?"

"Yes, dear. And good luck." At her signal, I released my hold on Brandon's artery.

The gush of blood from his armpit was immediately staunched by a clamp that looked like it could squeeze shut the doors of hell.

Lars pivoted, then marched us right out the door. Behind us, the doctor said, "Let's begin, people."

As Lars walked us back through the STAFF ONLY sign, the beeping, wheezing doctor-speak of the OR faded.

"Do you have a problem with your knee?" Lars asked me cheerily.

"I have an old injury," I admitted. "It's normally okay, but today…"

"Not your day," he said, dimples popping out on both cheeks. Really, he was quite a handsome man.

"Are you married, dear?"

He threw his head back, his laughter banging up against my ribs. I took a breath, then let some of his good humour roll over me.

"Where are we going?"

"I'm taking you to an exam room," he said. "Someone needs to look at that knee."

"I'm fine, dear."

"I totally believe you. Here we are."

He turned neatly at the door to an empty room, then deposited me on the examination table. I stretched my right leg, then bent it a few times. Stiff, but in fairly good shape. The left was more problematic, unfortunately.

"I'm going to give the staff a heads-up that you're here."

"Oh, please don't, dear. I'm just going to go home and have my family doctor look at me."

Lars crossed his arms. "Do you have a teleporter?"

"Not on me, no," I said with a grin.

"The ferry is offline right now, ma'am."

"Irma, please."

"Irma." He smiled. "You were outside in the sun for an extended period of time, and—"

"It's late afternoon, dear. The sun isn't even that bad."

"Actually," he said firmly, "it is that bad. The sun is still quite strong at this time of the day, at this time of the year, you weren't wearing a hat, you're bright red, possibly from sunburn, and I'm going to go get someone to take a look at you."

"Oh, I like you. I don't like the thought of staying here, but you I like."

He burst into laughter again. I held my hand out for him to shake, and he kissed it instead. Then he waved and was gone.

I slowly flexed my left ankle. Pain shot through my knee. *Drat.* I tried to bend and straighten my leg, but it was a challenge. *Double drat.*

A young woman in sky blue scrubs knocked lightly on the door. "Mrs. Abercrombie?"

"Yes, dear."

"I need to run a few tests on you."

"May I see some ID, please?"

The nurse had gorgeous wavy blonde hair that was loosely bound at the back of her neck. She was plump and pleasant and young, and very nicely showed me her hospital identification, which was on a necklace that had been dangling inside her scrubs. *Tish Riley*, it said.

"Sorry about that, dear," I said. "I'm just so discombobulated from what happened."

She patted me on the arm. "Don't you worry about a thing. I hear you're having some problems with your knee. And that you were in the sun for an extended period of time."

I put a hand on the back of my neck. It was warm, probably sunburned. I nodded, then produced ID of my own so she could register me in the system. After that, I let her do an examination of my knee that neither one of us enjoyed.

After plying me with electrolytes, she said, "Do you have anyone to come pick you up after we're all done, Mrs. Abercrombie?"

"Uh..." Who should I call? Violet would—in her words—*freak out* if she found out I'd had another brush with a violent event. Julian was probably working. Geraldine was frolicking in the Maritimes with her new beau, Mack. Stuart was playing poker tonight. Plus, the ferry was inoperable at the moment.

Boris.

No. I did not want to become dependent on him.

"Yes," I said. I'd have to sort out who to call later.

Tish nodded and promised she'd be back with my results soon.

I closed my eyes briefly, opening them when I heard a knock.

"Mrs. Abercrombie?"

"Yes?"

The uniformed officer from the ferry landing stood in the doorway. She was in her twenties or thirties, trim and short-haired, with plump cheeks and impressively large ears.

Drat.

Briefly, I missed the Pickle. In my former line of work, it had always been important to steer clear of local law enforcement. Technically, we were all on the same side, but the methods used by intelligence workers were sometimes frowned upon. Plus, it was never good to get yourself embroiled in a lot of civilian paperwork. It was even worse to get your picture taken.

"Can I speak to you for a moment?" the woman said.

I appraised her again. She looked like a standard-issue uniformed officer, all of her gear shiny and well-maintained.

"Of course."

She stood instead of taking one of the seats available, a quirk of law enforcement that I normally approved of. Sitting could get you killed in more ways than one.

After showing me her ID at my request, she said, "Could you please tell me about what happened on the ferry this afternoon, Mrs. Abercrombie?"

I nodded and gave her a brief summary of what had transpired.

"So you never saw the motorcyclist who was talking to Mr. Ott?"

"Just from the back."

"Beaver Island is a pretty small place. You didn't recognise her?"

I shook my head. "I wasn't paying much attention."

She brushed something off her shirt. "And you didn't see Mr. Ott get shot?"

I shook my head while she scratched in her pad.

"Could he have driven onto the ferry, already injured?"

I blinked a few times to gather my thoughts. "No. I was in the car with him."

Her eyebrows rose, and the pen paused in the air. "How's that? Do you know him?"

"He's a friend of a friend."

"And why were you in his car?"

I wiped some sweat from my brow. "Sorry, dear, I'm feeling a little tired."

"We're almost done, ma'am."

"I was in his car because he needed directions to the ferry."

"Why couldn't you just show him on Google Maps?"

"He's a bit of a Luddite, dear. As am I."

"Uh-huh. And how were you supposed to get home?"

"I put my bicycle in his back seat. I took it out on the ferry, then went to speak to Asif, the ferry master."

"In his cabin?"

"No, he came down to speak to me," I said, then added, "and I suppose my cycle is still on the ferry. Drat."

"And neither one of you saw or heard what happened?"

"Unfortunately not," I said with a sigh that wasn't manufactured at all.

She tapped the notepad with her pen. "And did you know the man who was shot on the island earlier this week?"

"No."

"But you found him." Her tone was flat. I was impressed. Up until now, she'd been treating me like any member of the public, but all along she'd known that my week had already been somewhat eventful. And now I'd been in close proximity of a second gunshot victim. I could only hope that the Pickle wouldn't catch wind of all this.

"Would you be willing to submit to a gunshot residue test?"

I took a moment to calculate how long it had been since I'd shot a gun. I got in some regular target practice on my own property—along with sniper drills from my third-floor widow's walk from time to time.

I knew gunshot residue could stay on one's hands for up to five days after discharging a weapon. But I always used a specially made hand sanitizer that whisked it all away.

Edward, my gadget friend and Stu's fishing buddy, had developed the sanitizer some time ago, and I always kept my larder well-stocked with it. I'd last shot a gun three days ago, but since I'd followed all of my normal precautions, chances were excellent that the residue from that event was all gone.

Plus, it would help the young officer with her investigation to rule me out. I, for one, had no idea why—or how—young Brandon had been shot almost in plain sight and left for dead. And I wanted some answers, too.

"Yes," I said. "Please go ahead."

"It's nothing personal."

"You need to do your job, dear. I understand," I said. Belatedly, I wished I'd put on my nice little old lady persona from the start. Of course, it hadn't occurred to me that I'd be seen as a suspect, an obvious miscalculation on my part. Perhaps I was more rattled than I had realized. "Do we need to go to the police station now?"

"We have all we need here."

"Goodie."

"Plus, we're going to do some imaging on that knee," Tish said cheerily from the doorway. When the officer glared at her, she retreated back into the hall.

"We're also going to need your clothes for evidence," the officer said, handing me a bag. "I've got some scrubs for you to wear home."

I'd suspected this was coming, but I didn't want my clothes in the hands of law enforcement, especially my left shoe, which held a small but energetic blade that I was quite fond of, also courtesy of Edward. But the hidden compartment required a few steps to release the catch, and if the shoes were X-rayed, the soles would look solid. Of course, if someone decided to take them apart, then I was definitely sunk.

"I'm going to need some privacy, dear."

She shut the door, staying inside the room. "I'm sorry, Mrs. Abercrombie. I have to be present to ensure chain of custody. Your clothes are evidence in a crime."

"In that they'll help prove I wasn't the one who shot Mr. Ott?"

"Something like that."

I pressed my lips together to hold in a sigh, then nodded. If they asked for my shoes, I'd just have to take my chances.

I changed into the scrubs—yellow, with little bunnies bouncing all over them—dropping every item of clothing except for my undergarments into a brown paper bag, which was a welcome development, as I'd just remembered that there was some piano wire in my brassiere that probably would have raised some eyebrows. Even better, I was able to keep my shoes.

The gunshot residue test was quick and painless: a cotton swab run over my hands and up my arms to my elbows, which was perhaps a tad over-dramatic.

The officer stepped out the door, probably to run the test, and I tried not to feel irritated that she was such a go-getter. That might not bode so well for me.

Twenty-Six — Violet

My cell rang about five seconds after Julian and I had finished dinner—a sumptuous mushroom-beef risotto alongside a garden salad with a champagne vinaigrette so sweet that it had been like a dessert. Actual dessert had been tartufo in tiny bowls. The man could cook.

"You going to get that?" Julian nodded at my phone.

My thumb hit the *answer* button, and I put the call on speakerphone.

"I just want you to know that everything is perfectly all right," Irma cooed.

"Uh-huh," I said.

"But I did I run into a bit of a snafu while dropping off our friend."

"Why doesn't that surprise me?" Julian asked.

"Julian, darling! How wonderful to hear your voice."

I rolled my eyes, and Julian stifled a laugh.

"What are you two up to?"

"Dinner."

"At Julian's place?"

"Uh-huh."

Irma took a deep, satisfied breath. "Isn't that nice. And here I thought nothing good was going to happen today."

"Did you get Brandon off the island?" I asked.

"Um...yes."

Julian and I looked at each other.

"Did you kill him or something?" I asked.

"Um...no."

"That's something," Julian muttered.

"I have to say, I'm a little insulted—"

"Irma," I said, a warning in my voice, "what's going on?"

"Wellllll...*I* didn't try to kill Brandon, but someone certainly did." Irma briefly detailed the shooting on the ferry, her trip to the ER courtesy of an enormous Swede named Lars, and how her hand had been stuck inside a stranger for the better part of an hour.

"An hour?" Julian said, sounding horrified.

"I used a glove, dear. And disinfectant, of course."

"Oh, of course," he echoed faintly.

"Do you need me to come get you?" I asked.

"Have you been drinking, dears?"

"Nope. We're just high on life," I quipped.

"Good for you!" she said before whispering, "They don't actually want me to leave, so we're going to have to have our wits about us."

"Should I stop the car when I pick you up, or just slow down?" I asked.

"Who's *they?*" Julian asked.

"The staff here," she said.

"Where's here?" he asked.

"St. Rita's."

"And why don't they want you to leave?"

"Potential heatstroke, blah blah blah." More quietly, Irma added, "Plus, I've bunged my knee up somewhat."

I closed my eyes for a minute, trying to push down the worry that was descending on me. If Irma was admitting to heatstroke and knee problems, which were survivable, that meant something much worse was probably going on. Plus, she'd gotten sucked into all this because she was trying to help my friend. This was all my fault.

"I shudder to think of what you'll do to the staff if they try to keep you there," I said, trying to force an upbeat tone into my voice. "I'll come pick you up."

"That's going to be a little complicated," Irma said. "The ferry is not currently operational."

"Why?" I asked.

"It's a crime scene, dear. Julian, do you have any boats at the house, or are they all at the club?"

I shot Julian a look.

He reached out and put his hand on mine. "Our powerboat is at our dock, Irma, but I'm on call tonight. I can't leave the island."

"Can Sidney pilot the boat?" she asked.

"Yeah," he said thoughtfully. "But tomorrow is her day off and she's going to see her sister really early, so…"

"Could someone drive Violet home so she can get *Vitamin Sea*?"

"Irma…" I looked out the window. "It's dark outside. I've never piloted alone at night."

"Just put the lights on, dear, stay close to shore, and go very slowly. It's not far, and the conditions are dead calm right now. You've captained the boat for much longer. And if you start out and you're not happy for whatever reason, just return home."

"Okay."

"I'll send someone to collect you on the mainland, and I'll pilot the boat home myself."

"Can Stu do it?" Julian asked.

"It's his poker night, dear. He's not answering the phone. And neither is anyone else. But I can organize something else if this isn't going to work."

"It's okay," I said, fiddling with the hem of my shirt. "I can do it."

"Wonderful! Julian, dear, make sure Violet has all the marine charts, please."

"Will do."

"I have a go-bag in the closet of my bedroom. It's the one on the top shelf, on the left. Could you please bring it with you, Violet?"

"No problem."

"And could you arrange a way to copy—or whatever—a cellular telephone?"

"Irma," Julian said slowly, "did you steal someone's phone?"

"I'm giving it back, dear. And that's the important part."

We all hung up. Julian walked me through some of the aquatic charts around the pier on the mainland, which I sent to my phone, and then we headed to the car. The driveway seemed even longer on the way out, and now there was another horse in that field.

We were quiet most of the way to Irma's.

"You don't have to do this, you know," Julian said eventually. "We can find someone else to go get her."

"Irma messed her knee up because she was helping my friend."

"I know, but she doesn't always have to get her way, Vi."

"Probably not," I said, "but it's just so much easier on everyone else if she does."

Julian laughed.

"And it's okay."

"I just worry because you used to have so many problems on little boats."

"Those vertigo exercises I've been doing have helped a lot." I put my hand on his. He was warm. Solid. A little weird, too, but that was okay. Weird was never boring. "Thanks," I added softly.

"For you?" he said, equally as quiet. "Anything."

Maybe that was why we kissed in Irma's back yard for a few minutes before I hopped into the boat to go rescue her, go-bag in hand. Julian, who'd spent a lot of time behind *Vitamin Sea*'s wheel, gave me a few tips and suggested I slip into a particularly poufy lifejacket, which I did with enthusiasm.

"Call me when you're coming back," he said as he pushed me off from the dock. "I feel like I'm owed the second half of our evening."

"Doing what?" I called.

"A nerdy night in front of a fireplace," he said. "I have to do some reading for a conference that's coming up."

"How could I resist an offer like that?" I said, and he laughed. Then I pointed *Vitamin Sea* toward the mainland. Julian waited on the dock until we couldn't see each other anymore.

I had been a little nervous, but Irma was right about the conditions: the lake was like glass, lights from the estates that ringed the island dappling the water and making it easy to see. So I opened the boat up a bit. Not too much, just enough to put a little oomph into my day, as Irma would say.

I'd worried things were going to get complicated when I was docking, but Julian had directed me to a marina with a nice-looking restaurant attached to it, and there were people everywhere.

Someone grabbed the lines I threw and helped me dock without even pausing her phone conversation. After that was done, I secured the boat and grabbed my knapsack. The computer that was pretty much always inside it now was a roughneck laptop a buddy of mine had asked me to beta test for him. It was getting a great workout, courtesy of Irma.

A sixty-something woman in scrubs who was standing on the dock approached me when I jumped onto land.

"Violet?" she said. Her voice was husky, like she'd spent a good part of her life smoking. She was petite, with laugh lines around her eyes, deep red lipstick, her hair a dead ringer for Farrah Fawcett's.

"Hi."

"I'm Nora. I'm a friend of Irma's. She told me to come get you."

I froze on the spot. Irma was always warning me about the danger of imposters, especially ones in uniform. On the other hand, she had friends and well-wishers squirreled away pretty much everywhere.

Nora held up a hand. "It's a perfect Beaver Island day," she said, which was one of Irma's code phrases. Of course, someone could have easily cracked that code. So I was still rooted in place.

A grin broke over Nora's face. "Yeah, I don't blame you. But I'm really her friend, I promise."

"Tell me something embarrassing about Irma."

"Why? Is that another code or something?"

"No, I just want dirt on her."

She grinned again. "I hear ya. I don't know anything embarrassing, but I can tell you that Irma and I met because she punched my jerk of an exstepfather right in the kisser when he was about to start beating on my ma. He never touched her again."

"Sounds about right. Okay, if you're going to try to kill me, can you do it quick? It's been a really long day."

"Is that why you're still wearing a lifejacket?"

I looked down. After slipping out of my enormous yellow vest and sticking it in a cockpit locker, I followed Nora to a beat-up Volkswagen sporting a bunch of Greenpeace bumper stickers that seemed to be holding the car together. She drove like a normal person, chatting about her day. She was an orderly at St. Rita's.

"Any word on Brandon's condition?" I asked.

"He's stable for now," she said. "But I'm no doctor, so I don't know all the details." She looked uncomfortable.

"What's wrong?"

After tapping a hand on the wheel, she sighed.

I was starting to get uneasy again. Maybe I should have made Julian come with me—maybe—

"Irma would probably kill me if I tell you," she said.

"Uh-huh?"

She looked around, like someone might be listening to us. "It's probably not a big deal."

The hospital loomed in the distance, a few ST. RITA'S signs appearing on the road. It was a multi-building complex with utilitarian architecture, tiny windows, and an airless feeling about it. Pretty much the polar opposite of Julian's place. Julian's *parents'* place.

"What is it?"

"Some of Irma's test results have come back abnormal."

"What? Why would anyone need to do tests on Irma? She wasn't the one who was shot."

"She was in the sun for over an hour, kneeling beside the victim, with her hand inside him, and she's elderly. At the very least, her electrolytes are out of whack."

"Don't let her hear you call her elderly."

"I'm three years younger than her," she said with a grin. "I can call her whatever I like."

"Good luck with that."

She burst into laughter that soon faded. "There's something else."

"What?"

"The cops think she might have shot that guy."

Twenty-Seven — Irma

When the mainland officer finally came back, I was expecting her to tell me the results of my GSR test.

Instead, she'd brought me a surprise.

"Hello, Mrs. Abercrombie," Mavis Pickle said from the doorway. If pressed, I could not have determined exactly what tone the Pickle was using, what expression was currently on her face.

I tried to keep my countenance equally neutral, even though I was not thrilled by this turn of events. "Hello, Mavis, dear."

A wry look was quickly replaced by a more serious one. Mavis shut the door behind her, and she and the other officer took a seat across from me while I adjusted the ice on my knee.

"What happened there?" Mavis asked.

"I might have injured it a tad during all the excitement."

"Uh-huh."

"Mrs. Abercrombie, Chief Bloom and I are going to be working together to get to the bottom of all this," Mavis said.

"Wonderful." I wondered if it would be inappropriate to ask for some tea. Perhaps a few nibbles as well.

"Because this is all very serious," she continued.

I supposed it *was* a bad time for snacks. I nodded. "Of course I agree with you completely. Gunplay in aquatic environments is always quite serious."

Chief Bloom shot a glance at Mavis, who looked like she had some sort of indigestion. It was too bad that I didn't have a protein muffin to offer the poor thing.

"Can you please catch Chief Pickle up on what's happened?" Chief Bloom asked me.

I did so, wincing when I moved the ice pack again. For some odd reason, all that cold wasn't improving things, knee-wise. And I detested pain tablets.

"So you saw nothing," Mavis said flatly.

"Correct, dear."

"Mrs. Abercrombie," Chief Bloom said softly, "I have some news for you."

I blinked.

"Your gunshot residue test came back positive."

I shot a glance at Mavis, whose expression had not changed one whit. Or were her nostrils flaring? I'd spent quite a bit of time trying to sort out what her *tell* was, but hadn't yet succeeded. But nostril quivering was definitely a contender.

I smoothed down the front of my pants to grab a moment to contemplate the situation. Eventually, I settled on, "Good heavens, dear. That can't possibly be true. Can we please run another test?" as a response.

"We absolutely will," Chief Bloom said. "But I was wondering if there was anything else you wanted to tell me about your trip with Mr. Ott."

"No, thank you."

She made a strange noise in her throat. "Perhaps I'm not making myself clear. I'm wondering—"

"You're making yourself perfectly clear, dear," I said, trying not to get snippy about it. "You want to know if I shot our young victim. No, I did not. You're wondering if I threw the gun I shot him with overboard. No, I did not. I had no reason to shoot anyone"—at that exact moment—"and so I did not." I adjusted the ice on my knee again. "I'm just a retiree, dear. I like to putter in my garden and crochet—"

Mavis held a hand up, and I shot her a glance. I did not want her referring to my former line of work in any way whatsoever. It could be dangerous for both of us, but more so her. And I had become fond of her, in my own way.

"Sorry," Mavis said, obviously reading my facial expression. "Please go on, Mrs. Abercrombie."

"I don't really have anything to add, dears."

"Ma'am," Chief Bloom said. I could tell I was trying her patience. She and Mavis had more in common than they probably thought. "Have you discharged a handgun recently?"

"No."

She referred to some of her notes. "I see here that you have a registered gun range on your property."

"Yes, but even without that designation, it's perfectly legal to discharge a firearm on private property, dear, as long as one is not in an urban environment." I sank down in my seat to make it appear like I was small and feeble. It was time to really transition into my sweet little old lady persona. "Dad was a military man, you know."

"And we thank him for his service," Chief Bloom said smoothly. "But I can't understand why your test would come back positive if you haven't discharged a weapon recently."

"Perhaps your field test isn't as accurate as one would hope."

"It is very accurate," she said firmly.

I closed my eyes for a moment. Really, I was out of my depth here, investigating murders and armed robbery and tractors running amok. I'd had a lovely career in…let's call it *harm prevention*, but most of the intel I'd relied on had been gathered by nerds in back rooms with big juicy brains. I'd always been more of a do-er, really.

Plus, I was quite aware that local law enforcement were allowed to lie to people. Civilians. Me. And I was fairly certain that the bright young officer in front of me was doing just that. It was hard to believe that Edward's magical disinfectant had failed me. He'd once constructed a pair of tap shoes that would shoot an explosive dart if you tapped an E sharp with them. That was talent.

"Chief Bloom, is it not possible that when I put my hands on—and inside—that poor young man's gunshot wound, the residue on his body rubbed off on my hands?" I smiled sweetly, even though I was actually starting to feel somewhat unwell.

Bloom responded by frowning at me, while I could swear that the left side of Mavis's mouth briefly curved up. I took that as a sign that Chief Bloom had no imminent plans to throw me in the slammer, which was nice, as droplets of sweat had just broken out across my forehead.

"You okay, Irma?" Mavis asked quietly.

A hint of nausea rumbled deep inside me. "Might I have some water please, Mavis?" I leaned forward to try to steady myself. And I wished I'd brought a real go-bag with me instead of my useless pocketbook. Well, useless except for Brandon's cellular telephone. Too bad I couldn't eat it. Really, I should have had a bigger lunch before confronting young Brandon.

"I'll get some," Chief Bloom said, then briskly walked out the door in search of a cup.

"You up to something, Irma?" Mavis asked after she was gone.

"When will the ballistics report be done, dear?" I asked. "Can you try to match the bullet from Brandon to the bullets you took out of poor Mr.— that other poor man?"

"Thanks," she said drily. "We'll definitely be doing that."

"Both small calibre, yes?"

A nod. "It can take weeks for that analysis to be done, Irma."

"Of course. Tell me"—I glanced at the door—"do you have any suspects in that gentleman's death yet?"

She frowned. "I can't comment. And you aren't interfering in my investigation, right?"

"Of course not, dear. You know how I get."

Mavis glanced at the door. "We're following some leads at the moment, Irma. But we're not close to an arrest at this time."

The nausea was starting to burble around in my insides. So much so that a little belch escaped me. I put my hand over my mouth and shook my head. "Mavis"—*belch*—"can you please be a dear and see if you can get me some nausea tablets?"

Mavis frowned. "What's wrong?"

"I'm not quite sure. It could just be the adrenaline whooshing out of me. Or it might be that I got too much sun after all."

"I thought you had a stomach of iron," she said, walking to the door.

"I normally do," I said. Right before I vomited on the floor. "Oh, dear."

Chief Bloom, who'd finally procured that glass of water, stopped in the doorway and looked at the mess I'd made. "What did you do to her?" she asked Mavis.

"Nothing. It's just been a lot of excitement for me today." I held up a hand. "Chief Bloom, dear, can you please see about getting me some medical attention? Between my knee and my stomach, I'm really not feeling all that well," I said, putting my hand over my mouth and covering up another burp. "And sooner would be better than later, dear."

Chief Bloom found enough hospital staff to cough up some anti-nausea meds, and get the room's floor mopped clean while shooing away any looky-loos.

Then a young medical tech strutted into the room with a rolling cart of supplies, some of which looked positively medieval. "I hear you've had an interesting day," he said cheerfully. He was young and lean, with a shock of red hair and enormous hands. I decided not to tell him he would have had an excellent career strangling terrorists.

"Quite." I let him run his tests and talk me into taking an anti-inflammatory for my knee, gnawing on a cardboard-tough power bar, and submitting to some IV hydration.

He excused himself when he was finished, and returned with a willowy Persian woman with a ring in her nose and fire-red lipstick. She was forty-something, with eyes that were both sharp and weary at the same time.

"Mrs. Abercrombie," she started.

"Irma, please."

She nodded. "Of course, Irma. I'm Dr.
Daghestani. I hear you were the one who hung on to
that young man's axillary artery. What made you
think to do that?"

"I watch a lot of television, dear."

"That makes sense, at your age."

I swallowed down some bile that was either
leftover from my recent stomach upset, or directed at
the young doctor.

From the doorway, Mavis made a coughing noise.

Dr. Daghestani scrolled through a tablet
computer for what felt like forever.

I detested lying in bed, doing nothing. And while
I was here doing all that nothing, Brandon was
probably out of surgery. Possibly even in danger. I
had a sinking feeling that I had misjudged Maura's
ex, which meant that what had happened to him had
been at least partly my fault.

"Do you know how Brandon Ott is doing?" I
asked.

"I can't give out that kind of information," the
doctor said.

Drat. I knew I wasn't going to be able to sleep
tonight without knowing what Brandon's condition
was.

"Your EKG came back abnormal," she added.

"Abnormal how?"

"It looks like you're experiencing a few
arrhythmias."

I waved a hand. "That's not a big deal, dear. EKGs are not the most precise of instruments. Plus, adrenaline can make everything go a little wonky."

She sat back in her chair and crossed her arms. "You seem like a real Renaissance woman, Irma."

"I have a houseguest who watches a lot of Discovery Channel shows," I said sweetly.

Another strangled cough from the hallway. To be honest, it warmed the cockles of my heart a bit to have Mavis back in such fine form.

"Excuse me." The doctor hopped to her feet, then closed the door quite decisively in Mavis's face. "You're correct, Mrs. Abercrombie, but we do have to take your advanced age into account as well. Which is why I'd like to admit you for a few more tests. After they're completed, I'd like you to wear a heart monitor for a few days so we can follow your cardiac activity."

Advanced age? I mean, really.

I cleared my throat. "Is all that really necessary? All I did was kneel for a while and hold on to something slippery. I mean, kindergarten teachers do worse every day, and they all seem fine. Apart from being criminally underpaid, of course."

"Um, yes. I understand where you're coming from." She scratched her arm. "I think. We're just going to move you into the cardiac monitoring unit for observation overnight, and we'll do some more testing tomorrow. That means no wandering around the hospital, especially with that knee. We're going to do some imaging on it tomorrow, too."

Drat. That would definitely put a damper on my burgeoning plans to watch over Brandon in the ICU so no one could finish him off. When I'd arranged for Nora Driver to collect Violet, she'd told me that the hospital had bumped up security precautions in the ICU lately. That was very nice, but she'd also told me that the overnight security guard was running late this evening, which was less so. Plus, I would need to return that cellular telephone to Brandon at some point, so no one would realize I'd pinched it.

But I said, "Of course, dear."

The doctor called a porter, who showed up promptly. After getting his marching orders, he smiled and helped me settle into a wheelchair. I wasn't a fan of not using my legs, but he was quite muscly and insistent, so I let him roll me out of the room.

Mavis came to my side. "I have to go for now, but I'm going to follow up with you later, okay?"

"Okay."

She put a hand on the wheelchair, and the porter stopped rolling me. "You sure you're all right, Irma?"

I put my hand over hers and squeezed. "I'm fine, dear. Really."

She arched an eyebrow at me but eventually nodded.

"Ta," I said. She waved as she walked off, and the porter resumed his duties.

"What's the charge nurse like on the cardiac ward?" I asked.

"Total battle-axe," he said cheerfully, mashing all the buttons on the elevator. Apparently, we were going both up and down at the same time.

"Does she like donuts or muffins? I know of some terrific protein-fibre muffins, she'd probably love."

"Not a muffin lover."

"Drat," I said, letting my head hang. "Fibre is such an important part of one's diet."

"It sure is." At this, he started humming something tuneless.

"Does she like flowers, or—"

"Mrs. Abercrombie, you are gonna spend tonight in bed. There's just no way around it."

"I see." I was hoping he was exaggerating, but after we rounded a corner and neared the cardiac nurses' station, I spotted the charge nurse in the midst of a gaggle of medical staff.

She looked like a cross between angry puffin and an Irish bulldog. Her reading glasses were perched on her nose, not unlike Snookie's—Snookie, who was potentially somewhere in this very same hospital. Hopefully, my island nemesis wouldn't sneak into my room in the middle of the night and try to smother me with a hospital-issued pillow. I really was starting to feel like I needed some rest.

The charge nurse's hair was white and no-nonsense short, her shoes were straight out of the

1950s, and the rest of her looked like she hadn't said yes to anything in years.

I gulped.

"Is this Mrs. Abercrombie?" she asked the porter. After a nod from him she said, "Bed five, please." Her tone left no room for negotiation, which seemed fine to the young man shuttling me toward my little prison. Bed five was right in front of the nurses' station. It was practically *in* the nurses' station.

"Are you going to be moving me again?" I asked the porter quietly.

"Nope," he said, passing some paperwork to the charge nurse, whose name tag said only: WILHELMINA.

"Mrs. Abercrombie," Wilhelmina said sternly—like I'd just taken a candy out of her handbag without permission.

I tried not to let it frazzle me. "Yes, dear?"

Closer up, it appeared that a few of Wilhelmina's chin hairs had escaped her tweezers. "My name is Nurse Wilhelmina."

"Nice to meet you, Nurse Wilhelmina. I just wanted to ask—"

"No."

"Of course. It's just— "

"No."

"I have a friend here who's quite ill, and—"

"Your job right now is to focus on you." She turned her head slightly and pointed at the hallway I'd just been rolled through. "What in the world…?"

When I turned to look, she slapped a red wristband on me.

"Hey!"

"You're at risk of falling, Mrs. Abercrombie. You are to stay on this ward until you're picked up for your imaging tests tomorrow. After that, you will convalesce until you're discharged. Do I make myself clear?"

I slowly took in a breath. "I suppose."

But then her face softened and she stepped forward, taking my pulse in a way that felt a little like a reassuring pat on the arm. "Everyone is quite concerned about you, Irma. You are a hero for what you did for that young man. Now we need to make sure you're okay, too."

Suddenly, tears felt like they were welling somewhere deep in my innards. That happened, sometimes, after a crisis.

Then she patted my arm for real. "We're going to take good care of you, ma'am."

"Thank you, dear, even though you played a dirty trick with that misdirection. Well done, you."

"Thanks! And you're going to promise to follow your doctor's recommendations, right? And do what I tell you?"

I bit back a laugh. "Has someone been talking to you about me?"

A ghost of a smile appeared on her face before her stern countenance returned. She nodded, then said, "Of course not."

"Understood."

Another pat, and she returned to the nurses' station, still right in front of me. She started reviewing charts, pausing periodically to flick her eyes at me over her reading glasses. The only time I'd seen this sort of setup was in the ICU. Or prison.

And where on earth was Violet? I was going to need some kind of a diversion, or else I was never going to get out of here.

Twenty-Eight — Violet

"You want me to *what?*" I asked. Irma was looking pretty chipper for someone whose hand had been inside someone else most of the afternoon, but if you looked closer, you could see that her normally flawless complexion was now red. Too red.

"The charge nurse is watching me like a hawk," Irma whispered. "I'm going to need you to build me a bomb in one of the closets down the hall."

"No."

"Please? Just a little one."

"No."

"Pretty please? There are so many chemicals in this place, it would be easy! Plus, it's the only way to get me out of here. We need a diversion."

"You didn't tell me you'd been admitted—to the cardiac ward, no less. You have an IV stuck in your arm! You aren't going anywhere." My voice rose on the last words, and the charge nurse glanced up, fixing Irma with a *No, you certainly are not* look.

"See what I mean?" Irma hissed.

I threw my hands up.

She scowled. "All right, let's forget about that for now. Why don't you wander on over to the ICU and make sure that Brandon is still among the living, then sit with him quietly until security shows up, please and thanks? Apparently, the ICU guard who's coming on shift has been delayed a little. Plus," she whispered, "I need you to return Brandon's cellular telephone after you copy it."

"Clone it."

"I've had enough nonsense this summer with all the drones, dear. Don't tell me I have to deal with clones too."

I pulled up a chair beside her bed. This was going to take a while. "It's a digital clone, Irma. It can't hurt you."

She made a *you never know* noise, so I decided to leave that one alone.

Irma slid her purse open to show me Brandon's phone, a battered Nokia Android. I snapped a USB cable into its port and started to clone it to a backup drive.

"Thank you, dear. Now, I have some spare scrubs for you."

"Howdja get *those?*"

"You brought them to me." Patting the sports bag she'd told me to grab before coming to the hospital, she smiled sweetly.

I gave her a look. "No, I mean, why do you have scrubs in my size? I'm like a whole person bigger than you."

"I felt like getting some new ones after my trip to see Camille in Toronto, and they were on sale, so I picked some up for you."

I gave her another look.

"They're really very good for wearing when you clean the house," she said. "You could even use them as pyjamas. Wouldn't that be nice?"

"No."

"Well, you can't please everyone, dear."

"What would please *me* is knowing what's going on with your heart."

"Perhaps you could just roll me to the ICU in my bed," she said slowly. "Then you could be my cardiac nurse, and I'm an elderly lady who—"

"I mean this nicely, Irma, and also because I am someone who is rooted in reality—no one is going to let you anywhere near the ICU while you're in a hospital bed. And I don't think you stand much of a chance of getting away from Nurse Ratched over there."

She made a *hrumphing* noise. "Things were so much easier when I had a team to smooth the way for me."

"I shudder to think of what that entailed, exactly. And you still haven't told me why you've been admitted." When she shrugged, I said, "Can you authorise me to get medical updates for you? Who is your emergency contact, anyway?"

"It really depends on the issue, dear. If it's pet-related, then Mrs. Sepp. If it's a money problem,

Roger Patel takes care of it. If I need worms for Stu, then—"

"Health, Irma. Health."

"Julian," she said promptly.

"Cool. Can you add me too?"

"There's really nothing wrong with me, Violet. Everyone sees someone with grey hair and they all become twitterpated."

"Not buying it, Irma." I swallowed. "And I don't like hospitals. What if I'm on my way to the ICU and someone walking past me has Ebola?"

"Do you often feel like people near you have Ebola, dear?"

"All right, fair, what about hepatitis?"

"Oh, that's definitely everywhere."

"Irma, you're not making me feel any better."

"Don't lick anybody and you should be fine," she said. "Look, I see your point. I'll go."

I held up a hand. "Are you going to tell me what's really going on with you, or do I have to call Julian?"

For a split second, shock blinked over her face, then a smile that looked a little eerie, frankly, started to take its place. "I must say, your ability to find an enemy's soft spots is certainly coming along nicely. Perhaps I shouldn't have shown you that documentary about CIA interrogation techniques."

"Oh, I really enjoyed that one."

"Fine. I don't want to worry you, but…" She fidgeted with the edge of her blanket. "My electrocardiogram came back ever so slightly not... normal."

I tried not to flinch.

"It's a minor issue, Violet, really. I was somewhat dizzy and nauseated when I got here, but I think it was most likely a touch of seasickness from the ferry, plus a little too much sun."

"You? Seasick?" Irma was like the postman, always reliable, rain or shine. And she was obsessed with being on the water.

She closed her eyes for a moment. "It happens sometimes, even to experienced sailors. I couldn't see the horizon from where I was kneeling, and that can help stabilise you when the winds aren't favourable."

"I mean...it's just hard to think of you as—"

"It's not a weakness to have bodily issues, dear."

"No, not weak." I held her gaze. "Human."

She laughed then, and it looked like a little of her spunk was returning. "They're going to take excellent care of me here, Violet, so I don't want you to worry."

I didn't say anything. Both of us knew that seasickness did not cause abnormal EKGs. And she and I were definitely going to talk about this more later.

Irma continued: "What I'm actually worried about is Brandon. When I spoke to him before everything went pear-shaped, he told me that *he* was the one who introduced Maura to Norman, and apparently Norman told him he was going to take her away from him."

"Wow. I wonder if Maura knows about that."

Irma shrugged. "What we do know right now is that someone is intent on doing Brandon harm. And someone who has the bollocks to shoot a man in plain daylight...well, it's just not good, dear."

"Yeah, I hear you."

"How was Brandon when he showed up at the estate to tell Maura about the private detective's death? Was he threatening?"

"No. He was worried about her."

Irma nodded. "When he finally agreed to leave, he asked me to look out for her."

"Ugh. What a mess. I wish I'd done things differently."

"None of this is your fault, dear. If someone wants Brandon out of the picture and has been framing him all along, they have the advantage. For now."

I crossed my arms. "Someone like Norman?"

"Perhaps. But if Norman is the culprit, why would he lock Maura in a garage like that? She could have died. And they're not even married yet. Why kill her before they say their vows?"

"Remember the fight they had at the house beforehand? He might have been punishing her, showing her who was boss. Some guys are like that. Plus, he refused to give me access into the security system to see what really happened. He's hiding something."

Irma threw me a sharp look, then nodded. "I really wish those bloody background checks were back."

"It's not like Camille to take this long."

There was a pause, and a troubled expression started to take over Irma's face. Finally, she said, "I didn't want to bother Camille, so I went to another firm for help."

"Did they say how long it was going to take?"

She shook her head. "They have a bigwig in town, so most of their resources are directed toward securing his person right now, I believe. It's a real bother. They keep saying they'll send me the info right away, but we've passed a few 'right aways' already with no progress. On the bright side, one of their staffers is going to send you an encrypted email shortly, with the hospital's layout."

"Why?"

"So I can show you a back route into the ICU."

"Irm*aaaa*!"

"I'd be happy to do it myself, dear, but I really will need you to build that bomb."

I looked at her again. She might be tomato-red and full of heatstroke, and her knee might be about to pop right off her body, but if I knew Irma the way I thought I did, she'd crawl through the building's ductwork to get to Brandon if I didn't agree to go to the ICU. And if she really did have something going on with her heart, that particular mission could go very, very wrong.

After a deep breath, I said, "It's going to be a no from me on that bomb, Irma, seriously. So, what's the plan?"

Ping. The email was in my mailbox already. Of course it was. Scrolling through the attached file, I said, "So, second floor, west wing?"

"That's correct, dear. You can use the D2 stairwell. The door will be unlocked."

"How could you possibly know that?"

"If I told you, I'd have to..." She made the universal *strangle the life out of you* gesture across her neck, then reached into her go-bag again. "And here's a hospital ID badge for you. If you're wearing an ID, you'll probably have an easier time when you sit with Brandon. You could say you're an employee who's a friend of the family. Oh, and leave your wallet here. You don't want to be found with two sets of ID, dear. Trust me."

I had both a small knapsack and a purse with me, and I took a moment to move my wallet to the purse, which Irma then stashed under her bed. "What do I do if someone spots me?"

"It's not a military or corrections facility, so they'll likely be more laid back. Someone might challenge you, ask why you're there and all that, although if you're just sitting quietly, they'll probably be too busy to bother with you. There's a shortage of nursing staff these days, you know."

"How nice that we can leverage that terrible state of affairs to our advantage."

"I agree completely! In any case, try to look natural. If you get challenged, tell them you came by to see how Brandon was doing, but that you have to get back to work or something like that. Just make sure you shove his phone somewhere non-crazy before you scoot. And if anyone comes in who looks dangerous, make yourself scarce."

"They have a million police downstairs and three metal detectors. No one's getting in or out without some serious ID checking. That's why it took me so long to get up here."

"And they've increased security outside the ICU, so that's all splendid."

"Except for that unlocked door."

"All the more reason to get a move on, dear."

I sighed before heading to the bathroom, where I shimmied into the scrubs. Of course they fit me perfectly.

"What do you think?" I asked when I emerged.

"Put these on," Irma said, pulling a pair of thick-framed black glasses from inside her bag.

They settled on my face heavily, but after looking at my reflection in one of the windows, I could see they changed my appearance enough that I looked more like a wannabe hipster than my usual self.

"Good luck, dear. Oh, and take your cellular telephone in case you need me for something. I have mine with me too," she said proudly.

"It's in my backpack. Where's Brandon's?"

She handed it to me, wrapped in a bandage to protect it from our fingerprints, and I checked to see if it needed a password or facial recognition to get into it. It looked like Brandon used an unlocking pattern to log into the phone instead, so I swivelled its screen in the low light until I could make out a sequence of smudges.

"What do you think?" I asked Irma.

She fiddled with it for a minute. "It looks like someone has been tracing an 'L' pattern on the phone's face, over and over again. How does that happen?"

"Brandon has a screen protector attached to his phone. You know, so it doesn't crack when he drops it? It looks like he uses a pattern to unlock his phone, and if you use your phone a lot, that unlocking pattern can get 'stuck' on some protectors. I noticed it a while back with a cheaper one on my own phone."

I cloned his cell, then downloaded some Android phone emulator software. After launching the app, I traced an "L" on the cloned image. Immediately, Brandon's phone unlocked.

"Well done, dear. They run a smaller staff in the ICU at night, but there might still be lots of people around. So do stay on your toes." She handed me a bright and shiny new ID card.

"This says I work in pediatrics. I know nothing about children. And how did you get my picture laminated into this badge so fast?"

"It has a lovely coating that can be removed and new pictures put in. A friend of mine developed it. Edward. He's going to be visiting soon."

"Yeah, that's awesome and all, but how do you have a picture of me that's just the right size for this ID?"

"It's your driver's license photo."

I squinted. She was right. "How did you—"

"It's really better to focus on the critical issues right now, please, dear. I just want to make sure Brandon is still among the living. All you need to do is sit there quietly beside him until the overnight guard arrives, put his phone back, and look normal."

"What if I don't look normal?"

"Just fake it, dear." Irma blinked a few times. "I'm having a certain amount of anxiety about Brandon's condition, to be honest. I allowed him to be shot right under my nose, so you can understand my concern. The hospital won't release any information about his status to a non-relative, so it would really help…ease my mind a bit to know how he's doing."

I nodded.

"I'm sorry to put all this on you, Violet. If Camille was in fine form, well…"

I put my hand on her arm and patted it, just like she so often did with me. She grabbed my hand in hers and gave me a little squeeze, her eyes shiny.

I swallowed down the anxiety that had kicked up inside me. Or at least I tried to. "What do I do if there's no good place to put Brandon's phone?"

"Bring it back. I'll tell them I accidently put it in my handbag."

"Are they gonna buy that? Especially since they think you might have done it?"

She waved a hand. "If they really thought I did it, dear, I'd have a guard watching me."

"And Nurse Ratched doesn't count?"

"Fair point, but I suggested that the GSR got on my hands while I was touching Brandon's wound, and Chief Bloom seemed to buy that. Plus, I'm very curious as to what the video footage from the ferry is going to show us. Unless Asif has moved those cameras around, then I should be visible throughout the trip. Visible not shooting anyone, that is."

I took a sharp inhale. "Do you have the video?"

"No, but I can get it. I was going to ask you to look at it when you got back…" She trailed off.

"I don't think we have that kind of time, Irma. The video probably shows everything! Whoever shot Brandon could be heading out west by now, for all we know. Or going for the border."

She looked hesitant. "I hate to bother Camille."

"Call Françoise and get her on it. She sent me a message the other day. They're doing okay, I promise."

"I know that, dear. But what happened to Camille is my fault."

"Then what happened to Brandon is *my* fault," I countered.

"Don't be ridiculous."

"Right back at you." I pretend-glared at her. "I'm the one who dragged you into all this. And PS, what happened to Camille was Igor Ivanovitch's fault. And you know that." I stood. "I'm going. Do I look convincing?"

"I am totally convinced!" Irma said, clapping her hands once, probably in an attempt to be cheerful. But under her sunburn, she looked a little…worn out.

I headed to the ICU, hoping that if Brandon's would-be assassin was skulking around the hospital, they'd at least leave Irma alone. She'd had a bad enough day. I couldn't even imagine holding someone together with my bare hands like that.

I shivered in the semi-empty hallway. Hospital staff passed me without another glance, wheels squeaking and voices hushed. As I started walking, I pulled up the map Irma's contact had sent. At first, I wasn't sure exactly which stairwell she'd been referring to, but eventually I found 2D.

At the top of the stairs, my knees almost buckled. I was going to get caught. I was going to get arrested. I was going to end up on the news.

But whoever had shot Brandon on the ferry had gotten away clean. And maybe that wouldn't have happened if I hadn't urged Maura to make Irma push him off the island. I owed him.

After a few calming breaths, I opened the door and let it close softly behind me. I heard the *click* behind me.

Immediately, I wanted to leave. I swivelled my head and the rest of me started to turn too, which was when I saw the sign. EMERGENCY EXIT ONLY. ALARM WILL SOUND.

Of course it would.

I took a deep breath and looked around. The ICU was set up with two nursing stations. Beds were arranged in a horseshoe configuration around each station, so every patient could be seen by every nurse at any given time.

There was nowhere to hide.

What had Irma said? *Just fake it, dear.* Wise words from a woman who'd spent her life convincing people that she couldn't kill someone with her thumbs. I'd spent my life trying to convince people to take me seriously. Not for the first time, I wondered why Irma and I got along so well. We were opposites in every conceivable way.

"Help you?" A middle-aged nurse with an armload of blankets stopped as she was walking past me. Her hair was short and blunt, and so was her manner. But she was smiling.

Instantly, I felt bad. How could I lie to a nice nurse? But I pushed on. "Uh, I'm looking for Brandon Ott. I work in ped-ped…iatrics and I'm a friend of the family."

She peered at my ID card. "He's in number five."

Same as Irma. "Thanks. How is he?"

"Stable. And lucky. It looks like his artery was only nicked, and the surgery to repair it was successful. Your friend is going to be okay."

A breath I hadn't even known I was holding exited my body. "Oh, thank you so much."

She grinned. "Gotta keep going. Take care."

I walked to bed number five. Flimsy cotton curtains made barriers between the little cubicles. An older man was snoozing on a cot beside one of the beds, which held a young woman attached to a tangle of lines and tubing. His grandchild, maybe?

Then, I was at five.

Brandon had an oxygen cannula under his nose, and a variety of tubes coming out of his body.

I didn't really sit down; it was more that my legs stopped working and a chair was nearby.

After trying to steel my nerves, I pulled the chair toward Brandon's bedside, depositing his phone in the plastic bag of his personal belongings that was on the floor beside his bed. Then I placed Brandon's hand in mine and held it. He was a little clammy, but he was alive. I closed my eyes for a moment to regroup.

When I opened them, two hospital employees were standing to my right. And one of them looked an awful lot like a security guard.

"Excuse us, ma'am. Can we please have a word?"

Twenty-Nine — Irma

Violet had been gone for an interminable amount of time, and I was so bored that I'd briefly considered faking a heart attack, if only to put a bit more pep in my evening.

Dinner had been a monstrosity of a meal, a skinless chicken breast dripping in a boxed gravy with frozen green and wax beans, along with rice that had most definitely seen better days, topped off by a demented-looking cobbler. It wasn't as bad as some of the prison food I'd endured over the years, but no Michelin guide was going to crown the chef of this particular meal. I deeply regretted not asking Violet to bring me back a sandwich and a nice fruit salad from the cafeteria.

After calling to inquire if the background checks I'd asked for had been completed and finding out that they wouldn't be done until next week—and that they couldn't take on any video-related tasks I needed help with—I sat back in bed to contemplate my situation. I needed Camille's help, or I was never going to put all this together. But I dreaded calling either her or Françoise. Their condo wasn't all that large, and Camille needed her rest.

Bloody hell. There was no other choice.

I stabbed at the numbers on the screen of my cellular telephone, and when I was connected to Françoise, I let out a sigh of relief. I'd assessed the patients around me earlier. At least some of the people here would speak French, which was why I decided German was the best way to go.

"*Gutten abend,*" I said to Françoise, who started giggling. *Good evening.*

"I can tell you're up to something again, Irma. *Et bon,* here we are."

I continued in German: "I need your help looking at some video footage."

"Details?"

"The footage is from the Beaver Island ferry."

"*Bon,*" she said crisply. "What are we looking for?"

I caught her up on what had transpired today— including the fact that the local police seemed to have their eyeballs on me—while she listened intently, asking pointed questions at various spots. "So you think this motorcyclist shot Brandon Ott, then drove off the ferry."

"I don't think he shot himself, dear," I said mildly.

"These days nothing surprises me, but I do see your point," she said. "So you want me to get access to the ferry footage how? The police likely have it."

"I've seen this problem before, actually, and the ferry master has told me that all the video footage is streamed to an offsite location. If you call him, he'll make a copy and send it to you." I rattled off Asif's phone number.

"Why do they stream the ferry footage?"

"Apparently, they were having issues with maintaining the files locally. Moisture and dampness problems on board, I believe. Violet could explain it better than I, but the essential point is that it's not going to be a huge pain in the patoot to get it, dear." I didn't know the right word for *patoot* in German, so I used *das hintern*, which was a bit of a miss linguistically, but it would have to do. "I'm sorry to bother you, dear. I know you're busy."

"Nononono!" she said, her beautiful Haitian-Parisienne accent ringing in my ears. "I am simply trying to understand the situation, Irma. Of course we will do anything to help you."

"The hospital security staffer for the ICU is delayed this evening. Violet is watching Brandon until they show up."

There was a silence. "Why did you not call me for this?"

"By the time any of your staff could arrive, the hospital's guard will already be here. And you have enough on your plate these days."

"We are doing quite well."

"Where is Camille?" I asked gently.

A sigh. "She is asleep."

"Because she's recovering. Which is what she needs to do."

Françoise made an *enough of that* noise. "What will Violet do if Brandon's attacker enters the ICU?"

"You're right," I said. "I really should have given her a whistle. But she has an excellent set of lungs. I always tell her to yell if something bad is about to happen. And then run away."

"I see a few holes in this plan."

"They've bumped up security at the entrances and the ICU guard should be here shortly, *liebchen*. Having Violet there is perhaps not a perfect situation, but I needed Brandon's phone returned to him. And his attacker must know that security will be heightened around the hospital for the foreseeable future. I don't believe that they will make another attempt tonight. And if we're lucky, the shooter might even think that they succeeded and Brandon is dead."

"*Bon*," Françoise said briskly. "Anything else?"

"Can you please do some digging about a private investigator named Harvey Allen? He was shot with a small calibre weapon on the island earlier this week. And apparently Brandon Ott, tonight's victim, recently hired him. Mr. Ott was also shot with a small calibre gun, perhaps the very same one."

Françoise made a whistling noise. "What are you thinking?"

"That Harvey Allen found out something he wasn't supposed to."

"*C'est pas bon,*" she said. *That's not good.*

"No indeed," I replied, still in German. "And can you please run background checks on all involved?" I rattled off Brandon's and Norman's names, along with the rest of Maura's family.

"*Bon.* The checks will take some time, but I shall get the ball rolling." After a discreet clearing of her throat, she said, "Irma, do you need some assistance with securing the party tomorrow?"

"It's short notice..." I said, but the fact was that I was not at my best. "*Ja, bitte,*" I said finally. *Yes, please.*

"*Bon.* I have two resources I will send out tomorrow. Possibly three. And I will get started on that footage." She made some kissing noises into the phone and rang off.

I tried to relax, although the malaise from that dinner wasn't making it easy. I needed my rest, since Maura's engagement party was set for tomorrow night and I had every intention of being there.

Eventually, I dozed off. I'd set my phone to vibrate, and that was what woke me up in the dead of night. I frowned. Where was Violet? She should be back by now.

"Irma Abercrombie speaking."

"I've reviewed the footage from the ferry, Irma," Françoise said, voice terse. "I must say, it is quite overexposed."

I refrained from expressing my irritation using some of the naughty German I'd picked up in East Berlin in the late '80s.

"The video will have to be enhanced, and my normal resource is dealing with a family emergency at the moment. Can Violet take a look at it?"

"I certainly hope so."

"I'll compress it and send it to her after we get off the phone. It will take some time to be delivered."

"Thank you, dear. Can you identify the shooter from the footage?"

"*Non.*"

"Bloody hell."

"The shooter—well, the motorcyclist on the Ducati—lifted the visor on their helmet when speaking to Mr. Ott, but put it back down when facing the camera. Their biker jacket looks fairly new, medium-sized, and is from a common national brand."

Drat. "Was it a man or a woman?"

"I cannot say. Their jacket is quite loose, and the rest of them looks average. Perhaps a smaller man or an average-sized woman."

"So there's nothing, then."

"The ferry footage might not be nothing."

"Oh?"

"First of all, it shows you not shooting Brandon."

"Isn't that nice."

"Also, our friend on the sport bike might have some sort of problem with their foot."

"Oh?"

"Yes, they had a metal loop on the bottom of their left boot. As you know, most motorcyclists wear footwear with a heel so their shoes don't get caught on the pegs. That is where the metal loops."

"It might be a fashion detail."

"Perhaps," she allowed, "but it looks like it could be a brace. And there is no such detail on the right boot that I can see."

"I wonder if she was with Women on Wheels and decided to pop off poor Brandon because he smirked at her."

"This is what I'm struggling with, Irma. If you ran Mr. Ott out of town on the fly, how would the shooter have known where he'd be and when?"

"He was texting someone when we got into the car together. I should have pinched a nerve in his neck and read the bloody texts," I muttered.

"Er, no, Irma, this is not something you should have done."

"That's debatable, don't you agree?"

She laughed, then said, "I will agree that you are quite right that we need the data from his phone. I cannot see how anyone would have known where he was otherwise."

"What if someone was watching him? I mean, I certainly was. Someone else could have had the same brilliant idea."

She made a French-sounding noise of surprise. "Did you get that sense when you were at his house?"

I bit my lip. "Yes, I did have a funny feeling. Dear oh dear, I do believe I have properly bungled all this. I was so focused on protecting Maura that I didn't give a thought to protecting Brandon."

"All we can do is move forward, Irma."

Since I was the one who had originally impressed the importance of that philosophy on Françoise, it was impossible to rebut her point, which was bloody irritating.

"I will do some more digging," she said.

"*Danke, liebchen.*"

She rang off and I was left to my own devices, which probably wasn't the best thing for me right now, frankly. And where was Violet?

THIRTY — VIOLET

The tiny room had a desk, two chairs, and absolutely
no windows, although it definitely held a faint
medicinal odour. I'd been plucked out of the ICU
and deposited here with very little fuss. My two
captors probably didn't want to make a scene in front
of all those deathly ill patients, and for my part I'd
been too petrified to say anything.

The closet-sized room was drafty and cold, and
somewhere in the back of my mind the lectures Irma
had given me about not talking to law enforcement
were buzzing around. But what story was I going to
be able to come up with to get out of here? They
hadn't taken my hospital ID from me, but they
hadn't seen it either. After they'd approached me, I'd
managed to unclip it from the bottom of my shirt and
squirrel it up under my left armpit, which was why
one of the corners was currently digging into my
sideboob.

Then, some noise in the hallway. A fresh-faced
Generation Zoomer wearing pressed slacks, a blue
dress shirt, and a colourful vest with a red and white

bowtie stood in the doorway, the guard who'd been with him earlier standing off to the side.

"Hello," he said, his expression one of stern professionalism.

"Hey." It could not be understated how awkward my response came out. Irma would have already bamboozled her way out of here. But I was no Irma.

I was dead meat.

"Looks like someone wandered out of bounds today." This was followed by a faint smile, like he was going to try to be friendly. I wondered if this was his way of distracting me from the fact that the police were on their way to throw me in the slammer.

I said nothing. Outwardly, my face was probably calm. I'd perfected my calm face with Phyllis, who liked to berate me about her poor life decisions after imbibing a bit too much. I didn't use the calm face often. It brought back bad memories.

But this was an emergency.

"Perhaps you'd like to share your version of events," he said.

I leaned closer and saw his name was *Jayden*. Then, for some reason I couldn't quite figure out, I put both my hands on the desk. "Hey, Jayden. It's nice to meet you," someone who looked and sounded like me said. And then a hand was stuck out. Jayden shook it, unsmiling. The stranger with my face kept talking. "I'm so sorry for the misunderstanding. I was just trying to visit my friend."

"Brandon Ott is your friend?"

"Yeah." When he said nothing, I nodded for emphasis.

"How did you know he was here?"

"Uh…my friend Irma called me?" I cleared my throat. "My friend Irma called me."

One of his eyebrows raised itself.

"She was on the ferry with Brandon when he was shot. Well," I added after seeing the look on his face, "not *when* he was shot, she wasn't with him then, if you know what I mean. She was on the ferry, and she's the one who saved his life. She was worried that…" Too much talking, too much detail. I finished lamely, "She was worried about him."

"I see. Do you have any ID on you?"

"I left my purse with Irma. She's in the cardiac ward. Do you want to go see her now?" I stood. "Let's go see her now." Irma would have this dude apologizing for bothering me in about 2.4 seconds.

"Please take a seat…what is your name?"

"Violet Blackheart."

Another eyebrow was raised, but I'd seen similar reactions to my name in the past. And don't get me started on what the kids used to call me when I was little.

"So, you came here to see your friend, Irma…?"

"Abercrombie."

His head tilted like he was searching his memory. But then he blinked. "I'm not familiar with that person."

"You didn't hear about the shooting on the Beaver Island ferry this afternoon?"

"Of course I did," he said in a not particularly friendly tone. "That's why we're concerned about Mr. Ott's safety."

Uh-oh. Did Jayden think I was the shooter, back to finish the job?

"Yeah, that's great," I said awkwardly. "I mean, that you're aware of the safety issues. Irma and I were worried about Brandon, so I wanted to sit with him for a bit."

"I see." He tapped his fingers on the table. "And why didn't you announce yourself to the nurses' station?"

"They looked pretty busy. I didn't want to bother anyone." *Plus, they wouldn't have let me in, since I'm not family.* I ignored the single bead of sweat inching down my spine. "I'm really sorry for the confusion. I don't spend a lot of time in hospitals."

He flicked his eyes down my torso, then back to my face. I could feel the heat from my back spreading to my ears. I was wearing scrubs. Why would I be wearing scrubs if I didn't spend a lot of time in hospitals?

"Oh, these?" I said with a laugh that sounded like I was strangling a duck. "I wear these around the house on laundry day. Irma actually got these for me. She said they're resilient and comfortable, and they sure are."

"Your friend bought you scrubs to work around the house?"

"Yup."

"Instead of sweats or something like that?"

"Yup." I swallowed. Then leaned forward. "You know how old people are."

"I...see." His fingertips grazed the short and artfully shaved stubble on his chin. "How did you get into the ICU?" he asked softly. "The entrance is secured."

"What does that mean?" I realized that I was grinding the nails from my right hand into the palm of my left.

"There's a security station outside the ICU. Everyone has to show ID and be logged in."

"Smart."

Now his hands were clasped in front of him. "So, how did you get in?"

"The stairwell."

He looked at his phone like he was confirming this data. "Right, the D2 stairwell. That's an emergency exit, Ms. Blackheart. How did you know it would be open?"

"Me? Oh, I didn't. I felt like getting some steps in today, so I took the stairs. I guess I just wandered in."

Now his arms were crossed. "You wandered in through a locked door?"

"It was unlocked."

He frowned.

"It clicked shut behind me, though. If it wasn't meant to be unlocked, you might have an issue with that door."

"You think?" he asked wryly. It looked like he might be starting to unfurl himself a little, which I really needed him to do. I was starting to get dizzy from the small room and his stern face, and about a million other things.

"I do," I said, taking in a long shaky breath. "I'm just passing along some security information. Security is like a bunch of Swiss cheese slices, right? There are always holes, but hopefully those holes are covered up by the next slice." I'd given this speech a dozen times, so my material was pretty solid here. "I'm an engineer, but don't worry, I won't charge you." I pulled out a businesslike fake smile, which he did not return. "But everything's okay now, right? Brandon's safe?"

"Yes. We brought in more security."

I let out a sigh of relief. "That's awesome. Anyway, I don't want to bother you anymore." I stood again, hoping that this time I would have more success at leaving.

"I'm going to need you to show me some ID," he said.

"You betcha. Let's go see Irma," I said.

"Not quite yet," he said before leaving the room, closing the door firmly behind him.

I let out a breath. He was probably going to verify my story with Irma. But if she got fancy explaining who I was with Jayden, then we were sunk.

THIRTY-ONE — IRMA

The young man in front of me was wearing
uncomfortably snug pants, a red polka-dotted bowtie,
and a checkered vest. I didn't quite know where to
look. It was almost worse than Boris's shirts.

"Mrs. Abercrombie?"

"Yes, dear?" I said over a pair of faux reading
glasses that I liked to use in situations like this. With
them in place, along with the frumpy bed jacket
Violet had brought me in my go-bag, I looked like
someone's grandmother, which suited me just fine.

Even better, I'd been moved into a private room,
a lovely state of affairs as I did not care much for
sleeping in close proximity with strangers. One never
knew quite what they would get up to under cover of
darkness.

"I'm sorry to bother you this late, ma'am, but I
was wondering if we could talk for a moment."

I closed the magazine I'd been flipping through
and folded my hands in my lap.

"Are you familiar with a woman named Violet
Blackheart?"

"Of course, dear." Then I gasped. "Has something happened to her? Is she all right?" Bloody hell. It looked like Violet's reservations about potentially getting nabbed during her little caper in the ICU had borne fruit.

"She's fine."

"Are you sure? Where is she?"

He held up both hands in a *calm yourself, old lady* gesture. "There was a little misunderstanding in the ICU. Do you happen to have her purse with you?"

I pushed the glasses up so I could use the little snippet of time to think. If he knew Violet's real name, and she and I both knew she'd left her purse with me, that meant she'd felt it was acceptable to show him her identification. What had happened to her fake hospital ID was a tad more mysterious, but it was likely not our biggest consideration at the moment.

"I do." Then I waggled my finger at him. "But I'm sure you know that looking in a woman's purse is a big no-no, dear."

His grin bore dimples. "You're right, ma'am, but I need a picture ID to confirm her identity."

"Why on earth would you need that?"

"If I could just see it, then I can answer more of your questions."

I made a harrumphing noise, then reached beside the bed for her purse. I rustled around until I found her driver's license, which I handed to the young man.

He gazed at it so long, I was surprised he didn't pull out a loupe. Then he nodded and handed it back.

"Will you tell me what's going on now, please?"

"Everything is okay, Mrs. Abercrombie. Your friend used a stairwell entrance to get into the ICU, so we were a bit concerned. There's heightened security in the unit because of your friend, Brandon. They still haven't caught the shooter."

"Oh, I see. Well, I'm quite sure Violet used the stairwell door because she's trying to get some exercise." I leaned forward conspiratorially. "I've been nagging her lately to do more physical activity, if I'm being honest about it. It's nice to see it's paying off."

He nodded, but he didn't seem convinced. On the other hand, this was no trained security official. If he had been, Violet would already be in a police car.

"Where is she, dear? She was going to stay with me tonight. I'm quite frazzled from what happened this afternoon, and I really need my sleep."

"Of course, ma'am," he said, then typed something into his cell phone. "She's on her way now. Did you want us to set up a cot for her?"

"That would be lovely, dear. Tell me, how's security in the ICU now? Has the night guard arrived yet?"

The beginnings of a frown started to form between his eyes. "How would you know about our staffing?"

"I heard one of the nurses talking about it."

"Gossip is never a good thing, Mrs. Abercrombie. I'd counsel you not to put a lot of stock in stuff you overhear. And the ICU is fully staffed now."

"I'm sure you're right," I said sweetly, relieved that Brandon would be in good hands overnight. "Will Violet be back soon?"

"Yes," Violet said from the doorway. Her face was a good deal pinker than normal, but she also seemed pretty chipper, all things considered. Her left arm was held against her body at an odd angle, and I'd bet that was where her phony hospital ID had ended up.

"Hello, Violet, dear! I missed you."

"Didja?" she said flatly. Oh dear, she seemed a little cross.

"I'll let you two ladies rest," Jayden said, nodding to Violet before he left.

Violet took one step into the room, then closed the door carefully behind her. Her ears really were red.

"How are you?" I asked softly.

"Considering that I've spent the last half-hour in baby jail, I've been better, Irma."

"Good heavens, there's a jail in the hospital?"

"Okay, it's just a really small room."

I snickered, and she finally smiled. "What happened?"

"I went in that stairwell door and sat with Brandon for like ten minutes before they bounced me."

"How does he look?"

"Like he was resting comfortably, I guess? The monitors attached to him weren't going off or anything. And one of the nurses told me he's going to be all right. His artery was only nicked, and they were able to fix it."

"That's excellent news," I said, feeling something ease deep inside my chest. "I wonder how security flagged you?"

"Someone must have been watching the video feed and noticed me coming in a door that nobody was supposed to be using."

"That happens sometimes. Don't beat yourself up about it. And speaking of cameras, Françoise is going to be sending the footage from the ferry over to you, if you're able to take a crack at enhancing it."

"No problem."

"Oh, and Françoise had a brilliant idea—she's going to send over two or three security personnel to help with the party tomorrow. Just in case."

"Whew," Violet said with a small smile. But she looked relieved. "And I had an idea of my own while I was walking back from baby jail. Do you know any biker chicks from WOW who might have seen something on the ferry?"

"I certainly do," I said, reaching for my cellular telephone and dialling. "I could kick myself. I should have thought of that before."

"You've been kinda busy," Violet said.

My call connected. "Simone, darling, how are you? Sorry to call you so late, but I know you're a night owl like Violet."

Simone Summers laughed. "No problem, Irma. What have you done now?"

"Who, me?" I said with a little laugh. "I'm wondering if you happen to know who was riding the Ducati this afternoon."

"Oh…right. I noticed her before we got to the ferry, then she buzzed off when we reached the mainland. I've never seen her before, though."

"Are you sure it was a woman?"

"Nope. I just saw the Ducati, to be honest. Beautiful bike."

"Can you see if anyone else on the ride noticed anything?"

"Is this about the guy who got shot on the ferry?"

"Yes, dear."

"Okay, I'm online on the WOW forum. I'll poke around until someone gets back to me."

"Do you want to call me back?"

She laughed again. "Uh, no. Someone has already replied. A few of them saw her, but they don't know who she was, either."

"Anything more specific? Did anyone notice if she had a limp?"

"Why?"

"We believe she was wearing a brace of some kind on her left foot."

More typing.

"They say she never got off the bike on the ferry, never walked around," Simone said.

"No," I said with a sigh. "I didn't think so."

"I'll keep my eyes open for you, Irma."

"Thank you, dear."

Mr. Tight Pants organized a cot for Violet, who decided to stay, since she was not comfortable piloting the boat back alone so late at night. Plus, I could see tiny gears grinding away in her head, so I decided to leave her to it.

I had some noodling of my own to do. What if someone had set up young Brandon, first to ruin his relationship and then make it appear as if he was stalking his ex-girlfriend? I thought back to what he'd said to me earlier in the day, that I'd be sorry for running him out of town. He'd been right on the money with that one.

I glanced over at Violet, who was pecking at her laptop's keyboard. "How long will it take you to enhance the footage from the ferry?" I asked. "I wouldn't normally ask at this time of night, but Maura's engagement party is tomorrow, and it looks like a storm is coming, so we need to get all our ducks in a row."

"It'll take me a bit to figure out how long it'll take, Irma. This isn't my area of expertise. Plus, I'm

very interested in going through Brandon's phone."
And then she bent over her laptop again.

I had more questions for her, but my eyelids were too heavy for me to pester her anymore.

Tomorrow was a whole new day, of course.

Thirty-Two — Violet

It was late and the hospital was quiet-ish. Perfect time to do some research, plus the video from the ferry had finally shown up. Because it was so large, Françoise had uploaded it to a secure internet server.

I started watching it with high hopes. Unfortunately, it was impossible to see who the unknown biker might have been, or even what they'd been doing at times. The video was grainy and overexposed, the Beaver Island sun pixelating everything and everybody on the ferry. No wonder Irma hadn't been feeling well after her little boat ride. If I'd knelt in the sun with no hat for as long as she had, I would have dropped dead from heatstroke.

I glanced over at her bed, where she slept silently, unmoving, like she was trying to camouflage herself, then back at my screen. The biker had been stopped right beside the driver's side window of Brandon's car. The other members of the WOW gang had parked their bikes and mingled between the cars and at the ferry's rail, looking out on Lake Ontario and the shore ahead of them. They seemed like they were having a blast.

As the ferry neared the mainland, the biker on the Ducati flipped up their face protector and gestured to Brandon, whose windows were so tinted that it was impossible to see his expression. The footage didn't contain an audio track, so we were never going to hear what they had been saying to each other. Plus, the ferry was always crazy noisy.

There. I leaned forward and squinted at my screen. There was a long moment when the biker leaned over and stuck their hand inside Brandon's car. It looked like the boat hit a wave at the same time, making the video wobble out of focus. Brandon's arm tensed, then...flopped? It wasn't a big *she's trying to kill me movement,* but it wasn't nothing either.

Then the biker flipped their visor back down and looked forward, prepping to disembark. When the ferry's gate lifted, the rest of the bikers swarmed past the cars, with that Ducati at the front of the line. Its license plate was a blur, which was odd, since the rest of the bike looked like it was sparkly clean.

Irma rolled onto her back with her arms clasped over her midsection, still creepily silent. I couldn't even hear her breathe. Had her spy training included silent sleeping? So an enemy couldn't find her if she needed some rest while she kept the world safe?

I downloaded the video-enhancing software that a friend of mine had once recommended, but as soon as I tried to run it against the footage, I realized that the little laptop I'd been carting around in my knapsack wasn't up to the job.

The only thing to do was to transfer the footage to a secure server I kept in Toronto that had a lot more juice, then run the video enhancement software from there. We needed to know what was on that license plate, and any other details that might identify the shooter.

But I didn't hold out a lot of hope that what was I was doing would actually work—they might press the "enhance video" button all the time on TV, but that's not how things worked in the real world.

Then I scrolled through the cloned image of Brandon's phone, feeling torn. Part of my job as someone who dealt with private and confidential data was to safeguard that information. Until my visit to Beaver Island, I'd never snooped on anyone's data. It my world, it was wrong.

But Brandon was in danger. And that was partly my fault, no matter what Irma had said.

So I scrolled. The last text he'd written was a reminder to his building super to fix a broken doorknob, sent two days ago. *Huh.* Next, I checked his email, which was equally empty. Unless Brandon was in the habit of deleting his personal communications, he hadn't reached out to whoever had ended up shooting him in broad daylight.

I sat back on my cot, trying to think. I didn't want to walk back into Harbour House if the security system was going to lock me in the basement and throw away the key. Especially if there was a cellphone jammer on the premises, so I couldn't call for help. All the research I'd done so far seemed to show that jammers caused a complete communication block when they were in use, which wasn't what Maura and I had experienced; my phone had been able to get my small messages out to Irma. But 911 hadn't been working, and it should have. So I still had doubts scratching away at the back of my mind.

But what could I do about it? A little more research popped up with an app that could help track down jammers. If I showed up at Harbour House tomorrow early and did a little walkaround, I'd be able to know for sure if there was one in use and disable anything nefarious I found.

I closed my eyes for a minute. *Keep going.* I did another search of Brandon's phone for mentions of Maura or the PI he'd hired to find her, but there was nothing. A little more digging showed that Brandon seemed to do most of his communication via email and eschewed social media. But if he was a Luddite like Maura had said, he might be in the habit of calling people instead of using electronic communications. There were a few personal calls logged in his cell, but none from around the time he'd left the island. The phone was a dead end.

I decided to ship the cloned phone data to my server in Toronto along with that footage and see if a few other tricks I had up my sleeve would bear fruit.

If Brandon had an encrypted folder on his phone, none of the information I was looking for would pop up in the searches I was doing now.

I checked back on the video enhancement software, which was at a whopping two percent. After that, I emailed Julian to tell him where Irma and I had ended up.

Then I rolled over and closed my eyes. I was absolutely sure I was going to need every ounce of sleep I could get before Maura's engagement party tomorrow.

Thirty-Three — Irma

Saturday morning was spent in a whirlwind of activity. Not for Violet, who was passed out on her cot, the earplugs I'd given her rammed into her ears. I supposed that was why she couldn't hear herself snoring, bless her heart.

I was taken for a battery of tests on both my knee and my chest, which I was quite certain would not produce any useful information, as I was in excellent health, although I did get a very nice cortisone shot for my knee, along with an ultrasound treatment. After that, my knee was swaddled in a tensor bandage. Happily, when all that was over, I bumped into Nora, who offered to take me to the ICU so we could visit Brandon. Mostly, I wanted to verify that he was still alive, and squeeze some intel out of him if he was. I was still concerned about the person who had shot him turning up at the hospital to finish the job.

"Good night?" Nora asked, commandeering my wheelchair.

"Yes, dear. Thank you so much for all your help."

"My ma says for you to come to Sunday dinner next week."

"Please tell her I'll be there with bells on."

We chatted pleasantly all the way to the ICU, where we discovered that Brandon had *not* been throttled to death overnight by the individual who had shot him right under my nose. In fact, he'd been moved out of the ICU to a room on the urgent care ward, which Nora assured me was for less critical cases and meant that Brandon's condition had improved overnight.

Once we had the room number, I had Nora wheel me back to my room, as she needed to get on with her work day. Violet was sitting up in bed when I got back, her nose buried in her cellular telephone.

"Good morning, dear."

She glanced up, and I spotted the industrial-sized coffee in her hand. "Morning," she mumbled, like she'd been hibernating for the past decade and had forgotten how to speak. Of course, that was how she always was in the morning, so I didn't take it personally.

"Remember Nora?" I asked.

"Hey."

"Mornin'!" Nora said cheerfully. "I'm going to get to work. You guys have a nice day."

After Nora left, Violet put down her telephone, took a long sip of coffee, and looked at me. "I don't even want to think about what you've been up to."

I burst out laughing. "Nothing, I promise. A lot of people have been looking at my innards, and we tried to visit Brandon but ran out of time. He's in a private room now. Perhaps we could go together?"

"Let me finish my coffee," Violet said.

"With a cup that big, dear, we could be here a while."

She snorted, then finished her drink in one long swallow. "Where are we going?"

"Acute care. Right near the ICU."

"Okey dokey."

Violet caught me up about the slowness of the video enhancement software she was running against the ferry footage—only twenty-seven percent completed so far—as well as the lack of information she'd been able to glean from Brandon's phone. I tried not to huff in irritation.

After that, there was some debate around whether or not I should be allowed to use my God-given legs to walk to Brandon's room, but it was eventually decided that we'd look less threatening if it was obvious I was a patient.

The stern-looking security guard stationed outside Brandon's room looked like he was eight marines squished into one person, which was delightfully reassuring. He gave us a bit of lip, but thankfully Brandon was awake and told him that he wanted us to come in, so we did exactly that.

"I guess I have a lot to thank you for." He looked paler than he had when I'd been head-butting him in his rented living room, with darker circles under his eyes. He was tall enough that his legs stopped only inches from the bottom of the bed, but he still looked small, somehow. The tubing and monitor lines that snaked out of his hospital jimmy hinted at more serious concerns as well.

"You look amazing," Violet said.

He smiled faintly. "Not exactly, but I'll take it." His voice was rough, possibly from being intubated during surgery.

I parked myself beside his bed.

"What happened yesterday?" Violet asked.

After adjusting his bed so he could sit up a bit more, he said, "I'm a little unclear on all the details, to be honest." He shot us a rueful expression. "The doctors say I must have hit my head."

I let out a sigh. "I'm sorry, dear. I did whack you around somewhat when I pulled you out of your car."

He nodded, then winced, patting the back of his head. "Yeah, I'm okay, though. The doctors say everything will come back to me, that I've been through a trauma and had anesthesia, and things can be a little muddled for a few days after that."

"Wonderful," I said, patting his arm. "What do you remember?"

"There was a woman on a sport bike outside my window when we were on the ferry," he said, frowning. "I thought she didn't speak English, because she just kept gesturing at the song on my radio and giving me a thumbs up, that kind of thing."

311

"What song was it?" Violet asked.

"I don't know. Your friend changed my radio station."

Violet flashed me an *Irma, no* look.

Brandon held up a hand. "But it sounds like I owe her my life. You some kind of cop or something?"

"No." I smiled sweetly. "Can you describe this woman, please, dear?"

He shook his head. "Not really. All I saw was her eyes."

"And you didn't recognize her at all?"

"I mean…I don't think so. The helmet covered most of her face, and the visor was tinted. I just thought it was some weirdo."

"What colour were her eyes? Long eyelashes? Eye makeup? Any moles or birthmarks?"

"Dark eye colour, longish eyelashes, normal eyebrows. I think. I mean, I was kind of distracted and not really paying attention, to be honest. And I've been racking my brain to try to remember more, but everything is still so fuzzy."

"But you're sure it was a woman?"

He nodded.

"Was she young or old?"

He paused. "Young-ish, I think."

"Do you remember being shot?" Violet asked.

Brandon went to touch his forehead, but his arm got snagged on an IV line. Violet helped him untangle it, and he laid back against his pillows. He looked like the small movement had exhausted him. "No," he said finally. "And I think I might have...lost some time when it happened. I remember thinking I'd gotten stung by a bee, or punched in the side. And then...nothing."

I patted his arm encouragingly. "Dear, did you text anyone before you left the island? Did anyone know you were leaving?"

"No."

"What were you doing on your phone?"

"Playing Candy Crush." When he saw the look on my face, he added, "It's a video game. It distracts me."

"It's a good game," Violet said.

"Can you think of anyone who would want to harm you?" I asked Brandon.

"Norman. Maybe Stassi, Maura's mom? She's never really liked me."

"Why not?" I asked.

"I don't think I made enough money for her. She's all about appearances. I mean, look at her Instagram feed. It's like she's a teenage influencer. It's nuts."

I threw a look at Violet, who nodded confirmation.

"And she sure likes Norman and all his money," Brandon said.

"I can't imagine Stassi on a Ducati," Violet said slowly.

Brandon snorted, then winced. "Not really."

"Did you ever notice anything odd about Ryeleigh's behaviour when you were with Maura?" I asked. Mrs. Sepp's comments about Ryeleigh being spoiled still bothered me. She'd been so timid when I first met her, friendly, even. Which meant she'd been putting on a show when we met. I did not like that.

Brandon closed his eyes for a moment. "Ryeleigh was always kind of flirty with me and stuff, but she's just a kid."

"She's almost two years older than Maura," Violet said.

"I always forget that. It's just that she acts so young." His eyes widened. "She's been in my neighbourhood a fair bit lately. She texted me a few times, and we've had dinner once or twice."

"Any chance she might have thought more was going on between the two of you?" Violet asked.

"You don't think…" Brandon looked horrified.

"When you were talking to Ryeleigh, did you ever mention Maura?" I asked casually.

He closed his eyes for a moment, then nodded. "I told Ryeleigh I was getting a PI to help me prove I wasn't stalking Maura, and that someone was messing with my financial stuff."

My heartbeat quickened. "And what did she say about that?"

"That I should fire the PI, that Maura had moved on and there was nothing anyone could do about it. She got pretty insistent with me, actually."

Violet met my eyes.

What if *Ryeleigh* had set up Brandon financially? She was an accountant, Violet had told me that night at the club. She might have contacts who could help her futz a few credit card bills. Maura and Ryeleigh were both staying at their mother's house at the moment, so Ryeleigh would have had access to Maura's belongings. What if Ryeleigh had stitched that AirTag into Maura's handbag and made a copy of her automatic car starter?

As a resident at Harbour House, Ryeleigh would have access to its security system. And if Ryeleigh had been flirting with Brandon, then perhaps she wanted him away from her sister so she could have him all to herself.

But why shoot him on the ferry, then?

"Brandon, have you spent any time with Ryeleigh while you've been on the island?" I asked.

He closed his eyes again, then nodded. "I ran into her at the club that night, just as I was leaving."

"What did you talk about?"

He blinked a few times. "I mean, nothing. She realized I was there to see Maura, and she said it was a bad idea." He looked at me. "Which it was. I can see that now. But I knew Harvey had some evidence that would exonerate me. That's all I could think about."

"Did you tell Ryeleigh about that?" Violet asked.

"Yes, I said that my PI had proof that I hadn't done anything wrong. She asked me a few questions, but like I said before, Harvey never had the chance to tell me anything. I took off after that."

He closed his eyes then. Our talk was obviously tiring him.

"Dear," I asked quietly, "did Harvey ever happen to mention that he had a problem with anybody? A client, or perhaps someone whose affair he had exposed or something like that?"

Brandon's eyes flickered open. "He didn't take those kinds of cases. He seemed like…"

"Like what?" Violet asked.

"Like a nice guy," Brandon said simply.

"Can you think of anything else that might be helpful, dear?" I asked. When he shook his head, I added, "Did they say how long you'll be here?"

"A while."

"You rest up. We'll be in touch."

Violet rolled me to the door, then went back and said a few quiet things to Brandon. After that, she gave him a careful hug and rejoined me. The security guard tipped his hat at us on the way out, and we headed back to my room.

"I feel terrible about all this," she said as we rolled.

"I don't feel fantastic about it myself, dear."

"Did I tell you that Ryeleigh was the one who pushed Maura to go out the night Norman and Maura re-connected and started dating?"

"How very interesting," I said slowly.

Happily, when we got back to my little prison, the battle-axe told me I was being discharged. Unhappily, I had to be rolled out of the hospital via wheelchair by an employee, with a cardiac monitor pinned to my chest like a scarlet letter. That was how I ended up being whisked out of my room to the hospital's rotunda, thoughts about our discussion with Brandon whirling around my head. I could have kicked myself for not thinking about Harvey's enemies before now. I'd have to ring Françoise and add that to my ever-growing list of requests.

A number of people were sitting listlessly in wheelchairs, all grouped around the exit doors. Hopefully they weren't sleeper agents gearing up for another assassination attempt on Maura's ex. On the bright side, the security guard assigned to Brandon seemed top-notch, so I could leave knowing that he was being taken care of, at least while he was still here. Getting him some security protection after his discharge was another thing I'd have to discuss with Françoise after tonight's party was over.

I closed my eyes and took a deep breath. What was that smell?

It was musty attic and old celery.

It was Snookie Smith.

I made sure not to twitch or move with haste as I turned my head to sweep the room. I found her in a corner beside a potted palm that looked like it was on its last legs. With any luck, it would fall and hit her on the head and that would be the end of Snookie Smith.

But just as I was turning away, I caught her scrawny little shoulders heaving. She held her glasses away from her face and dabbed at her eyes with a tissue.

Snookie was crying.

I had a bad moment after that. Part of me wanted to burst out of my chair and berate her until she cried some more. The biggest part of me, really.

Her shoulders quivered.

Bloody hell.

I plunked my handbag on my lap and girded my loins. Then I rolled myself to the information desk.

"Excuse me, dear," I said.

The twenty-something receptionist raised her face with a smile.

"How long has that" —I gestured at Snookie with my head— "woman been waiting?"

The girl put down her pencil with a frown. "Are you a family member?"

"Friend of a friend."

"Since early this morning," she said quietly. "And the sooner she leaves, the better. Not that I said that."

"I understand completely," I said, then thanked her. After that I rolled myself toward Snookie, clearing my throat from a good distance away so she'd have enough time to hide her tears from me.

Violet almost collided with me in my chair.

"Irma, no!" she hissed. "There are too many witnesses here for you to…" She mouthed *kill Snookie.*

I put my hand on hers. "It's all right. I suspect she's stuck here because the ferry is not yet functional."

Violet started pulling my wheelchair in the opposite direction.

"I'm not going to kill her," I said softly. "I'm going to offer her a ride home."

Violet stopped so quickly, I almost catapulted out of the wheelchair. Then she bent down, closer to my ear. "I infiltrated an ICU for you and got thrown into baby jail. I am not about to help you chuck Snookie's body overboard in the middle of the lake. It's too much for one week. Seriously."

"Understood," I said, then backed the wheelchair up and out of Violet's reach. "I promise not to kill her. We will take her home. Alive."

"I still don't like her."

"Neither does anyone else, dear. But since the police have not bothered me today about that GSR test, I'm assuming I hit the jackpot there. And sometimes you have to share your good luck with your neighbours, even if you normally want to kill them."

So we rolled toward her.

THIRTY-FOUR — VIOLET

I was starting to think Irma had hit *her* head while saving Brandon's life. As someone who'd recently been concussed, I could testify that it did some kooky stuff to you.

Regardless, Irma was heading toward Snookie with a grim determination that did not bode well for Snookie's health. I decided to follow from far enough away that I wouldn't be hit by any blood spatter.

"Snookie, darling," Irma trilled.

Snookie, who looked like she'd really been through the wringer, had her hands folded in her lap. "Irma," she said quietly.

"I was wondering if you needed a lift home. Violet and I are just leaving."

"No, thank you," she said stiffly. "My niece is coming to collect me."

"Awesome," I said. "I'll go get a cab, Irma."

"That won't do you any good," Snookie said. "The ferry isn't running. Where will the cab drop you, the middle of the lake?"

I decided to re-think not helping Irma throw Snookie overboard. And I'd bet a jury wouldn't even convict.

Irma let out a fake laugh. "Don't be so silly. Violet brought my boat over. So we're going by taxi to the pier, then boating home."

Something lifted in Snookie's eyes. You could see for a moment that she was considering it. I noticed an empty Tupperware container in her lap and wondered how long she'd been waiting.

"Or not," Irma said cheerily. "We have things to do, so we're leaving now."

Snookie looked like she'd just eaten an enormous lemon. Then she stretched her neck from one side to the other. "I suppose I could go with you," she said finally, like she was doing us a favour. It took every ounce of effort I could muster not to roll my eyeballs right off my face.

"Smashing," Irma said. To me, "Can you please call that taxi, dear?"

I did, and we were picked up by an older dude who talked about curling the entire way to the pier while Irma sat up front, asking prescient questions. In the back, Snookie arranged for someone from the island clinic to meet her at the pier.

A short set of stairs led to the dock, and both Irma and I let Snookie go first. Not so we could push her down the stairs, although I was a hundred percent positive I saw the thought flit through Irma's head.

Personally, I held back because I didn't want to be anywhere near the woman, even though I realised Irma was only trying to be neighbourly in difficult circumstances.

Irma, I was pretty sure, was holding back because she didn't want to do anything that would make Snookie want to sue her for something new.

Snookie took the first few steps nicely, but got snagged on the fourth. She grabbed at the railing to steady herself.

"I think it has to be you who helps her, dear," Irma said out of the side of her mouth.

"If she decides to sue me too, you have to get me a good lawyer."

"Yes, of course. My treat."

"For the record," I said over my shoulder as I made my way to the stairs, "I prefer *ice cream* as a treat."

"Duly noted."

"How can I help?" I asked Snookie.

She looked like she was going to bite my head off, then pressed her lips together. "Thank you, Veronica. Can you hold my right arm? My left is fine with the banister. I just need a bit more stability."

"It's Violet, and sure." I held her elbow in my hand. She was cold, her elbow swimming in my grip. Maybe she was human after all.

We slowly made our way down the stairs to the pier. She seemed to be having some kind of real health issue this time, not a phony made-up one.

"Is it your leg that's bothering you?" I asked.

She shook her head, her mouth a thin line. "I hit my head when I fainted the other night."

"Oh." When the silence became awkward, I added, "I'm sorry to hear that."

"Thank you for asking. So many young people these days are only interested in their phones, not people."

"Uh-huh. We're over there."

I looked at the lake, which was placid, thankfully. All the better to get Snookie home and out of our hair quickly. I needed to be focusing on Maura and her party. At least Irma had the cavalry coming tonight. I wasn't exactly sure how we were going to sneak in two or three party crashers, but if I knew Camille's staff the way I thought I did, they'd probably be perfectly happy hanging from the ceiling or hidden behind curtains.

After I buckled Snookie into her seat, Irma took the wheel, and I slid a baseball cap over my ponytail, then added some sunglasses to my ensemble. Then I collapsed into the chair behind Irma. Just walking that short distance with Snookie had exhausted me.

Irma piloted the boat slowly toward town, pausing as we passed by the ferry landing. The ferry was docked on the mainland side of the lake, yellow tape flapping in the breeze. A little ways past it, a mega-yacht was anchored in a little bay.

"See that boat?" Snookie said, sounding almost proud. "That's where my housekeeper beats the pants off her little poker circle every Sunday night."

"Good for her," Irma said. "Who does she play with?"

"Some other domestic workers," Snookie replied with a sniff. "A few months ago, she took in a huge pot. One member of her group still hasn't paid her back yet."

"I've met your housekeeper," Irma drawled. "I'm sure she'll collect eventually."

Next, we motored past the area that Sisu Solar was turning into an offshore solar farm. Everything seemed to be moving ahead nicely. I felt a strange pang in my chest, looking at it.

Snookie made a *tsking* sound. "Such a waste, all those hippies with their solar nonsense."

I bit the inside of my cheek until my jaw started cramping. We were almost there, almost home. She'd be gone soon.

At the downtown Beaver Island pier near Main Street, one of the nurses from the island clinic was waiting for Snookie in yellow scrubs dotted with bumblebees. "I'll take it from here," she said. "C'mon, Snookie. We'll have fun walking you home."

"I doubt that," Snookie said.

"Ha! Such a kidder." The nurse winked at us.

Just before the stairs, Snookie stopped and turned around. "Thank you, Violet. And…Irma."

Irma gave her a mini salute.

"Perhaps I shan't sue you after all," Snookie said, a ghost of a smile at her lips. Then she turned around and the nurse helped her to Main Street.

Through gritted teeth, I said, "I hope she gets ingrown toenails for the next twenty years." Then I let out a breath. "Let's go home."

"I have to get some provisions in town, dear," Irma said. "You take the boat home and I'll walk or get a lift."

"What about your knee?"

"It feels better today. And there's a very serious compression bandage on it. I feel like a mummy. See?"

"Okay, but don't overdo it. We have an engagement party tonight to get ready for."

"We certainly do, dear." She stood in front of me and held up a tiny hand. "I don't want you to worry about tonight, Violet. Camille's staff will make sure that Maura is okay."

"What about tomorrow?"

"We'll take care of that too. I promise." She smiled kindly.

I let out a relieved breath. Irma's health problems had shaken me more than I wanted to admit—to myself and to her. I was glad she was looking so well today, even though there was still a hint of fatigue around her eyes.

"Okay," I said. "I'm gonna see if Julian is around, maybe grab lunch with him."

325

Irma's smile was beatific. "That sounds like the most perfect idea, dear."

"Irma..."

She zipped her lips, then wiggled her fingers at me before turning left. And I went right.

The clinic wasn't far. Kendelle Chang was at reception, wearing a green and white polka dotted dress. Her hairdo reminded me of a bird's nest.

"Hey," I said. "Is Julian around?"

"He went for a house call."

"Seriously? I didn't even know that was a thing."

"His great-aunt isn't feeling well, so he wanted to check up on her. Did you want to leave a message?"

"I'll text him, thanks."

Kendelle smiled, then returned to gazing lovingly at her phone.

I decided that something from Mandy's would hit the spot, so I headed over there. The sun broke out from behind a cloud, and I was glad I was still wearing my baseball cap to shield me from it.

"This food is cold," I heard a voice snap as I approached Mandy's patio, and I froze for a minute. It was Norman. Mandy's restaurant was sprawling and set on a corner, so I switched directions mid-step so I'd be shielded from his view by the hedge on the far side.

I couldn't explain why I'd done it if you paid me a million dollars. Why not walk up the front steps and order wings? Why not go elsewhere and avoid Norman? I'd skulked outside Maura's room when we were at the clinic, listening to her and Ryeleigh. I'd infiltrated an ICU just last night. Now I was eavesdropping on my friend's fiancé. What was *happening* to me?

"I'm sorry, sir," Mandy murmured quietly. "I'll get you a new one."

"If you can actually do it right this time, then make it to go." Norman made an exasperated noise, and Mandy's footsteps started to recede. I peeked through the hedge. Norman had a shiny brown briefcase sitting in the chair beside him and looked like he was having a working lunch, even though it was a Saturday and his engagement party was tonight.

I couldn't decide what to do; first my feet went one direction, then they went another. I glanced around, my arms crossed over my chest. Nobody seemed to notice me.

On the other side of the hedge, papers rustled and a phone rang.

"What?" Norman snapped. "Yes, Maura signed the papers. Yes, *finally.*"

What papers?

I risked another glance through the hedge. Norman's back was to me, papers spread out on the table. He searched through them. "The policy is—"

Then he read off a long number.

What kind of policy was Norman talking about? An insurance policy? A *life insurance* policy?

Norman hung up on the caller without another word and, standing, started throwing the papers into his briefcase.

I was suddenly glad I'd worn my baseball cap, and that my sunglasses were big enough to hide half of my face in case he managed to spot me through the hedge. I slipped away and walked back toward the main pier, palming my phone and dialing Maura. I needed to get over there before the party and help her any way I could. The first thing I wanted to help her with was understanding that people who were rude to waitstaff were unmarry-able.

The next thing I was going to do was track down that cellphone jammer. If we needed help tonight, I wanted all the airways clear.

Thirty-Five — Irma

After leaving Violet and the boat, I moseyed over to Luna's Café, where I procured a few Death by Chocolate cupcakes for Violet. She'd done some excellent field work last night, and even though we were going to be at a party tonight, it wasn't a sit-down dinner, and dessert might be something froufrou that she wouldn't like. The Death by Chocolate cupcakes, with their buttercream icing, really were her favourites.

Plus, after everything else that had happened this week, I needed to partake of some fresh air. So that's what I did, walking around outside, the wind in my hair. I felt wonderful. The sun was shining. Tonight we'd celebrate Maura's engagement, even if Norman was such a complete twerp. And Camille and Françoise's staff would be there to make very sure Maura was safe. Along with myself and Violet, of course.

And I was *so* looking forward to having a word with Maura's sister.

That settled, I picked up my little box of pastries and headed to Raymundo Epstein's deli. A smoked meat sandwich felt like a lovely afternoon treat, and I ordered several so Violet and I could have some for lunch tomorrow.

It was a perfect Beaver Island afternoon, even though the forecast said the weather was going to turn on us later. After paying for the sandwiches, I was back out on the street. I was feeling better.

Until the back of my neck started to itch.

I kept the smile on my face when greeting Agnes O'Muffin, whom I'd decided to have a sit-down with at some point soon. While I had no proof she'd been behind Snookie-gate, I was dying to know if it had been her.

After passing Agnes, I stopped in front of a local home decor store, Decumanus. Juliette DeWitt, the owner, scoured the continent for hand-hewn furniture, most of it scavenged from farmhouses and estate sales. She cleaned it all up and sold it to tourists for a mint. It was beautiful stuff, although that was not the reason I was currently looking at the weathered hope chest made from a pale wood, the corners softened by use and age, and maybe even hope. I wondered briefly who had stacked their trousseau in that chest. Mother had given me a good .22 and a hug when we talked about planning my future.

There.

The figure behind me had also stopped. It was a man in his late twenties, a robust beard hiding his features, along with a nifty pair of designer sunglasses and a Blue Jays baseball cap. Jeans, a t-shirt, and a weathered brown belt completed the picture.

He looked like any other tourist wandering around the main street of a town that drew people to its shores. Which meant that he'd been on the island long enough, and had gleaned enough intel, to disappear into a crowd here.

It was Igor. It had to be. And if it was, he'd definitely been taking steroids in his spare time. There were many reasons why this was a bad development, so it was hard to decide which to be more upset about. He'd be stronger, for one, and I vividly remembered his incredibly long legs from our encounter after Violet and I had captured him some time back. Now those legs would be ultra-long and ultra-strong, never good things when one was confronting an enemy.

Adrenaline started to unfurl in my veins.

Juliette waved from inside the store, and I tried returning the greeting in a way that wasn't friendly enough for her to venture outside for a chat.

The man was twenty feet behind me now. No one else was dawdling around on the sidewalk, which was heartening. He likely didn't have a partner who was helping him surveil me.

And on the bright side, steroids tended to cloud one's judgement. All I needed to do was use my noodle well enough to outsmart someone who was stuffed full of them.

I moved down the block, keeping Maybe-Igor in my sights.

The height was right. The slope of his shoulders was right. Too large, but a similar shape. As I walked, I tried to think about the last time I'd seen him: in the island's jail infirmary, handcuffed to a bed.

He'd been irritated that I'd caught him, and somewhat reluctant to chat, but he hadn't seemed to hold his capture against me. A quick phone call from Boris had convinced Igor to tell me a few things. His first name. His non-military employment. That his next trip was to rough up a Mickey Mouse impersonator at Disney World.

But he'd ended up escaping his jail cell with a little help from a friend on the Beaver Island police force, and he'd crashed a civilian's car into Camille and Violet to return the favour. Luckily, the two of them were going to be okay, but I still had a score to settle with Igor on their account.

And now I was getting cross, thinking about the whole thing again.

The man ducked into Raymundo's, and for a moment my heart clenched.

But the bell on Epstein's door jangled again, and Igor—or his bigger, meaner cousin—was back on the street in a few minutes. I took a moment to think about the best location to force a confrontation with him. I had to get it done and dusted so I could focus on Maura's party tonight.

Should I cross the street and get him closer to Spa Lala? They had lots of nice pointy things I could use to poke his eyeballs out. All of the restaurants would have a thrilling selection of knives, but borrowing one or two might lead to some awkward questions. A telescoping baton would also work nicely, but mine was back home in my Ficus.

Where to go?

Somewhere that didn't have any cameras, for one. Pausing in front of the ice cream shop that Matty and I had patronized the other day, I opened my purse and did an inventory. I had some new shuriken throwing stars, but they were all at home, along with my gun, and all I had with me was my little telescoping mirror. Well, it did have a flashlight at one end, and there was a very nice blade in my left shoe. That would have to do.

Time to get off the street.

Via judicious use of my mirror, I observed that my shadow did not wait to cross at the stoplight as I did, but jaywalked into the road, although there wasn't much traffic. And it was likely too much to hope for that Farmer Ezekial would appear on his Kubota tractor and run him down.

The man's steps were uneven as he followed me. A little ragged. It made me think of whomever had shot Brandon, the poor dear.

I turned onto Snookie's street, which ran parallel to Main. I did not plan to confront Igor on her property, although I had every intention of doing so at one of her neighbours' houses. Happily, I knew that the owners of the house two doors over from Snookie were currently on vacation in Tahiti. I'd always been one to keep my enemies close, and their neighbours closer, especially since the Paytons—a lovely couple—had hedges so high that it was impossible to see their back yard. With any luck, nobody would even notice Igor and myself in our little backyard tryst.

I picked up a folded newspaper that had been thrown on their lawn some time back and walked up the driveway, then around the corner of the house.

Several deep, energetic breaths sent some oxygen to my extremities. I tested out my left knee. It definitely felt better than it had yesterday, and that compression bandage really seemed to be helping, but if I wasn't smart, my tussle with Mr. Igor was going to do some real damage.

Time for a few more breaths. Then I had the knife out of my shoe and in one hand.

I waited, trying to keep my breathing even, my thoughts clear.

It sounded like he was at the side entrance to the house now, the one the Paytons used after parking their car in the driveway. It was a lovely house, really, a Craftsman-style design, the lot generously wide, Gerbera daisies blanketing the front garden.

And my favourite feature: a small alcove set right around the corner of the house. It used to have a statue of the Virgin Mary set there, but Mary had been moved to greener pastures in recent years.

Igor's foot crunched on a dry twig, and he stopped.

I took in a few deep breaths, cold blanketing my shoulders.

He started walking again, my shadow. But he was on my territory.

Don't let it get you cocky, old girl. Once he was done with me, he'd come for Violet and Camille. Thank goodness Camille hadn't yet accepted my invitation to visit.

Crunch.

Igor was on the move again.

A few more breaths.

I took off my cardiac monitor so he couldn't strangle me with it.

And then he turned the corner.

But he was looking at his eyeline, at least a foot taller than my usual height. And I was not there.

Thirty-Six — Violet

After docking *Vitamin Sea* back at Irma's, I took one last look at the horizon. The afternoon sun was hidden behind a bunch of clouds that were turning grey in real time. I knew a storm was forecasted for tonight, which wasn't awesome, since I'd spent the last big island storm on a sinking houseboat, but Harbour House was much sturdier, and it was actually on land, so I couldn't see how it could possibly sink.

I slumped into my office chair, looking at the monitors on the desk in front of me. My "enhancing" software was still chugging away on the ferry footage, but was only thirty-nine percent done. I tried to quell the nervousness that that realization kicked off inside me. We weren't going to get any evidence from that file before the party tonight, and I still had a cellphone jammer to find and disable. Plus, I needed some proof of what Norman had been up to before Maura would even consider dumping him. This was the problem with optimists. They couldn't see reality clearly.

I sat there racking my brain about what to do next. My earlier call to Maura had gone to voicemail. Should I just show up at Harbour House? No. I didn't want to Norman to throw a tantrum and have me kicked out. I left another message on Maura's voicemail and got a snack.

Just as I was finishing up my second pizza pocket, Maura returned my call, and asked if I wanted to come over for a late lunch before everything kicked off tonight, since she knew I wasn't a huge fan of big parties and strangers, and especially big parties full of strangers.

Perfect.

I texted Irma to let her know I was heading out early—happily—in my own car, which had been dropped off at Irma's while we were on the mainland. My poor little Honda hadn't been starting properly all summer, and the one time it had worked, someone had smashed their own car right into it.

After packing up one of my laptops and the outfit I was going to wear to the party, a strapless wide-leg pantsuit with wedge sandals, I hit the road.

But as I was backing out of the driveway, Mrs. Sepp waved at me from her front yard. She was wearing one of her fancy going-out dresses with a gardening smock over the front, Mr. P snuggled in a Baby Bjorn on her chest.

"Violet!"

"Hey, Mrs. Sepp. What's up?"

"I have to put the final touches on the floral arrangements for the Kent-Wong engagement party, but my ride had to cancel at the last minute. If I don't get there soon, I will be late, and the person who is assisting me today is also late, so we will all be late."

"Lucky for you, that's exactly where I'm going," I said. Mrs. Sepp and her little guy got settled in the car and Mr. P leaned over to give me a slurpy kiss, washing off half my sunscreen. I didn't mind.

"Do you want to call them and tell them you're running late?"

"Not really, no," Mrs. Sepp said carefully. "I have had some problems with this family."

"Not with Maura?"

"Oh my goodness, no. She told me that she used to work for you. She said you were the best boss she's ever had."

I laughed as I made a turn. "She's just being nice."

"She is very nice. And quite intelligent." After a pause: "Except perhaps regarding her choice of family."

"I don't think she was able to choose her mother," I said. "Although if there's a way to do that retroactively, I'm all ears."

Mrs. Sepp patted me kindly on the arm. "Ah," she said. "This is why your eyes look sad sometimes."

I was glad I was wearing sunglasses big enough to hide half my face. After a weird cough, I said, "Irma was telling me that Ryeleigh and Stassi were driving you up the wall the other day."

"A floral designer cannot talk about their clients, Violet."

Mr. P bonked my shoulder with his head, pulled back, then did it again. Mrs. Sepp rubbed behind his ears.

"I understand," I said. "It's just that Maura can be a little...naïve sometimes. I worry about her. Especially because Ryeleigh's always seemed a little jealous of her."

"Violet," Mrs. Sepp said, her voice a little wavery. "Do you solemnly swear not to repeat anything I ever tell you about my clients?"

"Even to Irma?"

"Violet, do you solemnly swear not to tell anyone but Irma anything I tell you about my clients?"

"Scout's honour."

Mrs. Sepp let out a deep breath. "Ryeleigh's relationship with Maura is not healthy. And Ryeleigh's behaviour is terrible. She even destroyed the first batch of centrepieces I made for the party. They were all succulents and could be done ahead of time. But she threw them out the window! Right out the window! And refused to clean the mess up. The housekeeper and I had to do it."

I turned a corner and sped up. "Why would Ryeleigh do something like that?"

339

"She showed me a picture of a design on Instagram that is supposed to be better, more popular. She seems very focused on the family looking a certain way for public events."

"Yeah, I got that sense." I stopped at a four-way intersection. "But Maura doesn't care about any of that stuff at all."

"Yes, this is what she has told me. But Norman agreed with Ryeleigh and Maura did not want to cause a fuss, so we redid them all. Plus, of course, they were all out the window."

"Huh." I tapped a finger on the steering wheel as I drove. I knew Maura didn't really care about appearances. That was why she was wearing an understated engagement ring instead of the honking rock Norman had probably gotten for her. But she was also the kind of person to let things slide off her back and not get bothered by anything. I took in a shuddery breath and tried to focus on the road and what I needed to do once we got to the estate.

Other than the occasional arm lick from Mr. P, the rest of the ride was uneventful. He was looking perkier than usual, and breathing less like an eighty-year-old asthmatic.

Mrs. Sepp called to announce our presence when we turned onto Harbour House's laneway. After she'd hung up and put her cell phone in her purse, she looked none too pleased.

"Something wrong?"

"Why are you so late?" she mimicked. "But I am not late. I am right on time. Thanks to you, of course."

"Who said that?"

"Ryeleigh. Sometimes I wonder if she is marrying Norman or if Maura is."

We were met in front of the garage by a veritable army of helpers who plopped Mrs. Sepp into the six-seater golf cart and whisked her away to the house, with Mr. P straining to look at me over her shoulder.

I was alone.

Alone enough to take another look at that garage. All its doors were flung open, the space empty. The digital lock beside the side door was dark and the system looked disabled. Good.

A quick circuit around the space revealed nothing I hadn't seen the other day, and my attempt to identify exactly what security system was installed resulted in nada. The door still had a broken window, but someone had cleaned the glass up. Of course they had; this was a place where they swept the outdoors.

I looked around to confirm I was alone, then sparked up the cellphone jammer app I'd downloaded onto my phone. If I couldn't find the jammer and something bad happened tonight, there would be no way to call for help.

But the app started beeping immediately.

And then I was glad I was changing later, because the shoes I was wearing right now, as Irma would say, were very sensible. Perfect for the uneven grassy area at the back of the garage and the wooded area beyond it, where the beeping was coming from.

I didn't want to go into those woods. I was not an outdoorsy person.

Ping.

But I had to help Maura. I straightened my shoulders. My app lost the signal for a minute, so I turned in a circle, trying to find it again. If this kept up, I was going to be very dizzy for the party.

Ping.

I found the cellphone jammer in a clump of bushes near the treeline. It was a boxy, square thing, powered by a car battery, which was actually pretty smart.

I used my phone's flashlight to take a closer look. The jamming device wasn't big, but I guessed it didn't have to be. And one of the cables connected into the battery wasn't seated properly, which meant that the jammer might sporadically lose connection to its power source. *That* was why I'd been able to get small messages out to Irma when we were locked in the garage.

Triumph churned inside me for a minute, and I was all jangly nerves and adrenaline. After I'd calmed down a bit, I disabled the jammer with a smile.

Then I squared my shoulders and started walking across the little causeway.

Thirty-Seven — Irma

I slashed at the back of Igor's knee with the knife, but my blade hit something hard and bounced off.

Maybe he was wearing body armour. Honestly, that was just cheating.

Instead of coming in for the kill, Igor stepped away from me. Five feet away, then ten. It was a curious decision, but I wasn't one to criticize good fortune. When he paused under a lilac tree, I got a better look at his face. He had terrible acne now, mostly covered up by the beard he'd grown. And he looked angry. Possibly because of all those spots on his face, or the steroids he'd been pumping into himself, or perhaps both.

I bumped into the pedestal that used to hold up the Virgin Mary. Too late, I realized I'd backed myself into a corner. But Igor's eyes were steady on my face, and I did not want to bring any attention to this state of affairs.

"Nice to see you again, Irma," he said in Novosibirsk-accented Russian.

"I wish I could say the same," I replied in the same language. "Didn't your mother ever tell you it isn't nice to bother little old ladies?"

He laughed, then crossed his bulky arms.

"I suppose not, then," I said. "I have to be somewhere, dear, so how would you like to do this?"

Another smile slid across his face. "I would like to talk to you."

"So talk."

"I need your help."

I took in a sharp breath, unease kicking up inside me. I did not like the unexpected, especially when it came from juiced-up non-military Russian operatives.

"There is a job I need some help on. And from what I hear, you would be perfect for it."

I let out a slow breath. "What kind of job?"

He smiled. Not a nice smile. "I will tell you after you agree to do it."

"I wouldn't help you if my life depended on it, dear. And while we're on the subject, I have to tell you how very unhappy I am with your recent actions."

"Like?"

"Like breaking out of your holding cell at our lovely island jail. Like smashing a car into...some friends of mine." I didn't want to name names if he hadn't figured all that out on his own.

"Camille and Violet?" he asked with a smirk.

I sent him an unblinking gaze.

He held up a hand. "That accident was just supposed to get your attention. It ended up being more serious than was intended."

"That might just be the worst apology I've ever heard, dear."

"If I was not telling the truth, Mrs. Abercrombie-Fitzhugh-Maddox...actually, you have many names, do you not? Names I'm sure you don't want your fancy neighbours to find out about."

"To be frank, I worry less and less about that every day."

"It might be dangerous if some of your old enemies knew where you are."

"Intelligence work has rules, dear. Manners." Softly, I added, "But you wouldn't know anything about that, would you?"

"I am more corporate," he agreed with a shrug. "Which is why I have stayed on the island."

"That's not the only reason, dear. Your neck now has the circumference of a wagon wheel."

"I have merely been getting ready for my next job."

"What about that Mickey Mouse impersonator?"

"Someone else took over that project. But I am not distressed about this."

"Nice to see you don't hold a grudge."

"I wouldn't say that." His wolfish grin unsettled something deep inside my sternum. "But I am not angry. I look up to you, in fact. And I need your help with a job."

"What kind of job?"

"A job that will pay very well." He reached into his pocket, and I held my breath. He smiled, noticing, then pulled out a keychain attached to a beaver-shaped bauble. They sold them in one of the shops on Main Street. I let the breath out slowly.

"I have all the money I'll ever need, frankly."

"Perhaps that money will unexpectedly disappear." He started fidgeting with the keychain.

"Do please give that your best shot, dear."

Another unsettling smile. "It is not a huge job, at least not your part. All I need is to borrow some of your expertise and a bit of your time. Then I will leave you alone forever."

"I don't like leaving the island in the summer, so I don't see how I could possibly help you, dear."

Another smile. "It will be on the island. So, no worries there."

"No, thank you," I said, trying to keep my voice even. "Now, would you like to come back to the police station with me, or shall I have them collect you?"

"Things will be so much easier for you if you just agree to what I want."

"One of my teachers always used to say I was a disagreeable sort. At this point in my life, I have to say he was probably right."

"I do not want to threaten you."

I squared my shoulders. "You almost killed one of my friends. So the threat has already been issued."

"It's disappointing that you refuse to listen to reason on this matter. Obviously, I will have to raise the stakes somewhat." Smile. "And you are alone here on this island, are you not? Whereas I already have some friends here who can help me persuade you."

"Oh, good heavens," I blurted. "Really?"

"Yes, really. Is 'no' your final answer?" He rattled the keychain in his hand. It was important that I not let him get close enough to stuff one—or more—of those keys into my eyeballs.

"It is." I started to inch to the right, out of my little alcove.

But Igor was making a move of his own.

Thirty-Eight — Violet

The sun had started to dim in the sky, those grey clouds quietly churning bigger and bigger. Water shot over the causeway a few times during my little trek, but I managed to keep dry enough.

Maura, who was helping Mrs. Sepp entwine flowers into the majestic banister gracing the enormous stairs inside the house, squealed when she saw me. She was wearing a headband with two antennae sprouting out of it, smiley little beaver heads stuck on each one, and a pink t-shirt and yoga pants.

"Violet! You won't believe what I found this morning!" To Mrs. Sepp, she added, "Is it okay if I go? I can send Jerrod to replace me."

"My helper will be here soon," Mrs. Sepp said kindly.

"Come!" Maura grabbed my hand and practically dragged me up the stairs. The inside of the house looked perfectly decorated and ready for the hordes of well-wishers who were going to descend on the house in about four hours. There were fancy balloons and streamers and flowers, all in warm shades of pink and taupe.

Maura pulled me through all that to the master bedroom.

It was one of the biggest rooms I'd ever seen in my life, with a sitting area and TV, and a fireplace adjacent to the bed. There was a treadmill pointed at a window with a lovely view of the lake, fluffy pillows that almost reached the ceiling, and not one but *two* ginormous ensuite bathrooms.

And closets for days. Maura dragged me into one of the enormous walk-ins. "Look." She ducked under some clothes, still pulling on my hand. There was an unusually large amount of space behind the clothing rod. And then, a door.

"What the heck is that?" I asked.

"I'll show you," she said breathlessly. When she opened it, a brand-new room appeared. It was sparsely furnished compared to the rest of the master suite, but it still looked pretty comfortable. There was shelf-stable food, water, two couches, and a TV set. There was even a DVD library, in case the internet was out, I supposed. And another door led away from the room.

"This is so much better than my apartment," I blurted.

"Mine too," she said with a grin. "And look at this." She closed the door behind us and attached a bunch of different locks. A small plaque on the door read, *Safe Harbour.* "We could live here for ages. Nothing could get to us!"

"Fire," I said. "A bomb, maybe."

She laughed. "I didn't realize you had such a vivid imagination."

"Where does the other door lead to?"

"After I found this room this morning, Jerrod told me that there are a bunch of secret passageways in the walls. Can you believe it? You should come over next week and we'll go exploring."

"Sounds good," I said with a smile.

"You hungry?"

"Yup."

After a Harbour House staffer had set us up in a bedroom nook that overlooked the water, we settled in to stuff our faces. As we ate, I tried to think of a delicate way to tell Maura to cancel the party and run like a maniac away from Norman.

I tried to keep my face still while I sorted through my options. Norman might want to marry Maura so he could control her, or he might want to bump her off to collect some life insurance money, or he might want both. And if he'd set Brandon up to make it look like he was stalking Maura, and Brandon's PI had figured that out, Norman would have had ample reason to bump the two of them off. Either way, Norman was not the man for Maura, who tipped like she was a baller and generally ended her restaurant meals by hugging all the waitstaff.

But who had shot Brandon on the ferry? Norman was on the smaller side, but I didn't see how Brandon could have mistaken him for a woman, especially since they knew each other. Then I remembered what Irma had told me last week about eyewitness reports being unreliable. If Brandon had seen someone that *looked* like they were part of a woman's motorcycle club, could he have just assumed that the person beside him was a woman? Especially if he hadn't really been paying attention, like he'd told us?

"I am stuffed!" Maura said with a grin, her little beaver-topped antennae bouncing around.

"Maura, I have to tell you something."

Her famous smile faded off her face while I caught her up about Brandon being shot on the ferry. By the time I was done, her eyes were as big as saucers. "So, someone did all this in broad daylight?"

"Yes."

"Is he going to be okay?"

"I hope so."

She let out a sigh. "Wow." After a minute, she added, "And he still says he never did any of that creepy stuff?"

I nodded.

She put her head in her hands. "This is a nightmare."

I patted her on the arm. "It's going to be okay."

"I'll just be a sec." Maura withdrew to one of the enormous ensuite bathrooms, and I sat back in my chair. I had a lot of suspicions about who was responsible for everything that had happened, but no proof, no data that would convince Maura to ditch her dud of a fiancé, and time was running out. It was infuriating.

From this angle, I could see a few bankers' boxes jumbled in the corner opposite me, beside the same briefcase Norman had been using this afternoon. I glanced in the direction of the bathroom. I couldn't hear any handwashing yet, so I probably had a minute or two. But should I really go through Norman's stuff?

What if the proof was in one of those boxes?

I practically leapt across the room. The briefcase was locked, so I dove into the first box. There were sample party invitations with different kinds of paper, and a few candles that might have been meant for party gifts, along with what looked like proofs of engagement pictures, Maura smiling like it was the smile Olympics. I dug under all that until I found a crumpled sheaf of papers. After a minute, I realized it was the guest list for tonight's party—but almost half the names were crossed out. Including mine. And the title at the top of the first page was NORMAN'S LIST.

I heard the sink and jammed the list in my pocket. As I plopped back into my chair, Maura emerged from the bathroom.

"There's something else I want to talk to you about," I said, meeting her eyes.

"Shoot. Do you want some coffee before all the madness starts?"

"I'd love some." After taking a deep breath, I said, "Maura, remember how I never got my invitation to this party?"

"Yeah. I'm so, so sorry about that. There must have been some kind of mix-up. I really haven't had anything to do with the invitation side of things. Norman wanted to take care of all that."

"I don't think there was a mix-up," I said, passing the invitation list to her. She scanned it with one eyebrow raised. By the time she was done, she was wearing an expression I'd never seen on her face before.

She cleared her throat. "You know, after all the stalking stuff started, I kind of...withdrew. I haven't talked to some of my friends in months." She met my eyes. "I think everyone thought that Norman and I were in a love bubble, and left us alone for a bit. We never announced the party on social media or anything, to make sure my stalker never saw anything about it. I bet some of the people on this list never even heard about the party."

"I sure didn't," I said.

Just as Norman walked into the room.

Thirty-Nine — Irma

Igor threw the beaver-shaped keychain at me. It caught me in the chest and sent a jolt through my body like it was a mini-Taser. For a moment I marvelled that they could make these kinds of things so small these days. And then I slithered down, my back against the brick until I was sitting on the pretty interlocking stones, my legs thrust out in front of me. I had not landed gracefully.

I could still breathe, I could see, but I could barely move. And I definitely couldn't talk.

Across the path, Igor was gazing intently at me, and my heart skipped a beat. I was a sitting duck.

Or a dead one.

Igor was right that I was alone. Camille was out of commission, Edward was too far away to be of assistance, and so was Violet, who'd texted me earlier to tell me she was going to head over to Harbour House early. On top of all that, I'd failed in my assessments of young Brandon, who'd been shot right under my nose. I kicked myself for not connecting that Ducati with the noise I'd heard at the club the night of the banquet. I'd heard a sport bike revving in the parking lot shortly before Harvey Allen's death, and I'd done nothing with that intel.

I was losing my touch.

And if Igor came much closer, I'd lose a lot more.

I could hear my heartbeat pounding in my ears. Sensation was starting to return to my limbs, but it was going to take more time until I was re-combobulated, I could tell. More time than I had.

I let out a long, loud sigh. Then peace flooded into me. This was always how it was going to be. This was always how my ending was going to come. And when I was gone, Camille and Violet and Stu and everyone else would be safe.

Igor bent down and carefully pushed some hair off my face, sliding it behind one of my ears. It was an almost gentle act that turned my blood cold. "You'll feel better soon," he said softly. "And you have some time to re-consider my offer. We'll be in touch."

Then he turned and walked toward the road without looking back, while I sat on the ground like a fish out of water.

I most certainly did not feel better soon. In fact, it took almost fifteen minutes for my senses to return, and if I was being honest with myself, they weren't all back then, either.

Groaning, I got to my feet and collected myself. Anger had started to burn inside me. I had a headache, and I'd hurt my bottom when I fell.

As I made my way back to town, I thought good and hard about what I was going to do with young Igor, but those thoughts kept being interrupted by my realization that Maura's engagement party was fast approaching. I had to get there and help her.

...if I was still able to, that is.

Forty — Violet

Norman was already in a designer summer suit, his short-ish hair slicked back, shiny dress shoes reflecting the light.

"Yes?" Maura said. She looked calm. Serene. At least one of us was. Under the fake smile I was wearing, my heart was clanging against my ribcage.

"When are you going to take off that headband?" he said. "And why are you wearing a headband with beavers on it, anyway?"

"We're having our party on Beaver Island," Maura said evenly. "It seemed like a fun idea."

"None of this is supposed to be fun," he said.

I felt irritation bubble up inside me.

"Exactly," Ryeleigh said, stepping into the room and heading toward Maura, her gait uneven. Was she *limping*?

Maura waved both of them off. "My hair and makeup person isn't even here yet. I have a few hours. I'm just catching up with Violet."

"No time for that," Ryeleigh said, her voice snippy. She was already in her party dress, a sequined pink mermaid style that looked like it was cutting off the circulation to her feet. And possibly her head.

I squinted at her. Where was the nice, shy girl I'd met at the club? Exactly who *was* Ryeleigh, anyway?

Was she the kind of person who could have helped Norman orchestrate a rift between Maura and Brandon—or done it all herself? As a resident at Harbour House, she'd have access to the security system. What if she'd figured out how to manipulate the estate's security software into keeping those garage doors locked, even if there was a car spewing poisonous gas into the air?

But would she have killed Brandon's PI—a stranger?

If she was capable of locking me and her sister in a garage full of poisoned air…well, she was capable of a lot. And if Harvey Allen had found out Ryeleigh had been the one to break Maura and Brandon up, that would definitely be something Ryeleigh wouldn't want anyone to find out. So maybe she'd bumped Harvey off before he could spill the beans to anyone.

Why shoot Brandon on the ferry, though? Did Ryeleigh think his PI had told him what he'd found out? And why hadn't Brandon recognized her? Had he forgotten who the shooter was because of all the drugs they'd pumped into him at the hospital?

"Violet and I are going to have coffee now," Maura said, then picked up a walkie and ordered some from the kitchen.

Ryeleigh let out an exasperated noise. "I need to know about the flowers—"

"I'm sure Mrs. Sepp has all that in hand," Maura said.

"Nothing is in hand!" Norman snapped. "Half our guests for tonight have cancelled, and the ferry restarted this afternoon only to be shut down again because of high winds."

I gulped. What if Irma's security buddies couldn't make it here in time for the party?

"And I really need some 'getting ready' poses for Instagram, Maura," Ryeleigh said. "I'm going to shoot some video. And you need to put on your real engagement ring for all that."

For some reason, Ryeleigh had the ring with her, and she plopped it on the table between me and Maura. It was nestled in a pool of pink satin, and its diamond was so big, it momentarily blinded me.

"No, thanks," Maura said.

"You really need to do what Ryeleigh tells you," Norman said. "I have some very important people coming tonight. People I have to impress."

Maybe it was the tone he used, or maybe it was the glower on his face, but that was the moment all the air went out of my friend.

"And is that all you care about?" Maura asked quietly. "Impressing people?"

Norman paused and shook himself. Then he ran his hands through his hair, although not anywhere near as adorably as Julian did. I made a mental note to call him later. I could really use some quiet sitting in front of a fire time after all this was done.

"Sorry, babe," he said finally. "It's just all the pressure of the party. Things will be better after it's over."

Maura held a hand up. "Violet and I are going to have coffee now. I'll be out in a bit."

"But—"

"In a bit, Norman."

Jerrod entered the room with a silver tray and started clearing away the plates from our snack and setting up the coffee service for us. After he was done, he raised the tray with one hand, then leaned forward, his other hand on my shoulder. "I'm very glad to see you looking so well, Miss Violet," he said kindly, then made his way out of the room. I wanted to ask him a few questions about the current state of the security system, but not in front of Maura's fiancé or her sister.

After Jerrod was gone, Norman threw up his hands and left. Briefly, Ryeleigh looked like she was about to explode, before she stomped out after Maura's fiancé.

Or perhaps I should say: limp-stomped.

FORTY-ONE — IRMA

I spent a few moments organizing myself in Harbour House's parking lot. I had a small valise full of supplies, and I'd zipped tonight's ensemble into a carrying bag that was flung over one shoulder. Françoise's security detail had not yet arrived, and I did not want to leave Violet and Maura alone on the little island.

Lake water crashed over the wooden bridge that attached Harbour House to the mainland. The wind had kicked up while I was getting myself together at home, and tonight's forecast had turned even grimmer. There were some doubts in my mind that the party was going to happen at all, which was fine with me, frankly. I wasn't in much of a party-going mood.

After greeting Mr. P, who was frolicking inside the house in a very smart formal ensemble, I caucused with Mrs. Sepp, who asked if I could take him with me for a bit. I had him follow along while I searched for the girls.

During my trek, I spied the catering kitchen, which was bustling with activity and things that smelled absolutely excellent. Theresa, the head bartender at the club, was running through a list with some waitstaff, and she smiled and waved at me. Two young chefs were debating the merits of one type of crabcake versus another, and Jerrod was loading the dishwasher in a dress shirt and slacks, his coat probably still on a hanger until the guests started showing up in a few hours.

"Hello, Jerrod," I said.

"Good afternoon, Mrs. Abercrombie," he said warmly. Professionally. But something in his manner felt a bit rushed. Worried, even. Well, that's what happens when one is putting on a large event. "Might I get you a beverage?"

One of the chefs, wearing a starched white jacket with her purple hair pulled under a cap, did a little jig, her shoes slapping against the polished oak flooring.

"Water, please," I said with a smile.

"Of course."

"I bet you'll be glad when this party is over."

Jerrod filled a glass with bottled water and added a spritz of lime to it, then handed it to me. "I certainly will be," he said with a friendly smile. "May I be of any further assistance?"

"Do you happen to know where the girls are?"

"In the master suite," he said, pointing.

"Thank you," I said with a smile.

He nodded before making his way to the formal dining room, his shoes tapping an uneven pattern on the hardwood before picking up speed and smoothing out. I squinted at his retreating figure. The heel on his left shoe was higher than his right. Odd that I'd never noticed it previously, but domestic staff on the island often wore sneakers because they spent so much time on their feet. I supposed that plimsolls wouldn't really go well with formalwear.

I found Maura and Violet in the master bedroom, a tray of coffee and snacks on the table in front of them. "Hello, ladies," I said.

"Close the door," Violet hissed. After I'd done so, she detailed how Norman had struck most of Maura's guests from tonight's list, as if we didn't already have enough on our plate.

"Well, my dears, if something goes horribly wrong tonight, just retire to the panic room."

"How do you know there's a panic room?" Violet asked.

"Is something going to go horribly wrong tonight?" Maura asked.

"There's two, actually," I said. "And a number of secret passageways."

"This place has *two* panic rooms?" Maura squealed.

"I do agree that the architect got a bit carried away, but yes. Along with a network of secret passages."

"How do you know all this?" Violet asked.

"I got hold of Wendy Wilson, the estate agent. She walked me through the design."

"Hold up a minute. What horrible thing do you think is going to happen tonight?" Maura asked.

"Dear, someone has shot your ex and the private investigator he hired."

"But this place has great security. It's a safe harbour!"

I put a hand on her arm. "If the bad guys are already inside, then there is no safe harbour here."

Maura looked horrified. "Bad guys like who?"

"Maura, have you signed any life insurance policies or anything like that lately?" Violet asked.

She fidgeted in her seat. "Yes. Norman wanted all that done before the wedding. He handles all our finance stuff."

"And how much is your life insurance policy worth?" I asked gently.

"Uh...five million," Maura said.

Violet made a squeaky noise.

I squeezed her arm, then looked at Maura. "That's a lot of reasons to—"

"There's no way that Norman is capable of shooting Brandon," Maura said. "He's very squeamish."

"Brandon says he was shot by a woman," Violet said.

"A *woman?*" Maura crinkled her nose.

"Possibly someone with a brace on their leg," Violet said. "Or, you know, some other sort of mobility issue. Hey—why is Ryeleigh limping?"

Some other sort...

"I don't know," Maura said, shaking her head. She was wearing the most darling beaver-accented headband.

...of mobility issue.

My stomach clenched like it was a fist.

If one of Jerrod's legs were longer than the other, that would definitely qualify as a problem that might require a brace in some circumstances. I hadn't seen one on the shoes he was wearing today, but they were probably custom-built and designed so he could walk as perfectly as possible. Then I wondered if the real reason he'd fallen when the girls had been locked in the garage was because that physical detail made him unsteady on his feet at times. Certainly, the estate's grounds were pristine, and there had been nothing for him to trip over that day.

"Jerrod took the afternoon off yesterday, with no advance notice..." Maura said, her voice sounding funny.

"Around the same time that Brandon was shot, right?" Violet said.

"Maura, dear, I do believe you need to cancel your party," I said, cold blanketing my shoulders.

"Norman isn't going to like that very much," Maura said.

"Marriage is about compromises, dear."

"I don't know if we're going to make it that far."

"Even better. When is everything supposed to start tonight?"

"Cocktails are at seven. In two hours."

In my lap, Mr. P growled, and I patted him on the head. He did not care for storms, and the one hovering above us was about to start crashing down. He wiggled in my arms, then jumped to the floor.

"He really seems perkier lately," Violet said.

"Mrs. Sepp says he might have a gluten allergy. She's been feeding him a different kind of food. I wonder if that's made a difference," I said.

"He's such a sweetheart," Maura said.

"Maura, dear," I said. "Have you ever seen Jerrod limping?"

"No."

"Have you ever noticed him wearing a leg brace?"

"Uh, yeah." Her eyes were wide. "For his left foot. I didn't want to ask any questions, though. He's a pretty private guy."

A private guy who, as a moonlighting butler, didn't have a lot of ties. That could indicate nothing: Violet wasn't a people person and she was perfectly normal. Ish. But sometimes people who didn't put down roots had other problems that kept them on the move.

"What's wrong, Irma?" Violet asked.

"Why would someone lie about who shot them?" I asked. "Why would *Brandon* lie about who shot him?"

"Because he was up to something bad with the shooter, and decided to double-cross him." Violet's eyes widened. "You can't mean—"

Mr. P sprang off the floor and landed partly on the couch, partly on Maura's leg, his bottom not quite making the trip. She pulled him onto her lap and started patting his tummy.

His ears turned to mush the way they did when he was being petted. But after a moment, he snapped himself out of it. First his ears went back, then he rolled off Maura's lap and onto the floor.

And I saw something I'd never seen before: His hackles went up. Then he started growling at something deep within the room's closets.

I looked around the luxurious room. I couldn't sense any danger. And Mr. P, while adorable in that delightful little tux, was not an accomplished guard dog, no matter how many lessons I'd tried to give him.

He growled some more, then glanced back at me, before sitting down.

Was he...alerting me?

I focused on the little lad. He certainly had been behaving oddly lately. Could it be that some of my training had actually sunk in?

He twirled in a circle, before sitting down again.

Then the cold came for me, finally, wrapping around my shoulders, and I took a moment to cover one of my shuriken throwing stars in a hanky and slip it into the side of my brassiere.

Of course, that was when the power went out.

Forty-Two — Violet

In the dim light, Irma stuck something under her
shirt and kicked her go-bag out of sight before laying
her hands primly in her lap. She was wearing her
usual daytime uniform: a white collared short-sleeve
shirt with pedal pushers, ballerina pink today, tennis
shoes completing the outfit. Her heart monitor was
nowhere to be seen.

She cracked her neck to the right, then to the left,
straightened and bent both knees. After a few deep
breaths, she looked ready.

Mr. P was full-on growling now, and the fur on
the back of his neck was standing on end.

"*Beschermen!*" Irma said. Incredibly, Mr. P
trotted forward, taking a position between us and the
closet. Like he was protecting us.

"What language is that?" I asked nervously.

Dutch, Irma mouthed.

The room stood still.

Then Brandon stepped out from the closet
attached to the panic room. He looked good for
someone who'd just climbed out of a hospital bed.
His colour was a little off, and he was favouring his

left side, but he was on his feet, which was pretty impressive. He also had a gun in one hand, one big enough to make holes in a whole lot of people.

Thunder erupted, close enough that I could feel it in my stomach. I stopped breathing.

"Irma," Brandon drawled. "Hey, Violet. Maurie."

"Don't call me that," she said softly.

"Don't make me mad, Mo," he said, equally quiet. Something cold ran up my spine, hearing it. "What's in that bag you brought with you?" he asked Irma. His voice was so pleasant, it was surreal. I'd had Christmas drinks with Brandon. We'd entered an oyster-eating contest together one year. And now here he was with a gun.

My stomach started to churn.

"Private lady things," Irma said.

He snickered. Keeping the pistol pointed at Irma, he picked up her bag with a quick movement and dropped it off beside Maura. "Open it," he said to her, "and lay everything on the ground."

Maura closed her eyes for a moment, then unzipped the bag. The things on the top were innocuous: water bottles, some power bars, a set of keys. As she kept digging, the items became more and more Irma-like: plastic cuffs, two knives, a pair of walkie-talkies, and what looked like a Death by Chocolate cupcake that I'd bet was supposed to be for me.

"Quite the night you have planned," Brandon said drily, before eating my cupcake.

"My goodness, whoever raised you failed horribly," Irma said, her tone equally arid. Mr. P was growling again, and she rubbed his head for a moment.

Brandon threw a glance over at me. I hoped my face was showing him exactly how I felt about him.

"Why?" I snapped.

"You're gonna have to be more specific, Violet." Brandon was wearing a lopsided grin that I wanted to slap right off his face.

"Why kill a PI that *you* hired?"

"It was his own fault. He should have just done his job."

"What job did he think he was doing, exactly?" Irma asked.

"Finding Maurie, like I told you. Which he did. But then he found my burner phone and a bunch of AirTags, and he realized I'd been keeping an eye on Maurie after all. I guess he was a suspicious guy. He went to the club that night to tell Maura everything, so..." He shrugged.

"Why did you need a PI to find Maura if you had an AirTag in her purse?" I asked.

"She doesn't always use that fancy purse, does she? And the AirTags were great for following her in a big city, but things get a lot more complicated in the country, don't they? No iPhone users around means no network to get AirTag information from. Once Maura left Toronto, I lost her. Harvey was nice enough to find her for me."

"How the heck did you get that AirTag into Maura's purse, anyway?" I snapped.

He smiled. Not a nice smile. "After Maura changed the locks at her old apartment, she gave a key to Ryeleigh, and I borrowed it to make a copy. I liked to go there when Maura wasn't home. I saw a thing on the news about AirTags, and I decided to put a few in her stuff."

"But why try to kill Maura in the garage?" Irma asked, rolling her ankles the way she did when she was warming up for a fight. My breath was trapped somewhere in my throat.

"It's simple," Brandon said, his eyes glued on Maura. "It sure looks like she's going to go through with this whole Norman thing. So why not make it look like Norman was out to get her?"

Irma *tsked*.

Brandon's smile slowly took over his face. It was a creepy, soul-less smile. "Plus, if I can't have Maurie, nobody can."

Maura inhaled sharply.

I tried to breathe, but my chest hurt. I'd punched a killer in the liver a few weeks back, and Irma had been giving me self-defence lessons whether I liked it or not, but I had no idea how to disarm a murderer with a gun—plus Irma wasn't exactly at her best these days. And I was the one who'd dragged her into all this.

"How are you still standing?" Irma muttered. "You're supposed to be half-dead."

Brandon grinned broadly. "That's the thing with hospitals. There's so many good drugs."

I looked closer. His pupils were enlarged; sweat dotted his brow. He was going to crash soon. He had to. All we needed to do was keep him talking until he fell over.

I took a long, shuddery breath. "How did you do it?"

"Do what?"

"Lock us in the garage."

"Oh, that was Jerrod. He has full access to the security system. I threw a few bucks his way, and voila!" He smiled.

Maura looked like she was in a trance, and I was definitely going to hurl on Brandon, probably sooner rather than later.

"Why did you lie and say that a woman shot you on the ferry?" Irma asked quietly. "Why didn't you say it was Jerrod?"

"Because I want to take care of Jerrod myself." Brandon laughed. Not a nice laugh. "He had no clue what I was up to. He thought I wanted to lock you guys in the garage as a practical joke. He had no idea I was going to turn that car on." He saw the question in my eyes. "I had a copy made of Maura's remote starter fob back when we were dating."

Irma said sharply, "And you want us to believe that Jerrod would do a thing like that?"

"He has a gambling problem." Brandon let out a creepy little giggle. "Poker, I think. He lost a bunch of money in a game a few months ago and couldn't pay it back without a few jobs off the books. He *threatened* me after he realized that Maura's car was running when you guys were in the garage. Can you believe that?"

"Threatened you with what?" Irma asked quietly.

"He said he was going to go to the police." Another smile. "I told him if he didn't want to end up like Harvey Allen, he'd keep his mouth shut." He hiccupped, his weight shifting.

"Why would you leave the island with me?" Irma asked.

"Oh, I was going to come right back, trust me."

"And Harvey?" Irma asked.

The gun didn't waver. "I let some air out of one of his tires. Left just enough in it for him to get out of that club, away from witnesses. He got out to check the tire pressure, and I was following him in my car." He licked his lips. "I had him get down on his knees before I killed him, which is the exact same thing I'm going to do to Jerrod."

Lightning cracked across the sky.

Brandon held both hands out. "Get up," he said to Irma.

"I'd rather sit, if you don't mind. My knee is bothering me."

"That's because you're as old as shit," he said, his face twisted into a sneer. "I want to see what you've got in your pockets."

Irma stood, stumbling a bit as she did. I sincerely hoped she was putting on a show.

Irma pulled the lining of her front pockets out. They were empty. He had her pull her shirt up to make sure she didn't have a weapon on her waist somewhere. Satisfied, he nodded at her to sit again.

"So you were stalking me the whole time," Maura said.

"I was keeping an eye on you. Making sure you were safe."

"That's stalking."

"It's not stalking when you love someone, Maura. And I do love you."

"You sure didn't act like it."

"That's true. See? I can admit my faults. And I should have dealt with my financial issues better, too. I can see that now. But you shouldn't have left me for Norman. It was a test, introducing you to him. And you failed."

"I didn't leave you for him."

"You failed," he repeated. "After I'd worked so hard to make you happy." A smirk. "Although I can admit that maybe I went off the rails a little with all that stalking stuff. But I wanted to see if that big happy personality of yours was real or not. I mean, you've always had everything handed to you, so what's not to be happy about?" He smiled. "But I've done a lot of thinking, and I've decided that I can be good again. That's how much I love you. I'm not going to hurt you. I just need you to come with me. Right after I deal with Jerrod."

Thunder rumbled, closer now.

"This house is full of people," I blurted. "You'll never get away from here in time."

"From what Jerrod's told me, the house is also full of hidden passages," he said. "That's how I'm going to get Maura out of here. After that, it's over to the boat I have on the other side of the property."

"There's a storm coming, dear," Irma said.

"I ain't your dear, and it's a big boat. We'll be fine." He yanked Maura's arm. "We're going."

"I'm so sorry," Irma said, standing. "But I can't let you do that."

"And neither can I," another voice said.

FORTY-THREE — IRMA

Jerrod emerged from the panic room and stood behind Brandon, a gun in one hand. But Brandon was already turning with his own gun out, and shot him first. Jerrod hit the floor like a ton of bricks, and Brandon shot him again.

Things moved very quickly then.

Brandon yanked Maura's arm and snatched up my bag of goodies. I didn't care if he took them. I'd once bludgeoned a target with a Beanie Baby that had been lying around. I'd find something to get the job done with Mr. Brandon.

"I'm gonna go now," he said cheerfully. "Put Jerrod's gun in the bag, Mo."

"You'll never make it," Violet said. "We'll find you."

Oh, Violet, please zip it.

"I hope not, for your sake," Brandon said, pointing the gun right at Violet's frontal lobe. His hand trembled, but not as much as one would hope for. "I always liked you, Violet, and you sure can eat a lot of oysters, but if you follow me—actually, babe, can you please put those plastic cuffs on these two?"

Maura's hands were shaking, but she managed to hang on to the cuffs. At Brandon's instructions, she secured Violet's hands in front of her.

After Brandon directed Maura to do the same to me, he bound her hands with another set of cuffs and leaned close to my ear. "I sure am sorry about this, Mrs. Abercrombie, especially since you've been so very helpful to me." A giggle—a mad, crazy noise— erupted from him and I wondered exactly what drugs he had taken. "I sure did like how you saved my life, though. And that's why I'm not going to shoot you and Violet in the head right now. But don't you follow me."

He had my bag slung over one shoulder, and was yanking on Maura's elbow with his left hand. After pulling her into the closet and the panic room behind it, he clicked a series of locks into place.

Violet crawled toward me.

I listened to make sure those locks weren't going to clank open again, then tightened my cuffs by pulling on the plastic that was threaded through the locking mechanism with my teeth.

"What are you doing?" Violet hissed.

"The tighter the cuffs," I said, "the easier they are to break." I raised both hands and brought them down on the edge of an end table. A few whacks later, I was free. I cut Violet's off with some scissors from the bathroom.

"I'm going to need you to move all the civilians to the panic room in the basement. On the bright side, it's in the wine cellar."

"Got it."

The two of us went to Jerrod's side. He was breathing heavily, red dotting his shoulder—just a flesh wound—and there was a bullet hole in his right flank that didn't look terrible, but it didn't look wonderful, either.

"I'm all right," he said, trying to lift his head. "The keys are in my right pocket."

"Keys for what?" Violet asked.

"Everything."

"Good man," I said, handing him a throw blanket from the couch. "Put some pressure on your side."

"I never meant for any of this to happen," Jerrod said, wincing as he pressed down on the wound. "It was… supposed to be a prank. I needed…the money."

"Why did you shoot Brandon, though?" Violet asked.

"I didn't…mean to. I just wanted to talk to him. I was waiting for him to come home when Mrs. Abercrombie—"

"Irma, dear."

"—showed up. Then the two of them left together, and I followed. When Irma got out of the car on the ferry, I tried to talk to him. He had those tinted windows, so he was able to pull a gun on me without anyone seeing him. We struggled, and the gun went off."

"Is that the gun you had with you tonight?" I asked.

He nodded. "Look—if Brandon has locked that door behind him, no one will be able to get in. There's another entrance to the passageways in the linen closet next door."

"Good heavens, the architect must have been as mad as a hatter. But thank you." To Violet, I said, "I'm going to follow Brandon. You call the police, move the civilians downstairs, and then everything will work out just fine."

Violet reached forward and hugged me hard. I squeezed her for a moment, then thrust her away.

"Go, please," I said, and thank heavens she did. I squared my shoulders, took stock of my weapons, and entered the maze of passageways via the linen cupboard.

I could hear shouting from somewhere deep inside the house, and adrenaline raced through me. I took a few deep breaths. Time to go.

Ahead, to the left, I could hear a muffled woman's voice. Then an angry man's in response. I slid off one shoe, then the other, pausing to take my knife out of the heel. Then I crept forward.

"Stop it!" Maura said.

I peered around the corner, pulling my head back when Brandon started shouting again. He was so much taller that he towered over her.

"You're hurting my arm!" Maura cried.

Brandon pulled her down the hallway, but not before she spied the top of my head. Her eyes widened, and then she was gone, yanked so hard that it wouldn't surprise me if her teeth were rattling.

If I was interpreting what Wendy Wilson had told me about the passages correctly, we were near the main living area.

Thunder rang out.

I could hear Brandon dragging Maura farther down the hallway.

Wendy had told me that there was an exit from the passages into the family kitchen. If I could surprise Brandon as he was going through that door, I could get his gun away from him.

Maybe.

I moved quickly, my heartbeat thudding in my ears. Violet would get the civilians into the downstairs panic room soon. She had to.

The passage turned another corner, and there it was—the door to the kitchen. Brandon was fiddling at the latch. Ha! He was stuck.

So I moved.

I hit his left arm first, slashing at his wrist with my knife. Maura scrabbled to get away from him.

His eyes were wild as he turned toward me.

I ducked under his fist as he swung the gun at my head, and toggled the door so it opened.

The two of us burst into the kitchen.

Oh, so many knives in here!

And pots. I grabbed a frying pan off the kitchen island and swung it at his head, connecting with a satisfying clang.

Maura peeked out of the passageway, eyes wide.

"Go lock yourself in the pantry, dear," I said, tossing Jerrod's keys to her in case the lock was keyed. "And don't open it unless I say so."

"Oh, you're gonna say so!" Brandon kicked at my knee, I moved out of the way, and Maura ran.

Both Brandon and I heard the click of the lock.

"Turns out," I said, leaning on a counter for support, my breath coming hard and fast, "the architect for this house had a real penchant for panic rooms. The pantry is quite secure. Bulletproof, actually. How do you like those apples, dear?"

He bellowed like a werewolf. He was looking most unstable, his eyes darting everywhere.

Then a knife whistled past my left ear. I hit the floor, from which I had an excellent view of the expanding splotch of red on Brandon's gun hand. He'd dropped the gun, but it had fallen too far away for me to grab it. *Bollocks.*

"Good luck calling the police," Brandon said with a sneer. "All the cell signals are blocked, I've made sure of it. And the house has no power, no security system."

More thunder, followed by a flash of lightning. The sky outside was a jagged grey.

"Well, you can't have everything." I tightened my grip on the frying pan's handle and stood.

"You know," Brandon said, wrapping his gun hand with a tea towel and grabbing a cutting board with the other, "I talked to a few people about you, Irma." He let out a barking laugh. "You have a real nice reputation here. Everyone thinks you're so sweet. You donate to the ballet school, you're an upstanding community member, all that junk. But really, you're just a nosy old lady. And where the heck are all the knives?"

"You won't be needing any of those," I said.

He swung at me with the cutting board and I parried with the pan. He caught the side of my shoulder with the board and I stumbled into the counter.

The French doors to the balcony popped open from the wind, and Brandon turned his head in surprise. I took the opportunity to scoot around a corner and duck down. I was not fond of my predicament, but I knew that Brandon was not an experienced fighter. All I had to do was wear him down.

"Irmaaaaaa," he called softly, pulling out drawers. He must be looking for knives. Thank heavens the kitchen was enormous. With any luck, it would take him forever to find them.

I caught a glimpse of Jerrod. He was sitting with his back against the oven, breathing hard. He looked bloody terrible, pale as a ghost.

"Irmaaaaaa…"

The sing-songy voice made the hair on the back of my neck stand on end.

"Oh, there you are, Jerrod," Brandon said. I heard him scoop up his gun. "You know, I just can't decide which one of you to kill first." I popped my head up briefly. Brandon was standing over Jerrod, the gun pointed at his head.

I scuttled around a corner, then reached into the side of my shirt. Slowly, silently, I pulled my throwing star out. After unfolding the hankie it was wrapped in, I held it carefully. I was only going to have one chance.

"I guess I'm going to start with you, Jerrod," Brandon said with a giggle that rattled something in my ribcage.

I aimed my body in the direction of that voice and stood, the star already leaving my fingers.

It caught Brandon in the right side of his forehead and stayed there. He roared in pain and stumbled out to the balcony. I picked up another frying pan—cast iron this time—and followed.

Brandon started to back up, toward the balcony railing. He was stumbling now, perhaps from shock, maybe because the throwing star embedded in his temple was throwing off his gait.

He pointed at the outside wall of the house. Two cameras—no, three—were pointed at us.

"They're off," he snarled, backing away from me. And toward the railing. "So everyone will believe me when I tell them you attacked me."

Mr. P burst out of the house, Jerrod behind him.
Mr. P ran a figure eight between Brandon's legs,
tripping him up, just as Jerrod threw a heavy copper
pot at Brandon.

I held my breath.

It missed.

Brandon hoisted the gun up, and shot Jerrod in
the chest.

I let my frying pan fly, and Brandon stumbled as
it hit his head with a *clunk*. His head snapped back as
his rump slammed into the railing, and then he went
up and over it.

He was so tall, after all.

I limped to the railing, my heart thumping against
my ribcage. Brandon's body was lying, broken, on the
downstairs patio.

I heaved a few breaths before making my way to
Jerrod. "How are you doing, you old sod?"

"Maura...okay?" he said. He was starting to slur
his words.

"Everyone is okay," I said. "You did very well."

His eyelids started to flutter, then he lost
consciousness.

I went inside to liberate Maura, and the two of us
dragged Jerrod out of the rain. We set him beside the
pantry door that connected to the passageways.
That's when I noticed the little plaque mounted
beside it. *Safe Harbour*, it said.

"Safe Harbour, my arse," I muttered, then settled
in to wait for the police to come.

FORTY-FOUR — VIOLET

The cavalry came quickly. Jerrod was taken to the very same hospital that Brandon had escaped from while the security guard assigned to him was in the bathroom. He got the same excellent care.

It briefly looked like Irma might get pinched for killing Brandon, until the estate's camera footage was reviewed. The CCTV cameras had been running on a different network than the rest of the estate and hadn't gotten shut down when Brandon killed the power—the only smart thing in the whole design, as far as I could see.

The footage corroborated Irma's story, so the Pickle, instead of throwing Irma in the slammer, was forced to thank her for all her efforts. Irma celebrated with an extra strong pot of tea, obviously.

After Irma had pleaded Jerrod's case with the Pickle, it was uncertain whether he'd be charged with a crime related to Brandon's shooting on the ferry, or if the authorities would accept that he'd acted in self-defence. He was still a free man—for now, at least. And a hero, in his own way.

Some more investigation turned up the burner iPhone that Brandon had used to register the AirTag he'd hidden in Maura's purse, and a deep search of Brandon's phone revealed the secret folder he'd used to conceal all the stalker-y emails he'd sent Maura, along with a receipt for no less than three cellphone jammers. The gun that Jerrod had wrestled away from Brandon on the ferry matched the bullets from Harvey Allen's body, and so did the slug that had been taken out of Brandon after the ferry shooting.

The security company that had manufactured the system installed at Harbour House eventually admitted that someone had locked the garage door remotely via their software—and turned off the local emergency override capabilities. Apparently, they were working on a patch to resolve the issue. Since Brandon had admitted to having his own remote starter for Maura's car, the mystery of how she and I had ended up trapped in the garage was finally solved.

The video footage from the ferry was of too poor a quality to be used in court, but seemed to corroborate Jerrod's story.

"The sport bike I heard at the club the night of the banquet actually belongs to Perrie Kowalczyk. I had no idea she had a new Dodge Tomahawk. And that's it, I believe," Irma summed up.

She and Maura and I were sitting on the patio at Luna's Café a few days later, a plate of cupcakes in front of us. I was knocking back coffee, and Irma had been steeping her tea for about three hours. Maura was sipping a pink lemonade.

"I should have thought more about why Jerrod looked so worried the first time I went to Harbour House," I said.

"I think Jerrod felt nervous about his agreement with Brandon to lock us in there," Maura said. "He's a good guy."

Irma and Maura, the two strangest optimists I'd ever met, exchanged a sympatico look.

"But how did Jerrod know where Brandon was the day he was shot on the ferry?" Maura asked.

"Oh," Irma said, then blew on her cup of tea. "Jerrod was hidden behind an enormous wisteria across the street, waiting for Brandon to come home. When he saw that Brandon was leaving with a suitcase, he decided to follow us. He didn't want Brandon to leave the island without giving him a chance to turn himself in."

"Here's what I don't get," I said. "Why were you talking to Mr. P in Dutch?"

Irma laughed. "It's common to train guard dogs in German or Dutch. Many dogs are trained over there."

"If you think Mr. P will ever be a guard dog, then I don't know what to tell you," I said, grinning.

"I think the little lad did quite well," Irma said coyly. "And I'm very glad you decided to stay here until your vacation is up, Maura. My invitation to stay with us still stands."

"Thanks," Maura said, then slurped down the last of her drink. "I've gotten a rental in town. I think I need to be on my own for a while." She took a deep breath. "Maybe a long while."

I gave her a side hug. "You didn't deserve any of this."

"You certainly did not," Irma said kindly.

"I think I have some problems with men," Maura said. "I can't believe Brandon was such a complete lunatic, sitting right under my nose the whole time."

"Therapy's a lovely thing, dear," Irma said. "You get to talk about yourself the whole time."

Maura smiled, then said, "I can never thank you two for what you've done. But I'm sure going to try."

"We just want you to be happy," I said. "And on that subject, where is Norman right now?"

"Toronto. I gave him back his ring. Both of them."

"What did Stassi say?" I asked.

Maura took a deep breath. "She went with him. So did Ryeleigh."

"Let them, dear," Irma said. "You're better off without them."

"I'm sure I'll talk about all that in therapy." Maura glanced at her watch. "I gotta go. Barre class. Vi, you up for drinks later tonight? It's perfect patio weather."

"Wouldn't miss it."

Maura gave us both enormous hugs and headed to the barre studio.

Irma and I sat in silence for a while.

"Thank you," I said eventually.

She held up a hand. "It was a group effort, dear. And you were a big help. Speaking of help...I really did enjoy that contest you made up to help make me take your rent money."

"What contest?" I said, my voice wobbling. Man, I was a terrible liar.

"You ladies busy?" Agnes O'Muffin was standing on the sidewalk, wearing a mint green collared dress accented with an enormous matching purse, topped off with pristine white gloves.

"Never too busy for you," Irma said cheerfully, and I nodded.

The older woman carefully made her way to the chair Maura had vacated and settled herself in. "You seem to be up to your usual tricks these days," she said to Irma after a few pleasantries.

Irma smiled. "So are you, of course."

"How's that?"

Irma took a slow sip of her tea. "I hear that one of your nephews was on the crew that filmed Snookie's docudrama. You know, the one that was shown at the club?"

"That's true," Agnes said, pouring herself a glass of water from the pitcher on the table. "She drove him quite mental."

"You didn't encourage him to shoot all that extra footage, I'm sure," Irma said, a smirk hovering behind her smile.

"I most certainly did," Agnes said. "It was the truth, wasn't it?"

Irma pressed her lips together, like she was trying not to smile.

"In other developments, I had a nice long chat with Snookie recently," Agnes said, "and I think you'll find that she has withdrawn her complaints about you, along with her silly lawsuit."

Irma's mouth fell open.

"What?" Agnes said.

"You always do have something up your sleeve," Irma said with a grin. "Just like Violet."

"Who, me?" I said.

"She put together a fake contest to give me rent money," Irma said to Agnes.

The older woman set her eyes on me. They were wise and a little intimidating, but still kind. "You the kind of young lady who likes to pay her own way?"

I nodded.

"Take the money, Irma," she commanded.

"Yes, ma'am," Irma said with a smile that could be seen from space.

And that was that. My friend was safe, Irma was letting me pay rent, Julian and I had a hot date scheduled for tomorrow night, and Irma was planning a Friday night BBQ to celebrate our recent victory. All was right in the world.

"Excuse me," a dapper older gentleman said as he bumped into me in front of the snack table at the BBQ a few days later. He was on the short, round side, with wispy hair combed straight back, hazel eyes, and a lovely English accent.

"No problem."

"I'm Edward, a friend of Irma's."

"I've heard about you," I said with a grin.

"And I you. I'm here for a visit."

"Awesome."

After a few more hours, the party started winding down. Mrs. Sepp gave me and Irma truly spine-cracking hugs and headed home with Mr. P. Maura got a ride with an enormous Swede named Lars. Mandy McGuire did a hot sauce taste-off that I barely survived before she took her leave. The other islanders eventually drifted away.

At the end, it was just me, Boris, Stu, Edward, and Julian all grouped around Irma's firepit, with Camille and Françoise on Zoom and Geraldine Greenwood on Skype. And Irma, of course. We looked like an AARP version of the Avengers.

Irma passed out jiggers of scotch, then told us about her encounter with Igor the other day. I tried not to choke on my drink.

"You sure you're okay?" Stu asked gruffly.

"I am, thank you, Stuart."

"We really need to talk about that knee," Julian said.

"Indeed we do, dear. But not today," she said firmly.

"Did Igor give you any idea of what he wanted you to do for him?" Camille asked via encrypted video.

"*Non*," Irma said. "I will assume it is regarding one of my specialities."

"That covers a lot of ground," Françoise said with a smile, and I decided not to ask for clarification.

"Julian," Irma said, "perhaps it would be better if you skipped this discussion."

"I'll stay, if that's okay with you."

After a beat, I interlaced my fingers with Julian's.

"Finally," Stu grumbled.

Boris lifted an eyebrow, then nod-smiled at me.

"I think you should all leave Beaver Island until this is over," Irma said. "Whatever he's up to, he's going to do it here."

"Except me," Boris interjected.

"You too," Irma said. "We don't know what Igor is really capable of."

"He's capable of making his neck the size of a hula hoop, apparently," I said.

"No," Stu said.

Irma looked at him. "Is that a general no, or a—"

"No, I ain't leaving. If this joker wants to start a fight, let's fight," Stu said. "Who's with me?"

Irma held up a hand. "This is going to get messy. And dangerous."

Edward put both hands on his cane. "Oh, I know. That's why we're staying." His smile was radiant.

"You in, Vi?" Stu asked me.

Julian squeezed my hand.

"Yup," I said.

"So am I," Julian added.

"Good," Irma said, arms crossed. She looked like she was ready for a fight. So did we all.

Julian leaned over and kissed me on the forehead.

Beaver Island was a lot of things. It was weird, it was wet, it was dangerous. But it had ended up teaching me that you don't need a panic room to find safe harbour.

You can find it anywhere, if you're lucky enough.

ALSO BY THIS AUTHOR

Vitamin Sea: Book 1 of the Beaver Island Mysteries

Dead Calm: Book 2 of the Beaver Island Mysteries

High and Dry: Book 3 of the Beaver Island Mysteries

Water Town: Book 4 of the Beaver Island Mysteries

Safe Harbour: Book 5 of the Beaver Island Mysteries

Bon Voyage: Book 6 of the Beaver Island Mysteries

Irmageddon: A Beaver Island Novelette
(for newsletter subscribers only)

Peace on Earth: An Irma Saves Christmas Novella
(Ebook only)

About the Author

Maia Ross is the author of the *Beaver Island* mystery series, featuring retired spy Irma Abercrombie and couch-locked nerd Violet Blackheart, along with the spin-off series, *Irma Saves Christmas,* and the *Beaver Island* prequel novelette, *Irmageddon.*

Maia spent almost twenty years in the tech sector, and is an avid sailor. She makes her home in Toronto with her better half, John.

To be notified about new releases, contests, and giveaways, and to get a free copy of *Irmageddon*, please sign up for Maia's monthly newsletter. You can find her online at www.maiarossbooks.com.

Acknowledgements

A big shout out to all my editors for their terrific work and feedback: Dustin Porta, Kim from Brockway Gatehouse Literary Services, Lee from Ocean's Edge Editing, Marta from The Cursed Books, Elizabeth at Binocular Edits, and Lauren Elmore from Lauren Elmore Writes.

Copyediting and proofing services by the always awesome Carol Davis. Thanks so much for all your help! Extra special thanks go out to Shayna Krishnasamy and Carolyn Taylor-Watts for all their support and feedback.

Finally, thanks to my smismar, John. *Ma armastan sind*, babe (*ja Aprill tuleb parem*).

Maia
March 2023

Made in the USA
Las Vegas, NV
06 April 2025

20620477R00236